All My Precious Madness

MARK BOWLES

GALLEY BEGGAR PRESS

First published in 2024
by Galley Beggar Press Limited
37 Dover Street, Norwich NR2 3LG

All rights reserved © Mark Bowles

The right of Mark Bowles to be identified as the author of this work has been asserted by him in accordance with the Copyright, Design and Patents Act 1988

This book is sold subject to the condition that it shall not, by way of trade or otherwise, be lent, resold, hired out, or otherwise circulated without the publisher's prior consent in any form or binding or cover other than that in which it is published and without a similar condition including this condition imposed on the subsequent purchaser

A CIP for this book is available from the British Library

Paperback ISBN: 978-1-913111-56-4
Black-cover edition ISBN: 978-1-913111-57-1

Text design and typesetting by Tetragon, London
Printed and bound in Great Britain by CPI Printing, Chatham

ALL MY
PRECIOUS MADNESS

One night I had lain down in bed, ready to go to sleep. I'd put on the music, as I always did. But as I lay there in darkness, it struck me that the lights were still on in the bookshop. I had not switched them off. It was midnight. I wanted to check the lights. I didn't want him, the owner, the corduroy waistcoat, the fuckweasel, to come in in the morning with the lights still on. Only the week before, there had been a note on the desk saying I had left the place in a mess, a charge that was quite unjust, if not an outright lie. But I had been upset by this note. It had taken the wind out of my sails. So, I put on my slippers and went out into that cool September night. I remember that it was in fact unusually cool for September. For some reason I wore my slippers to go out. I'm not sure why I wore my slippers rather than my shoes, but I did. As if Oxford were only a series of rooms, as if Oxford wasn't quite a real city but only a grand house through which one could walk at leisure beneath a remote and sparkling ceiling. And I walked out in my slippers to the bookshop to check the lights.

In fact, they were off. I hadn't left them on at all. I'd misremembered or imagined leaving them on, as I lay in bed, in the dark, on the border of sleep with the soft notes falling and rising. And now, only half an hour later, I was stood outside the shop, in the cool air, wearing my slippers, looking in through the window. I decided to enter. It was a simple mortice lock and there was no alarm. Imagine. You find it improbable, but it's true anyhow. I went inside and turned on the lights, and I sat at the desk by the window. I took down a number of first editions from the Foreign Literature section, including the tragic Schulz, whose drawings are dug from the corners of our dreams, and also a 1972 translation of Paul Celan: *Inside the house, the drifting snow, of what was left unspoken.* Yes, *inside* the house, exactly. I had never read this book before, but each word glowed with meaning as it never would again. In fact, I have never since been able to fully access these poems, as if a gate had been placed in front of them. But that night the gate was open and I simply received them like a gift, a libation that irrigated my body and mind. Only later did I discover that Celan killed himself by jumping from the Pont Mirabeau into the Seine. But this is of no importance. I sat there reading the book, at what was well after midnight. Occasionally some drunk students would walk past and point or call out, but I did not listen. I sat there illuminated by my book. I sat there for three hours, at the desk in the bookshop. They were hours stolen from sleep and as luminous and vivid as a dream. It was not that three hours passed quickly but that no hours passed. Time was excluded. It had to wait in the alleyway across the street, like a beggar, for me to come out of the shop.

I can honestly say that this moment, or rather this whole divagation, from leaving the house in my slippers, to sitting in the bookshop reading, to returning to the house: this was one of the most enigmatic and mysterious experiences I have ever enjoyed. As if directed by an occult hand. As if interpolated from another life. An experience like this, that burns only once, unexpectedly, therefore burns forever: the light in the window still there and me at the table even now, exempt from time and harm.

But all of this, which occurred over twenty years ago, back in the 90s, is only by way of introduction, a kind of obscure and looping prelude, to the man in the café, the small Italian place on Berwick Street.

I used to go to that café every morning, up until maybe a month ago now, the month of the sad referendum. A pungent espresso in a thick white cup with navy piping. Espresso as it should be, as thick and as dark as arterial blood. I remember the first time I saw him, the slender man with the tanned long face. He reminded me of Claude Cahun, a sculpted androgyne from an era long gone. His movements were delicate and precise, his eyelashes long and dark; a beige moleskin jacket and open-necked shirt completed the portrait. In the early morning light, and viewed in his marmoreal isolation at the corner table, he would be thought beautiful. But then he answered his phone. He began speaking in a vaguely posh accent about his travels. He'd travelled to Thailand, Cambodia, Tibet, South Africa. And this had of course been an 'amazing experience', the 'experience of a lifetime' and other such phrases. That was pretty much all he had to communicate. 'The landscape, the culture,' he stuttered, too amazed to complete the sentence. He'd had a tattoo, he said, 'this awesome guy in Tibet. Practically a midget. What's that? No, not an actual midget. Didn't have the big head. Just really small. Really interesting guy. Mandarin? Why would he speak Mandarin? They have their own language. It's Indic script. Then a Tibetan knot on the ankle. Are you on FaceTime? Hang on, I'll show you…'

Some people, far too many these days, need to make a 3000-mile trip to have an experience. Their bodies and minds are presumably so anaesthetised that it requires the galvanising jolt of a trip to Thailand, being thrown out of a plane on a skydive or pushed off a bridge in the back of beyond on the end of a rubber rope. Just to have an experience. There was one thick-necked cretin back in the office, that zone of perdition where I wasted years of my life, where I poured hours and days of my life down time's omnivorous toilet, a thick-necked cretin called Liam, one among many, who told me that he'd travelled extensively in his twenties to 'get some experience'. As if *experience* were a kind of stock or pension fund you put in the bank for the subsequent stretch of ordinary years. He saw ladyboys in doorways, insects cooked in roadside stalls, the usual stuff predicted by guidebooks, surface perceptions that tickled his fancy. He wandered through distant streets or designated pathways, clocking the merely 'different'. He returned home, of course, unerringly, to the stubborn province of his own stupidity, to a life of money-grubbing and onanism, having 'seen the world', but blindly, lacking, in fact, the perceptual and sensory equipment to see or feel anything.

People fail to understand, I complained to Carvell, that you do not have to travel to meet with amazement. We might wake on a winter's morning in a stranger's house by the fields, the mist covering completely the earthly floor, and the trees like charcoal under tissue paper. A sunken world, the old barn like a wreck underwater, the bleak beauty arranged by nature for the wandering spirits. But you don't have to open a bookshop at midnight, you don't have to rise to the sleeping mist. You can sit in a café, raise an espresso to your lips, watch as the sun takes the floating dust and turns it into a column of tiny golden insects, and this moment, not noticed, not snatched by the camera as soon as it's born, is an experience of great depth and distance. But it requires stillness, it requires slowness. You need to stop. It's not about crossing the earth so fast that the boo! of novelty knocks you down. The endless bungee jumpers, the skydivers, those who've had their ankle tattooed by a Tibetan midget on the side of the Kunlun volcano... all they needed to do was sit at the table by the window and the world would unravel itself in front of their eyes. Carvell concurred.

Carvell was one of my few remaining friends from Oxford. Carvell, despite being a close friend, by male standards, was a compulsive liar. Every time we met, he said things that were obviously made-up. He told me his uncle had been 'sewn up the wrong way' after a bowel operation so that shit came out of his mouth. I remember this example because, metaphorically, it was also true of Carvell, who – when he wasn't talking about philosophy or literature – talked a load of shit. None of his stories, judged individually, were obviously untrue, for Carvell was perhaps careful to locate them within the radius of the possible, but cumulatively they added up to a wall of bullshit wherein each story was an individual brick. He told me that he had attended a Noam Chomsky lecture where Chomsky had replied in Hebrew to a hostile question about Israel. However, I wrote subsequently to the chair of the meeting, Professor Honderich, who verified that no such exchange had taken place. Carvell told me that he'd seen the Unionist leader David Trimble in Waterstones Charing Cross Road buying a copy of *Mein Kampf*. But he'd clearly forgotten this when, years later, he said he'd spotted Yoko Ono buying *Mein Kampf* in Waterstones Piccadilly. Ono had in fact been in London at the time, but the antecedent Trimble tale removed any plausibility, as did the fact that Waterstones did and do not stock *Mein Kampf*. Sometime before that, Carvell claimed that his grandfather was the man who banged the gong at the beginning of the Rank films, but by a truly bizarre coincidence, I'd gone to school with the actual grandson of the Rank man, a bow-legged boy named Burns. Carvell told me that he had a friend connected to the IRA, a one-armed priest, who we could call on should we ever need 'a favour'.

Other lies were pointless and banal, and by that token invited credence, at least from those unfamiliar with this tactic. So, for example, he reported that he'd been sat in an 'all you can eat' pizzeria in Covent Garden when Seamus Heaney walked in, unaccompanied. Carvell sat and watched Heaney eat a total of nine slices of spicy sausage pizza, one after the other, washed down with a pint of Coca-Cola. 'And was he just staring into space, was he reading a book?' I asked, hoping to trip him up. 'Yes, reading a book.' 'Oh really, what book was it?' – at which point Carvell's eyes widened with suspense... 'It was a biography of Mussolini!' But there is of course nothing in the Idea of Seamus Heaney that includes eating the equivalent of two large pizzas, alone, washed down with Coca-Cola, in a threadbare pizza chain in Covent Garden, whilst reading a Mussolini book. Each person's proper name is also a kind of Idea demarcating what they might do and say, a range of action and possible statements. I explained my theory to Carvell, who rebutted it by claiming that Heaney was well known in Belfast for his love of junk food, particularly kebabs and pizza. He added that there is always, with anyone, such an anomaly, a detail which does not fit the person's Idea and which not only makes them more endearing but is actually the back door to their soul. He cited also Picasso's love of wrestling as a further example, and, as I already knew, a well-documented one. But Heaney's love of pizza and kebabs is nowhere documented, and no such documentation will emerge, for the very good reason that it is pure fucking bullshit.

Nonetheless, I did not challenge him on these falsehoods, which never bothered me very much, for I am respectful of the fragile fictions people spin around themselves to make their lives tolerable, and it is not for me to unravel these intricate structures in the name of 'honesty'. In 'telling the truth', there is typically a motive which is questionable, which we fail to acknowledge and which we disown by saying, simply, 'but it's the truth'. The motive is exposure and humiliation. So I had no wish to expose, to catch out or humiliate Carvell; I had no particular wish to unravel my friend any more than I might destroy the web of a spider or a tortoise's shell. We are all creatures actually, with our webs, our territories, our nests and secretions, even though these are disguised as words and beliefs and habits. Many of our ways of speaking are in fact ways of crying, of scratching, of nuzzling or hissing. Hence my tolerance for Carvell's lies, which were in fact spun by some inner necessity as the silkworm spins its silk.

Anyway, as far is travel is concerned, it is true that I travel to Paris, to Rome, every year, with a view to living in one of those great cities, to escaping England, just as the estimable Berger escaped due to people finding him 'too intense', as he said, which is a code for simply being alive, being merely awake and properly sentient, states which are too 'intense' for the English. The English prefer to look at the world through the filter of irony and resignation. In the end it will be necessary to live in exile from the English, which would not be exile but homecoming. Berger, who is certainly an emeritus at the Academy of the Underrated, was compelled to move elsewhere rather than have his mind stop... and the same is true of all writers. The English hate anything which doesn't return them to the prosaic and the everyday. Grand passions and intellectuals are automatically suspect. They live under the sign of necessity: 'What can you do?' they burble. 'It's a funny old world.' They permit themselves the sole freedom of mockery. To a script written and edited by others, they make ironic additions in the margins. The English may have a 'good sense of humour' and a historic litany of many comedians, satirists, ironists of the best mettle. Fine. But the forfeit they pay is intellectual castration. The critical impulse, the philosophical force of the negative, which might once have fomented revolution or toppled the Monarch, is instead turned on themselves, shrivelled to mere carping and grumbling. The regime's faults are inevitable; such is the way of the world. Whereas the Gallic shrug says 'who can tell?', the English shrug says 'what can you do?' The former shrugs off the world to win a yard of freedom, the latter is an act of surrender. The laughter of the English is their measly consolation for a world beyond change. It is not the laughter of joy, of surplus vitality, like a baby's laughter when it discovers a new trick, but the laughter of deficit, life's perpetual deficit and defeat, life's perpetual falling short.

My American students, of course, are always hungry for insights into 'Englishness' and so forth. Let me first say parenthetically that I like my American students, and that I love America and, as importantly, the Idea of it, which it typically fails to live up to. This very failure is in turn part of its tragic mythology. 'The failure of the American dream' and all the consequent blather. Many Europeans who love America are precisely those accused of hating it, or are assumed to hate it. This is because they love the 'wrong' America: the America of jazz, blues, of Beat poetry, of the Black Panthers. Movements which, in their time, have of course been labelled as anti-American, even as they are quintessentially American.

As far as English and Englishness are concerned, I tell them that I have little interest in the subject and can speak only anecdotally and in a personal capacity. And this I delivered to the students only as a prelude to speaking of my father. 'Why is it,' my father once asked me, 'that in order to get anything done in this country, it is first necessary to make yourself an absolute pain in the arse?' He was right, of course, that one must turn oneself into a real haemorrhoidal discomfiture up the clenched arsehole of the official or operative to whom one is speaking, with whom one is dealing, and, thereafter, to insert oneself as far up the hierarchy of said organisation or company as possible.

I remember very clearly and fondly his battle with some tinpot orthopaedic sofa company, after I had advised him of course to buy from a major retailer. But no, he had identified a bargain and had been assured that their sofas were 'bespoke' and medically endorsed. This firm was confined to a single shop on the high street in Wetherby. The sofa, cheap and badly designed, placed him in excruciating pain. My father, of course, in complaining about this sofa, first of all met with the brick wall of 'company policy', the blank intransigence of 'company policy', which is almost psychopathically indifferent to particular circumstances and to bodily pain, so that those functionaries who identify with company policy effectively turn into psychopaths, their sentient interiors having been scooped out by this impersonal law. 'Company policy' allied with 'the system' presents the customer with a seemingly impregnable wall of inertia. And doubtless most pensioners would have simply capitulated to 'company policy', as to some final court of arbitration, as if 'company policy' preceded all individual wills and decisions. But my father merely viewed this as a challenge and a spur to his ingenuity. He stood outside their premises with a home-made placard advising people not to purchase anything from Southfield Orthopaedic Furniture and informing passersby of the appalling customer service and administrative uselessness of this ostensible furniture emporium. And it was soon apparent, after my father effectively picketed their premises whilst holding his placard, that 'company policy' was no more than a gossamer sheet of legal jargon, for within perhaps half an hour of him setting up his stall the sofa operatives scuttled out of their office with a cheque for a full refund and arranged to pick up the sofa later that afternoon. 'Like rats out of a trap,' said my father with evident jubilation after he returned home and danced a delicious victory dance and sang of his triumph whilst punching the air, repeating the words 'rats out of a trap', whereupon anyone hearing and seeing him could not help but join in and laugh, and trample on the now discoloured name of Westfield Orthopaedic Furniture following their humiliating climbdown.

All this I relayed to the students, who appreciated this digression, and I too enjoyed narrating this anecdote of my father, for pedagogical purposes of course, to grant texture and colour to the general drift, but to invoke also my father's ghost, to bring him briefly back to life, and to see him, as I spoke, walk slowly in front of the lectern in his green corduroy trousers and mustard-coloured pipe and take his seat at the front on the left.

My father, who was happy to sit in his solitude, whereas many people are never able to do so and can only stand, awkwardly, in the telephone box of their solitude, knocking on the window and shouting 'excuse me' in a strangled angry voice. This eccentricity of my father, I told the students, is perhaps something I share, this eccentricity which is neither his nor mine, but something we have both carried, and which does not have a nation or a gender or a religion, for it is a singular thing, and 'identity', if it has any meaning at all, which is doubtful, consists of such singularities.

So, I have a plan to live in either Rome or Paris. As yet no actual planning has taken place. It is enough for the time being to *call* it a plan. This is always the first step. The preliminary statement of intent. To say 'This is a plan.' Calling it a plan rather than a 'daydream', for example. Once you have the name, the name 'plan', the clock starts ticking, you have certain obligations. But no, the actual planning has not yet occurred. I joke that I divide my time between London, Paris and Rome, spending fifty weeks in the former and two in the others. For it is certain that one day I will live in Paris or in Rome. For only in those two cities can I be happy. And one day I will also die in either Rome or Paris, or I will move finally to Icaria, where, at the age of seventy, I will bloom again and live another thirty years, learning Greek in delicious increments.

In Paris I stay in a place near Montmartre, a tiny apartment on the Rue Lepic, above the city. From my window I see the whole city turn to gold and fall asleep. I walk down the hill each morning to that same café in the Rue des Martyrs. I ask for 'un café', the bitter 'medicine', as the French call it. I sit and write. The memoir about my father, which is *now* – finally – almost finished, or the monograph on Beckett and the summary refutation of everything written about Beckett by the philosopher of the moment, Badiou, who has understood nothing. My pen bleeds quickly on those café tables, round as planets, counterfeiting the sun with their own golden circles. Later I meander down to Saint-Germain, and to the Café de Flore for a second coffee. It's a cliché, of course, but I am listening to the spirits. It's a visit to the museum. The hubbub in the Flore is only the echo of another hubbub, another world whose promise has ebbed away even if its material shell remains.

In Paris, as in all the best places, the dead are still present. Pressing your ear to the pavement you can still hear Giacometti's footsteps. It's raining and he's covering his head with a summer coat. Elsewhere, your ear to the flaking wall, there's a burst of Jean Genet's laughter, his beady stare stops dead your small talk.

In Paris, as in Rome or Budapest or Prague, the fabric of the Old City shines forth and is the cause of civic and national pride. But in London it is under constant and sustained attack from wrecking balls and bulldozers, and it is impossible to turn a corner without seeing buildings covered in scaffolding and plastic sheets, underneath which the stonework or brickwork is being assaulted and corroded, destroyed and replaced by a predictable facade. Or else, where one expected a familiar sight, one instead bends one's eye on absence and can no longer recall what was there before, afflicted with the quick and useful amnesia that plagues all of us. Many old and revered institutions, such as the old Italian on Bateman Street with the 1930s espresso machine, are becoming extinct, driven out by the madcap rents of absentee landlords and replaced by whatever, indifferently, yields most profit. Had Café de Flore been in London it would now be a Nando's or an apartment block. All the great European cities, in fact, still have cafés that have been, for a hundred years or more, the engine rooms of intellectual and artistic activity. Prague has the Imperial, Budapest the Central, Florence the Giubbe Rosse, Venice the Florian – little more than a well-preserved museum, granted… All except England. The Gherkin, so-called, The Cheesegrater, so-called, Walkie Talkie, so-called, and other laughable grabs at iconicity. Money rips through the irregular fabric, indifferent to history, neighbourhood, culture, to the very idea of the City, in fact. Where there are old buildings there is melancholy; with the new blank buildings, melancholy has been wiped out and the ghosts and spirits made homeless. They won't let this happen in Paris.

I took my mother to Paris for her seventieth birthday, the year before last. We stayed in a small apartment in the Marais, a former atelier, a beautiful little place on a cobbled square behind the street. It had a thin tin roof on which the rain drummed crazily, a cacophony which eventually stopped to unveil a warm and glorious dawn. It was so hot that morning and we walked with slow steps, for her back was bad, along the Rue de Turbigo to the Louvre. My mother never thought she'd see Paris, she told me, such a beautiful city, and said how my father never wanted to go there, just as she had never wanted to visit Egypt, compelling him to go alone. She'd never actually been overseas until her late thirties, when my father took her to Yugoslavia, as it then was, just before the civil war, to see the golden glories of Zagreb.

At the Louvre, in the Mona Lisa room, I noticed an idiot taking photos of himself next to each painting with a so-called 'selfie stick', a term I refuse to use. There are certain terms one should always refuse to use, like the idiotic 'her majesty', which should also never be capitalised, referring to the nominal head of the Windsor clan. And likewise, though for very different reasons of course, 'selfie' should never be used in so far as it is too comfortable with the thing it describes, makes it seem familiar and obvious when in fact it is quintessentially moronic, and this very term 'selfie stick' ought properly to induce feelings of anger and depression. Therefore, for this anecdote I will call it a 'narcisstick', for these people who take 'selfies' are people who always have to be in the picture. The idea that the Mona Lisa or Big Ben or manifold other stereotypical 'attractions' might rest untagged by their gurning face is unthinkable. The image must be countersigned by their grinning and vacant head. And these images, in turn, are destined for their various 'social media' pages, which display not the variety of their travels but the unerring and moronic repetition of their head with various backdrops – the Florence backdrop, the Paris backdrop, the Taj Mahal backdrop and so on. This flattening of the world to wallpaper for the grinning head is the essence of narcissism, so that the term 'narcisstick' has no bias whatever but is purely and economically descriptive, whereas the term 'selfie stick' drags with it a whole culture, and winks indulgently at this culture, helping to legitimise what really should be ridiculed and destroyed. And so, as I was guiding my mother through the swarm of people, the swarm of idiots clutching their narcissticks, to see the Mona Lisa, it so happened that he, the gormless idiot, visibly giddy and rigid, pushed his way past my mother, elbowed her out of the way, so forcibly she scowled and released a muted 'Ow!', equivalent to a scream of agony in more expressive people, which he didn't hear of course, scrambling for his photo opportunity. And because this kind of rudeness cannot go unchecked, the reciprocating elbow he received from me in the small of his back was considerably harder, and, accompanied by a swift back kick, it meant that he went down and stayed down, narcisstick clattering to the floor, head swivelling around angrily, confused and undone. I couldn't decide whether it was amusing or annoying that he had no idea, no clue, why he'd been flattened. Anyway, inconspicuously, and arm in arm with my mother, I strolled into the next room discussing art in the usual whispers.

Of course, Paris is overwhelmed with tourists. They are happy to see the Eiffel Tower, Notre Dame: things that are only signs of 'having been to Paris' that just happen to be located in the city of that name. Similarly, they photograph St Mark's Square because it *signifies* Venice, the Colosseum because it *signifies* Rome, just as Big Ben is *the sign* of London. Nothing is photographed because it *is* that something but only because it signifies that something. Of course, there might be a photo of them at a small local café down a side street they somehow stumbled upon. But this is no exception, for it signifies and is there to signify only 'authentic Paris' and is on the same plain as everything else. They have only the signs of their own experience but not the thing itself. In fact, before any experiences can happen, they are intercepted by their own image. Drinking in a bar, a plate of food, travelling on a train, are snatched by robots before they can happen and drained of life. These images are always abstractions, for the simple reason that actual experience is distributed through *all* the senses, not just the sense of sight. The espresso sipped in Rome passes through the smell of the coffee, the noise of the machine, the morning light pausing golden by the door, the hum of voice and vehicles outside. It is perfectly sensible to say that the coffee *tastes* of these things, and whoever says anything different is wrong.

My students are constantly presenting images of themselves, stories about themselves on so-called social media for others to scroll through. I tell them that people who scroll through Facebook and Twitter are in fact ontologically bored. Facebook and Twitter are in fact methods for organising their boredom and lending it structure. Nor are they bored, these Facebook and Twitter users, in the sense of being temporarily without something to do, or in a state of waiting, as one waits for the dentist leafing through a soiled copy of *GQ* or *Woman's Weekly*. No, they are bored in their very being, they are made of boredom, as a house is made of bricks. Beneath the shining plaster of their 'feed' is a grey vacuum of boredom. I remember from my last visit to Paris a small street off the Rue Bizerte. There were two old men, two *golden codgers,* sat on a bench, talking about politics. They weren't tweeting about it, they weren't 'Facebooking' it. They were just living, as people used to do, unconcerned that their conversation would burn brightly and leave no trace, as with all beautiful things that are not art. An intensity, purely here and now, unconcerned with leaving some evidence or how things might look to that congregation of digital shadows we call our 'friends'.

As for Rome, they could never understand, those office cretins, why I repeatedly went to Rome. 'Haven't you been to Rome already?' they'd ask. 'Haven't you done everything?' As if one could. I've done some things, I said, and I'll do them again, and again. I'll eat the rich, salty carbonara at Da Enzo's. I'll stand at the bar at the Bar San Calisto and knock back a brief espresso, or sit outside in the sun and write, whilst the old men play cards around that small copper table, angry and disputatious as if deciding the fate of mortals, whilst the tame sparrows of Trastevere bob and flutter and wait for crumbs. I'll walk once more along the Via Giulia with its burnished cobbles, long and straight as one of the shining rails of eternity. I'll stand at the fountain in the Piazza Santa Maria and throw a coin and wish for my deliverance. There is a type of repetition born of joy and allied to joy, and a type of repetition which is the creature of habit, allied only to death, and they are exact opposites. Rome, which I visit in October, surely the best month to be there, is for me inseparable from Julia and our brief tryst in the Via Giulia, near the banks of the Tiber. I confine myself (except 'confine' is exactly wrong) to a kind of circle, with the Bar San Calisto at its centre. The Bar San Calisto is of all places the place where I feel entirely at home, and my only sense of patriotism is to this small area, where, were I exiled and put under district arrest, I would be entirely happy and count myself, like Hamlet, a king of infinite space. It was with Julia, eight months into my doctorate and shortly before the onset of my father's breakdown and my own illness, we went to Rome, and to the Via Giulia in particular, to excavate her origins and to stay in the hotel where she was herself conceived, or so she had been told. The hotel where we had sex.

The librarian and academician of the obscene Georges Bataille once said that in sex the spine is dissolved, by which he meant, I can only assume, that the whole body becomes as sensitive and as central as the spine; as the spine does when some slow angelic finger runs down it as if reading poetry in Braille. So it was with Julia. Having said that, nothing more can be said about sex with Julia, nothing. This is because the description of actual sex, as opposed to imagined or fictional sex, always fails. Any attempt to remember and describe is doomed. And sex words, or more accurately the words that are part of sex, likewise do not survive the scene of their enunciation. They cannot be repeated, cited, transferred or otherwise represented. They will always – like a jellyfish – be seen as ridiculous outside the water in which briefly they live. This is in part because sex is always, among other things, a crucible in which language is melted down and recast, words become caresses, and it happens also that the 'obscenest' of words, such as 'cunt' or 'fuck', are turned tender, the most innocent deliberately grubbed and soiled. In any case, they are ephemera. They are part of an arc that ends or begins in the body. Proper erotic literature, purely fictional and without an original, is never a description of something that has really happened but a form of arousal in its own right. It is a stimulant, a vial of language poured in the ear.

Julia called me by my nickname, 'Antaeus'. A couple of women, in fact, have identified me with the 'earthy' in some way, such as the fey upper-middle-class Emer, who regarded me as a 'Heathcliff' figure. 'Watch out I don't hang your dog,' I replied, but she hadn't in fact read *Wuthering Heights* in sufficient detail to get the allusion and looked merely apprehensive. In any case, all of this was probably only because of my northern accent and the round vowels which convention has marked as coarse and robust, certain words like 'pub' and 'bath' and 'us', which sound, to a southern or American ear, like the thwack of a spade. All of which of course is nonsense. Never lose touch with the earth, Julia said, by which she meant the north, or you'll lose your strength, your taut ligament of violence. But I have always wanted to jettison the north, except for certain rivers, such as the Nidd and the Ure and the Ouse and the Aire, of course, the magical Aire, the Aire which is in a category of its own – elusive, haunted by woodland spirits, by lights and breezes that play on its banks, the Aire whose name I wanted as mine, and which, despite being polluted lower down, and at one stretch canalised, despite running through some of the direst and dirtiest towns in Yorkshire, eludes them and finds the Ouse at Airmyn. Yes, I once thought of changing my surname to 'Aire', a word that has an uncertain etymology but that I choose to associate with the element air, 'aire' being the spelling we see in the likes of Spenser or Chaucer, of course: 'the aire ys twyst with violence'. But other than the Aire, and certain landscapes, such as Malham Cove, which is in any case the Aire's source, I have never thought of myself as a northerner, or only in the most trivial sense.

I have always believed that accidents of birth are to be discarded, and in retrospect it seems to me that Julia's desire to have sex at that hotel in the Via Giulia could and can be read as an attempt to rewrite her own origins; to revisit the scene of her conception and to replace it with a different scene, to reinscribe it with a new beginning. 'Ingenious but fatuous' was her verdict when I suggested this early last year, when she visited England with her child, William. But we all attempt to erase our origins, to revisit and to scrub out our past, to turn it into the mere pale tablet on which we write our own indelible destiny. This trip occurred shortly before her return to the US, where she had a fiancé, and within a year of our unannullable tryst she was married to a stockbroker. I invariably, on revisiting Rome, go first of all to the Via Giulia and walk down its cobbled surface to Trastevere, for the Via Giulia is the strait gate through which one re-enters life as it should be lived. It was in that square near the Bar San Calisto that Julia and I stood by the fountain, and I felt, throughout the day, the ripening of happiness in its pure state; for happiness in its pure state is always something that ripens or blossoms without ever reaching full bloom or becoming overripe.

Julia was, and is, one of a dwindling number of Americans of European ancestry whose mind bends heliotropically towards the sun setting in Western and Central Europe as much as it inhabits the smooth plains of the New World, their prognosis of limitless freedom. For certainly, the American idea of freedom is best signified by the open plain and the great sky above it – not by the word 'freedom' or indeed the words 'open plain' but by the plain itself or its cinematic or painterly equivalents. We spoke about this too, Julia and I, the plain and its place in the American imagination, the plain depopulated and unscored, save for the ghostly demarcations of the Indian dead. In such territory, Julia said, more or less said, you carry the origin in your knapsack; any place you pitch down might be a beginning. This is the landscape of Westerns, where the one-track towns are always only temporary constructions, interruptions merely of the plain, just as the main drag is only a limb of the plain, dusty and uncovered. They give the impressions, these towns, of being on wheels. And everyone is a drifter, a nomad, no matter how long they stay. But Julia's dreams are in Europe. They saunter through the Old Town, or sit at a café terrace, scanning the papers and reading the crowd. Her thoughts plunge into the maze of cobbled streets and open the heavy escutcheoned door that guards the apartment building. She ascends the winding stair that goes up to the library, where books like dozing birds are perched, and the gentle and delicate panels of light fall through the tall and dusty sash window. And beneath all this the cellar full of secrets; above all this the attic full of memories. And these dreams are mine as well.

It may now be dying, Old Europe, sinking like Venice itself. But whatever is dying is not on that account of less value than what is living, and may be of more value, or its value may become newly visible nearing the point of extinction. There is every reason to live in Old Europe at the point of its demise and disappearance, rather than sniffing after the zeitgeist, which is made of cables and clouds, brands and fragile exoskeletons amalgamated from images. There is every reason to garner everything that Europe possesses, before the eclipse, for things before they die often experience a kind of refulgence, as my father did, and swim back to brilliance. Perhaps the best thing would be to bathe in the refulgence and scribble down what we see as the sun still shines. I am not including, by the way, under the name Europe, the United Kingdom, which, although nominally and legally a part of the whole, is actually a shithole on the outer edge, spiritually and culturally removed. In any case, it was entirely appropriate that it was Julia who guided me through the old world. With Julia I went to Paris and Prague, to Rome and then south to Naples, Amalfi, and finally then to Thira. And through these places was my soul enlarged, exactly as the grip of England loosened.

In most of the places we stayed in Europe, Julia and I slept in the same room. Mostly in twin beds, but in Rome we slept together in a great queen-sized bed next to the window, warm with morning light. Anyway, Julia told me that every night, just before I fell asleep, or just after falling, presumably, I would cry 'Fuck off' in a tone both exasperated and triumphant. 'Fuck off, then fast asleep,' she said, clicking her fingers, 'and with such finality. As if consigning some vexatious object to oblivion. As if,' she said, 'the vexatious object had just that moment fucked off and you were slamming the door with your words.' It was news to me, this final 'fuck off', this triumphant exasperated sign-off. 'It's a shame you can't record it,' I said, as of course it would be easy to do today, where everything is recorded and made available. Today we would record it, and listen together to this voice directly from the subconscious, or from the soul, to use an older language. Although why would the soul say 'fuck off'. It's not, stereotypically, what a soul does, certainly. Anyway, I always wondered what it meant, this violent exclamation, or exhalation. Julia and I thought that it was it was a fuck off to waking life before disappearing back into the snug oblivious body, a 'fuck off' and free-fall into the dark. When I was ill, I took a different view; I took it to be a fuck off to life itself. There was life, a face at the carriage window, and me on the platform, pale, saluting its departure even then. As if already, when I was happiest, in Europe with Julia, I was secretly sick, the illness working underground. This is how one thinks when you are ill, of course, rewriting every episode as a portent of the catastrophe. But now I am inclined to think of it quite differently. Bearing in mind that this happened in Europe, continental Europe, I am inclined to think of it, although there is no evidence, but it suits me to imagine nonetheless, that I was saying fuck off – on an ongoing nightly basis – to England, to the English, and to Englishness. For when I move to Rome or to Paris, this is what I will surely say as the Eurostar or the plane pulls away or takes off. Fuck off England, fuck off you old vexatious object, finally now fuck off.

London of course is the least English part of England, and the only city with a majority of denizens born elsewhere, a majority of denizens who at least had the drive to flee their intolerable provincial origins, and therefore to flee England itself, effectively. And what London is to England, Soho is to London, a place where disparate realities collide and collude and form a new world. That old pot-bellied Greek with eyes like Sartre, the homeless man in the square playing ping-pong – punctuated by swigs of vodka – with the man who does the bins, the polyamorous dandy with his polecat on a string, media types like Cahun, the market traders on Berwick Street putting together their stalls as if, under the watchful sun, assembling the whole world again from scratch. It is only here that I can live, in the whole of England, in this small square that will no doubt soon be eliminated like all the rest.

I assumed that Cahun lived in Soho, as evidenced, I thought, by his dog. Towards the end of his call, he made the dog say hello to his interlocutor. Not literally of course. 'I've got Casper with me,' he said. 'Say hi Casper,' he instructed the dog, grabbing and moving its paw. It reminded me, this small Casper dog, of a dog from my childhood, the 'stub dog', I called it, a mere stub of a dog, as it were. 'Not a whole dog but the stub of a dog,' I used to intone as I went to sleep, banging my head on the pillow. It lived in the house opposite ours on the joyless estate, a giant cul-de-sac with a single road in and out, where we lived for many years when I was a child. On the first day we moved there I said hello to some children that were passing the house but they ignored me, an incident I still remember very clearly, for these seemingly innocuous incidents can in fact alter the course of a child's life. In this case it was a portent of the unfriendly and often brutal nature of the estate, where the school bully Tanner also lived. On my first day at school I realised that it was in fact Tanner who had passed me on the strect that day and ignored me. Yes, it was him.

Anyway, the stub dog, so named because it was a very small stout dog. One night this stub dog was at the top of the driveway of the house opposite, barking incessantly. It was around midnight. It wouldn't stop barking although there was nobody walking past and no cars. After a time, I heard my father get up and exclaim 'Right, I've had enough of this!' I was puzzled as to what he was going to do but excited that something was about to happen, excited by the sudden turbulence and instability, as I always am. I heard his feet on the stairs and a rummaging and clatter from the downstairs cupboard. The door slammed and I looked again out of the window. From the corner of the frame appeared my father in his bright white vest and some trousers. He was wearing his slippers and holding a piece of beading, which is to say a long thin piece of wood. He walked quickly over to the dog and hit it twice on the head. It yelped and ran off. For years after this I would recount this incident to my father. Over the course of the years, in telling this story, it ended with the fact that we never saw the dog again after that night, but I cannot say for certain that's true. But in any case, what is true is that I never saw Casper again.

Cahun, when he'd finished blathering, sat gazing at his laptop, beneath the mirror in which I could see what, I assumed, were the endless images of his so-called travels. In one image I could make out Cahun about to do a 'skydive'. He was trying to look 'up for it' but in fact looked like he was shitting himself, as I'm sure he was. I imagined him returning to earth with thick impacted shit all the way down his legs, terrified and bewildered. Cahun was drinking a large latte in a takeaway cup. It's a particular bugbear of mine, people who drink their coffee inside the café but with a takeaway cup, as Cahun did. 'Large latte for here but in a take-out cup,' he demanded whilst on his phone, trying to pay with his fucking watch. If you order a takeaway cup, then remove it and yourself from the premises, is my considered opinion on this matter. Staying at the café with a takeaway cup can only be seen as a desire to advertise the fact that you're on the move, that you might have to head off at any moment and so on. What they are holding in their hands, such people, is no longer a drink but only a symbol of their 'busy schedule' and of their need for a pit stop etc. These are people also, and I'm sure this is verifiable, who are likely to be on their mobile phones, the sloppy latte and the mobile phone being, as it were, parts of the same repugnant contemporary jigsaw. I have articulated this theory to Carvell, who half agrees but thinks they may also just want a bigger cup of coffee. But as I pointed out to him, decisively and irrefutably, one does not get any more coffee but only more hot milk, and this is actually the enemy of coffee, as are the people who drink sloppy lattes, whether from takeaway cups or not.

Fuck them. Sloppy latte-drinking fucks. And it pleases me to say that such people should in fact be banned from public space. I do not believe this, if pressed on the matter, of course, but it pleases me to say it nonetheless, and it is important, often, to say things not because they are true but merely for the pleasure they give us in saying them and the affects they help us discharge – in this case *annoyance* and also *sadness* as to what coffee drinking has become in some quarters. We harbour certain forces – anger, irritation, etc – which crave expression, and if it helps to say something 'extreme' then so be it. You can't replace this with mere description. If you say to another person 'You're making me feel angry' or 'You're making me feel sad' these are descriptions of a state of mind not *expressions*. Anger or irritation needs an exit, some form of words, or action of course, which allows it to be released. Or completed. It is therefore better to say 'you're going to get your fucking head kicked in', as the football fans used to chant, or some such thing. A vent. Conversely, many statements that we take literally, as reports or descriptions, are in fact the necessary verbal spell whereby some otherwise telluric affect seeks its proper daylight. This is the lesson of poetry. *April is the cruellest month* is in no sense a description of April; it is not a statement of either fact or opinion. It is the verbal formula unlocking and making audible some particular note of mundane desolation. Of course all of this will depend upon the etymology, the ring of connotation surrounding each of these words, but these words are only, as the great Celan more or less said, various keys to unlock the otherwise unspoken. Religions too are of course mostly vast fictional apparatuses for expressing and actualising affects. The litanies, gestures, rituals and so on are ways of organising and releasing what would otherwise never have come to light or been born. *Prayer*, said Pascal famously, *is a natural motion of the soul*. He was right in saying this. Prayer is an escape valve, and releases skywards all kinds of affect which rise and colour or stain the heavens rather than nibbling at brain and heart. Only this act of kneeling down, of chant and supplication, of whispered intimacy with outer space, can do this, and many people who know in their hearts that the heavens are empty have nonetheless performed this ritual without contradiction. Many, similarly, have cursed a God they never believed in, so as to expel the demons of rage, and have shouted and screamed, and threatened to rip God out of the sky, and trample him to death, while knowing he was never there to begin with.

You, or anyone, might wonder why I prefer to work in a café that is perhaps only five hundred metres, if that, from my flat in St Anne's Court, a courtyard above that dingy drug- and drink-addled street, which I was lucky enough to be given by the Soho Social Housing Coop some seventeen years ago, or so, when I was renting a friend's flat in Tottenham Mews and living off benefits, as it was once possible to do. It belonged to that brittle and enervating bourgeois Emer, whose parents had bought the mews flat some years ago. Before I moved in there, and when we both still lived in Oxford, she would sometimes go down for a weekend, and sometimes I would visit her. I associate Emer with the precipitous onset of my illness, which occurred on one of those weekend visits to London and which seemed to descend in a few hours over dinner. My mother could never quite remember the name Emer and referred to her instead as Emu, which was in fact a better and more apt name, for she was an awkward and flightless creature and an incidental emblem of my own plight no doubt as well.

I confess that I broke off all contact with Emer, in the most abrupt and cruel fashion, shortly after she too moved to London. It was just after I went to live in St Anne's Court, at which point she took up residence in Tottenham Mews and would invite me round frequently. Whereas she had never smoked at Oxford, she had now, shortly before coming to London, started smoking, and smoked thin roll-your-own cigarettes with untidy strands of tobacco peeping out of the end. She would light these small repellent cigarettes with matches, and always take three or four attempts at striking the match before it burned, and in turn two or three attempts before the cigarette was lit. Thus, even before the thick acrid smoke began drifting and curling from the bent cigarette there was already a sulphurous stink in the air from the matches. But it was less this stink I minded than the fact that Emer, because she smoked almost constantly, began to smell of tar and gas, and her flat also smelled of tar and gas, and her breath as well smelled of tar and gas and her clothes in turn. In Emer's presence, I was no longer able to listen to what she was saying or speak with any intelligence or focus, being overwhelmed by the smell of tar and gas as well as the residual smell of sulphur from the lit match and the insidious curl of grey and blueish smoke from the 'rollies', a word I found as repellent — if not more — as their stink. Some words seem to absorb, like gauze, particles of what they represent to such a degree that they become things in themselves. This is the case with 'rollies', a stinking damp thing-word. Anyway, all of these smells made me feel nauseous and even more mentally fuzzy, and even in writing these words I begin to sense these odours creeping upon me again and have to stop.

I should add that I was reminded, in the presence of this Emer, or Emu, of my childhood, wherein everything stank of cigarette smoke and it was impossible to avoid the smell of cigarette smoke — either drifting around the living room, or in shopping centre cafés, or mingling with fresh air outside, or stale on people's breath and clothing. Even on the beach, one never smelled the sea air, the pure breeze, but only cigarette smoke, yes, even there. It was for this reason actually that I escaped the living room and sought refuge in the kitchen, where I turned on the radio and listened to Radio 4. That's what opened the door in fact to my education, which had little to do with Shawcross School and everything to do with various early-evening dramas and documentaries, and Alistair Cooke of course. The voice of Alistair Cooke was a signal from another world. I am not talking about America, the ostensible subject of his letters, but another cultural world is what I mean, or another *place* from which to see the world. Here in the kitchen there was a semblance of clean air, albeit relatively clean, for if the window was open there was still very faintly the smell from the wool-combing mill near the playing fields. This smell was always around the corner, always around any given corner on the estate where we lived. And only with all the windows shut in the house could you exclude this smell completely, although in that case there was still the odour of cigarettes leaking out from the lounge. When my parents were out and the babysitter came round you could still smell it in the fabric of the green bobbly sofa. The babysitter sat silently sewing, with only the click of the needles and the hum of the gas fire and the residual odour of cigarettes sunk into the very fabric of everything. Emer reminded me of this, the childhood world, the world of gas fires and slices of white bread with pink jam, and ashtrays and endless cups of weak tea. Emer and her smell of gas and tar plunged me backwards into all this, which was not somewhere I wanted to be.

On the one hand, I love my flat in St Anne's Court. In it I am able to lead my eccentric life, to cultivate my eccentric life, to lead a life that is an odd life, dancing to a different jubjub and with my own forms of entertainment. For example, one St Patrick's Day. It was midnight and I had to teach in the morning. Ironically, I was teaching a course on Ireland, literature and political action, looking at the play *Cathleen ni Houlihan*. Picture it. I'm reading through my notes: 'The call of nationalism, like the call of art, removes one from the realm of practical calculation and utility. A kind of madness, a kind of death.' There were some drunks outside, with tall Guinness hats and green scarfs. Needless to say, they weren't fucking Irish and doubtless knew nothing about Ireland and its, her, history. Needless to say, they had not read *Cathleen ni Houlihan* nor *The Countess Cathleen* nor *Riders to the Sea* nor *The Plough and the Stars*, and nor did they know, I'm sure, these lines:

They sang, but had nor human tunes nor words, / Though all was done in common as before; / They had changed their throats and had the throats of / birds.

No, their throats were the throats of middle-class English cunts, who needed, not that they did *need*, another pretext for drinking till drunk; some fancy dress for their drunken project: St Patrick's Day, Halloween, Christmas of course.

So, there they were, outside the pub beneath my flat and below my green sash window with its peeling paint, a relic from another decade, and they were making a hell of a present-day racket. I turned off the lights in the flat and opened ever so gently the window, just enough to allow a hand to poke through. I took an egg from the fridge and on my knees crept to the window and threw the egg, and smash: it hit one of them on the back of the head. He was wearing a black donkey jacket. 'Fucking hell,' he shrieked, in some weird register of shock. 'Where the fuck did that come from?' I could see them looking up at the sky, confused, afraid, as if in the cross hairs of a sniper or errant angel – which of course I am (i.e. both). I lobbed another warning egg that smashed on the pavement. They started to run up Dean Street, unable to see their self-effacing assailant. How amusing I found all this, to have orchestrated this petty drama, to have dispatched these goons, to have redirected their everyday life and killed their conversation. This would be just one example. Another time, not untypically, I was still up at 3 a.m. The electric ran out. I had a small plastic key that plugged into the meter and had to be topped up from time to time. So I went out to the garage on New Cavendish Street, in the dead of night, walking proudly, along the quiet or almost quiet street, breathing the summer air, casually doing my errands as the world slept, reciting a poem by Yeats, 'Who Goes With Fergus?' of course, thinking of those figures who depart along *a line of flight* pursuing incalculable passion, answering a *call* from within or without, unsure which, departing – at cost and consternation – from everyday life and its constant concessions, moving towards a Beyond which is also deep inside. Yeats's Michael: *He has the look of a man that has got the touch*, the solicitations of everyday life dumb and derisory as never before.

I had no fear at that time, despite the adenoidal skinny heroin addicts and their malicious presence, for I was alive and invincible, walking through that concrete valley, shoulders back and primed with golden words which, if I didn't use them on some aggressive wretch, I would surely write down when I got back inside.

But anyway, I cannot spend my daytimes here, because my reason for working in the café rather than in the flat is that I prefer to be outside myself, if you like. One of my heroes, the great Walter Benjamin, wrote some of his most brilliant and aphoristic prose two feet from a jazz band in a noisy bar, or composed in his head while walking the streets, using his footfalls as a metronome. Benjamin, who died by his own hand escaping from the Nazis and whose portly but winged form, weak heart aflutter, still lingers by the shore at Port Bo, which opens onto infinity. It was Clarkson, whose family name had been Chernik, who told me the tale of Benjamin, and who introduced me to his work, in the arduous approach to the Oxford entrance exam, a recherche route to say the least, like the twisting vertiginous road to Sorano. The soft-voiced Marxist MacGregor certainly, and to a less extent the red and bibulous Connor were impressed by my citation of Benjamin's work in my Oxford interview.

And Benjamin it was who insisted it is best to be out there, in the street and among strangers, rather than cloistered in your apartment surrounded by familiarity and memories congealed into souvenirs. This was not simply a matter of personal preference, no, for Benjamin had eminently philosophical reasons for doing this. It was the city, Benjamin said, in its 'insistent jerky nearness', which provided the cognitive and creative sparks the thinker and writer needed, bombarding us and catching us off guard, ambushing us from unanticipated angles. All of which thinking should copy. He also recognised, Benjamin, that our thoughts and feelings dwell outside us, or come at us from the outside and not the inside. Proust of course taught us that our memories, and not only that but our past selves, are typically located outside us in smells and tunes, and he himself would not, by some effort of will and introspection, have been able to access his past but for a fluted cake in a café. In this cake did he find what he could not have discovered by straining at the stool of introspection. The songs of our past, most obviously, and in my case, for example, Bob Dylan or the Velvet Underground or Pink Floyd, which I discovered as a teenager, are a lozenge which when sucked release into our mind and bloodstream the very different flavour of the long-gone. Nor it is only memories which reside outside us in objects. My melancholy is revealed to me in the ruined abbey on the hill, my tears are in the music I listen to, I understand my inner calm and resilience when I stare at the slow deep river. *My peace is there in the receding mist*, Beckett said. Not in his head or his heart, but out there, outside him in the mist. And I am always outside myself in landscapes, songs, smells, objects. And of course people.

There are certain strangers who will illuminate our soul from such and such an angle unexpectedly and certain friends and family of course who, when we are with them, allow parts of ourselves to shine forth, parts which might otherwise have remained in darkness and unknown, or even unborn. When my father died, a facet of me died, a facet of me was deactivated and could not be activated again. There was a speaker who only lived when he spoke to my father, and a listener who only lived when my father spoke to him, and forms of speech that passed between us now long dead and buried. My mother thinks she knows me, she thinks the visible bit she knows is of the same substance as the bit she doesn't. In fact, she only knows the facet that is actualised by her, the facet that flickers into life when the two of us speak. The facet she knows lives only in this interval between us, and will die when she dies or I die. We live and come alive in our encounters with others, and also, if you're a writer, our encounter with language, and introspection never has the reach and clarity of our encounters with others.

Permit me a digression, a digression that is nothing of the sort of course but, like so many digressions, a pocket in which the truth can breathe ('method is detour', wrote the great Benjamin). Being hit by my father, thirty years earlier, hit round the head for being clumsy or whatever pretext it was, being hit on the leg or cracked with a belt, 'within an inch of my life', as my father said. For example, we were on a walk in the Dales and we had to pass through a gate with a catch. I opened the catch and the gate fell to the floor. Only the catch had held it in place. For this I was called a 'numbskull' and 'bonehead' and hit. 'I didn't know it didn't have a hinge,' I protested, but this was seen as defiance and I was hit again. He asked me to get something out of the hut for him. I turned the rusty key and it broke. This enraged him and he hit me repeatedly on the head. I curled up in a ball on the floor, but this was seen as resistance and I was kicked in the ribs. I knocked over a glass of orange juice or something else such as a cup of hot tea. Some of them I don't remember but have been told about, as for example when I was three: We were on the promenade at Scarborough. I'd been asked to carry a bottle of Coca-Cola by my father, but I dropped it and was hit with a sudden ferocity. Nobody intervened of course, as they might now. I don't remember half of these incidents, but there is a succession of them, over many years, each shadowed by the daily fear of more. A door slams and the weather changes, the rooms are loaded with silence. I remember also my mother time and again imploring him not to hit me on the head, or my grandmother similarly beseeching and being told to stay out of it. Their protests antagonised him. In any case, he wasn't just hitting me but performing an exorcism, allowing himself to be burst open with rage. It was something that happened to him, like being struck by lightning.

But anyway, the point is that in my thirties I thought I harboured no ill will, I thought it was safely, well, not even locked in the past but dispersed altogether by time's ministrations, and this would have been my conclusion no matter how much I might have thought about it, no matter how much soul-searching or how many psychotherapeutic interventions. But one evening, we were sat in a restaurant, a curry house in Baildon. He, as usual, had wolfed down his food in five minutes. 'Come on,' he said, 'I want that eating up quick. My programme's on at nine.' 'I'll do as I please,' I replied. And he: 'You wouldn't have said that thirty years ago, you'd have got a good thrashing.' These words, and 'thrashing' in particular, blind to their own reach and invasiveness, were in fact a kind of conduit, a funnel, that directly released into my brain and bloodstream the consciousness and feelings of a 10-year-old boy, namely myself, so that the humiliation, the fear, the powerlessness, the sense of being closed in, thrown back on his own resources in absence of parental protection, and an aggregate of other emotions, suddenly flooded my mind as some substances saturate our tissues. I wanted only to come to the aid of this child who was suddenly my contemporary, who had wriggled free of the past and sought asylum in my chest. He was crying, and only with adult strength could I stanch my own tears. But now this child had the body of an adult and the strength to avenge the impending relentless blows. And so I sat silent in the restaurant, overwhelmed by and harbouring this small escapee. I was primed with purest anger, a ravenous rage, a finger resting on a trigger. And later, when we returned to my parents', I had to leave the house, to walk it out of my system. I rang Carvell, as he had rung me after the death of Guy Debord – as I'll later explain – and began to curse my father in the foulest and most astonishing way. That is, I myself was astonished, as if I was speaking in tongues threatening murder and more. It was the child still hiding in my chest using me and my vocabulary, unavailable back then, as a vent, an accusation that splattered the sky. The point of course, the point is that only those chance words, spoken in the restaurant, unknowing, a careless conjuration, unpremeditated and arriving from the outside, could have accessed that child and set him loose in the streets of Baildon. Immediately before my father died, I kept returning to this episode, from which I was now estranged, except the source of that rage was buried within and doubtless inexhaustible. But this was in turn intercepted by my father's death in 2006, which released also the sap of sadness which never stops. Anyway, the point of this little diverticulation, the point is that we know how we feel and think not by turning our gaze inward but rather when an object or event knocks on us from the outside. Everything is there on the outside or meets us from the outside, and we know very little until the outside intervenes.

Nevertheless, it is true that for long years I worked in my room, wrapped in secret studies, and equally spent long years trapped in 'introspection', as it is misleadingly called. For introspection does not simply reflect on the self; it produces a second self which monitors, supervises and doubts the first, and this in turn breeds anxieties, clumsiness, paralysis, as in Hamlet. Hamlet, as I always tell my students, is changed by a deed, not by thought. The rapier, operated by a synapse, that kills Polonius, also dispatches the procrastinator and pitches Hamlet into the world of action. The alliterative flourish that signs off the courtier's demise – *dead for a ducat* – signals that wit must now chase action. There are no more soliloquies. It is seldom observed, but true. The second self, quizzing and questioning the first, is gone. Hamlet sends Rosencrantz and Guildenstern, the two goons, to their death with the cleverness and economy he previously reserved for language. He heads back to Denmark for death-dealing combat and, at the graveside, snatches grief from the mouth of Laertes, mocks it with fatal hyperbole, and points the way forward to combat. Time, which the procrastinator put to sleep, and Death, have entered his veins like a virus, engorging the heart and allowing him to release his strength, which is all that any of us want.

And all this, in short, is why I prefer to write and work in cafés, and why for many months I worked and wrote in Café Amato, with the sun slanting in and the gentle Italian chatter percolating around me.

A couple of weeks had elapsed since I first saw the numbskull Cahun jabbering about his travels and volcanos and midgets, but one morning, as I was writing in my notebook, little metallic flakes of noise began to scratch and scrape my ears, little particles of noise which only gradually coalesced into a human voice:

How's tricks? Keeping busy?
   Dave? Do you know Dave? Yes, yes... he's a good guy. He runs the UK office for Pandigital... we're gonna end up partnering up with them... Harif left, yeah, yeah... Headhunted... What? Yeah, some of them are talking to us... Yes, Rob and Melissa... Do you know Rob at all? When I was in LA, there was him and Melissa at Flash, yeah got a lot of love for that guy... Anyway, been speaking to Ali, we'll all be working together... that's what we're doing, partnering up with people like Rob. I'm moving away, doing more international stuff... We're changing up the style... There's a lot of potential, and it's getting traction... It's just a case of capitalising it... see how it works out mate... Yeah, Kim's excited, really excited.

Only then, glancing up (and doubting, though I had never heard of her before, the genuineness of Kim's excitement), did I realise that the voice belonged to Cahun, who was ordering his latte whilst chatting on his phone. I should say that I do not demand silence. No, what I prefer when writing in a café is a hubbub, a bubble of hubbub around me, a bubbling amalgam of animated voices. I love the very word 'hubbub', and that other word, 'brouhaha', both words being as much noises as words. 'Hubbub' is a bounce of the lips, and 'brouhaha' is chimpanzee laughter. Both words contain that chattering animality which accompanies all human communication, an element which is non-semantic, which approximates to the squeaking and screeching of chimps or even the sonorous code of dolphins. A hubbub, and even a brouhaha, can be ideal backgrounds for writing, but what is altogether intolerable is a solitary man speaking on his phone, addressing himself to a person who is absent, chucking around random names and fragments of conversation...

> We've just launched a beta site... Yeah, got a pretty good evaluation... Guess, no guess... thirteen! Thirteen mill. I'll send you the details when it goes live... our funding success at the moment is about 90–95%... we're getting very good at, y'know... cutting through the crap. Right, they don't just provide capital... it's about introducing digital disruption to councils... yeah gets people to pitch their ideas. We're doing a pitch-off, which should be fun... Government are really backing tech right now... yeah, we build a portfolio according to their criteria.

Carvell thinks that some law should be introduced regulating, and in fact banning, the use of mobile phones in certain public spaces. While in sympathy with the irritation behind this point of view, it is fundamentally flawed and ultimately insidious. In general, we need to operate by tact and discretion rather than impersonal laws, by free and spontaneous courtesy rather than prescriptive legislation. By way of example, people ought to express gratitude, just by way of example, and it is good to express gratitude, and to feel it, but this cannot be made an object of law. It would be not only ridiculous to make gratitude a legal requirement, but actually impossible, for the Law would directly destroy gratitude in demanding it, in so far as gratitude is, *in its essence*, a free movement of the heart. And so, if we take this fellow Cahun, it is true that his behaviour violated certain basic rules of tact and discretion, respect and mutual awareness, and his inane shouting, his blather and voluble effluent of pre-masticated buzzwords, was directly destructive of these subtle and in some ways delicate guidelines, which have not been devised by a committee or a judicial body, but have evolved connaturally with human society and are congruent with the benign contours of our nature. All of this is true. But were Cahun subject to statutory laws restricting his uncouth and inhuman shit-speak, were he simply obeying such a law in keeping relatively quiet, under the stern eye of a policeman, as it were, then this would be equally destructive of that tact and judgement which is, in fact, the very substance and soul of our humanity.

His name was not Cahun, of course. It was Seb Johnson. I gleaned this fact from the second time he answered his phone, except I initially misheard this as 'Seth Johnson' and could find no information about him on Google later that day, except regarding a mediocre footballer whose foolish signing by Leeds United in the early years of the present century, at an inflated fee and with extravagant wages, heralded that club's precipitous fall into the lower leagues of English football. They have, it seemed, never recovered, cursed by their impatience and hubris and doomed forever to snatch failure from the jaws of success. Nonetheless, I will continue to refer to Johnson as Cahun, a name which – despite being shared by that pioneering artist whose enjoinder to live otherwise resounds across the century and is still tucked somewhere in the whorl of my ear – has stuck, an act of 'primal baptism'. As such, it is very similar to the nicknames my father would always give people, such as our two next door neighbours, 'Herbert Ferret' and 'Gutner', whose actual surnames have now been irreversibly buried, although he stopped using Gutner after the man had his leg amputated due to smoking. He had a nickname even for his belt, which he called

Montgomery and which hung on a hook in the hall. It is interesting, incidentally, that he called his belt Montgomery, after Field Marshal Montgomery, just as at Shawcross School we nicknamed Mrs Lancaster, the head teacher, 'Bomber' in reference to a war that had happened thirty years previously. The Second World War was still ready to hand as a point of reference and still very much present, whereas now, at this moment in history, it is true that whatever happened thirty years previously is sunk in oblivion and beyond the reach of the popular imagination.

In applying to Oxford, I did not want to take my A levels at Shawcross, which was a laughable institution staffed by the dull and defeated, people bullied and beaten into submission by the pupils, their tormentors, who were interested only in cash and cigarettes and sex, or imagined sex. There was Cuthbert, tormented on account of his enormous feet; Sergeant, for his initials, D.K., and their aptness to his old and scabrous face; Babbalegs (his real name escapes me) for the veins in his forearms; Monsieur Oliver, a French teacher, mercilessly lampooned because of his nose and penumbra of garlic; Glassman, who was confused and half deaf and who responded to a very loud fart with the angry question 'Who threw it?!?'; Kilburn, to whom we sang in unison a Beach Boys song at low volume until she rose from her chair and snapped; Stephens, the German teacher, tormented for his alleged homosexuality; Borden for his glass eye; Hayes for no particular reason; Peterson, for his face like the surface of the moon; Webber, his eyes bulging out of his head and his pot belly likewise distended; Hartson for her squawking dinosaur voice; Sugman because he had slipped a disc; O'Leary for her dark oily hair and soft Scottish accent; and Healy of course, whose skin was tight and shiny, as if tied in a bundle at the back of her head. Only Clarkson was exempt, and Clarkson it was who advised me to take my A levels elsewhere, to escape Shawcross, which he described as an egregious cackhole. I had told Clarkson that Hayes, the English teacher, had not only denied my story with her judgement but defined irony as 'another word for sarcasm'. After surfing our waves of laughter, we washed up on the beach disgusted and appalled, and it would have been impossible to study English under this Hayes dummy, this professional dunce. Clarkson himself was looking for work elsewhere, and possibly overseas, he said, for he could endure it no more, and felt he had served his penance 'teaching working-class kids', which had left him disillusioned and politically listless. He was one of the few teachers, perhaps the only one, who did any teaching, who was not reduced to a bouncer or policeman, as the others were. Of course, as regards these bouncers and policemen, their bouncing and policing was constantly held up to ridicule, for the pupils *wanted* them to be bouncers and policemen, and in attempting to discipline the teachers were fulfilling the pupils' desire. The antics of the pupils were in fact addressed ultimately to the teachers, as an ongoing and orchestrated provocation, with the sole aim of driving them to the point where they were reduced to bouncers and policemen, or even better to Great Dictators filled with spitting rage and stripped of dignity. The pupils were able to engineer this whole process with almost somnambular ease.

It was Clarkson who introduced me to philosophy and to Samuel Beckett. Although he was himself a maths teacher, he had a deep knowledge of philosophy and modern literature, and offered to tutor me for the Oxbridge exam whilst I took my A levels at

Bradford College. I studied in the evenings whilst working part-time cleaning dishes in that cavernous bar on Piece Hall Yard, a crepuscular chamber of smoke and pounding music where businessmen lounged not only at noon but also every evening, emptying their glasses and hearts and souls and bladders and wallets of course, until last orders were called and the lights went up on their ugly ill-lit faces made malleable and cock-eyed by alcohol. And then afterwards, I returned home unable to sleep, reading Pound and Eliot and Joyce, dictionaries and reference books at the ready for the allusions scattered like the leaves from the trees of a wood now cut down and covered in concrete.

The tutors at St Catherine's, at my interview, were doubtless impressed by my autodidactic flights of fancy, reciting and speaking about Pound's *Cantos* at great length but without having read a single one of Shakespeare's histories, my fardel of arcane philosophical references to the paunchy but winged refugee Walter Benjamin, which had been decanted to me by Clarkson and, like everything else, half-metabolised and half-invented by me. The *Cantos*, I announced, start so confidently, keel to breaker, ploughing the dark waves, but enter too quickly into a region of mists and fragments; the journey is shipwrecked almost at once. And this might serve as an emblem of modernism as such, I announced. A literary culture of the smashed and the fragmentary, the ruined and the anachronistic, and ideas and passions constructed upward from a bed of pieces. I advanced also my theory of Joyce's *Ulysses*, rubbishing, as I thought, the received wisdom about Joyce uncovering, beneath the surface chaos of the Hibernian metropolis, the deep and reassuring contours of myth. *Au contraire*, I explained, myth has been shattered into a thousand husks, which are now delivered to the modern writer as dead materials for a completely new construction.

Melancholy nostalgia for the epic world and a ruthless futurism are two sides of the same coin, I declared, as if throwing them some glittering curveball. Modern literature, I *explained* to MacGregor and Connor, surfing my own zeal, is predicated on the recognition that the epic world is lost, that the Holy Centaurs of the hills have vanished and we no longer know how things work, only how they appear. 'Modernist creation is haunted by the destruction it presupposes,' I said, a maxim I'd coined on the train. Our modern writers are stranded in a world where money and bureaucracy (rather than the gods) have become the ghostly intermediaries of all human communication. This is the situation from which all modern literature springs and which it cannot avoid. I presented myself as a precocious Mercury delivering this momentous news to these two chuckling lively elders, sitting on their bench on the side of Olympus.

I expect that my interviewers, the bibulous and red-faced Connor, wobbling with hops and jocularity, and the soft-voiced Marxist MacGregor, were impressed not so much by these various theses but by the guileless enthusiasm with which they were delivered. For what is expressed in the voice, in its cadence and reverb, is certainly as important as what is said.

This was one of the few philosophical lessons I learnt when I worked, years later, at the telesales office. One of the very few oases of insight in that philosophical and moral wasteland. All our business was done over the telephone. There was only the voice. We all read the same sales script, and the same scripted replies. We read out our script to various company directors, head teachers and so on. We called them 'leads', but a more accurate word would have been 'marks', as a professional conman might say, or, even better, to our 'victims' – except they were never quite that, for they were accomplices in their own deception. The point is, for the time being, the point is that despite the same script, the same answers, some of us sold a lot and others not so much. And certain people, despite uttering the same form of words as the top sellers, nonetheless sold nothing and were sacked. This tutored me in the magic of the voice, the mesmerism, the telekinetic power of the human voice. Some voices had in them authority, reassurance, optimism, excitement, whereas others had only trepidation or boredom. Only the force and intonation in the voice changed from person to person, and this made all the difference. A part of them, a primitive but more persuasive part, wanted what the voice contained, and for this they surrendered their money. This was the secret transaction beneath the surface of propositions and discussion. In short, they did not know what they were doing, these buyers, they were unaware of what truly motivated them. The case is not so unusual, I might add. *Au contraire.* Think most obviously of the Nazi crowds stupefied by Hitler. For these massed supplicants, however much they assented to the so-called Fuhrer's so-called message, were enchanted by the impotent rage in his voice. They responded to the hysterical rising tones, stolen from Wagner, which threatened to give in to madness without ever quite doing so; the tiny man winding himself up before the vast crowd and simultaneously winding up his audience, an audience fuelled by the same impotent rage that rose and rose in woozy tides. This audience, following the voice, were only too predisposed to give over their own anger, like a gift, to the barking tiny demagogue, funnelling their collective rage through the gaping mechanical mouth, the puppet face. I thought of this example partly because Hitler, it seems to me, was himself like some sacked salesman who finally snaps and delivers to his boss, liberated now from etiquette and office politics, a furious wild peroration, drowning the office in spit and expletives, wherein for the first time he feels truly alive, the whole office agog and avid with admiration, wishing that they could do the same.

When I first arrived at Oxford – in what was called 'Michaelmas', 1990 – I was overwhelmed, like one that had stepped through the looking glass. I lodged next to two others, Will and Ollie, neither of whom had ever questioned that they would go to Oxford or Cambridge. Oxford was cut from the same tweedy cloth as their domestic life. They had in no way stepped into a brave new world but had only inherited an old one from their parents and their parents' parents; they had, through the avenue of trees, walked through their garden into the quad, as it were, and stood now in this same quad that was little more than an extension to their garden, sipping Pimm's and discussing mutual acquaintances. Will was a gluttonous choirboy with short curly hair, untouched by the rough edges of the world, a creature of pews and manicured lawns, for whom the word 'Housemaster' was nearer than 'Hammer'. 'Pitted olives are for lazy people' were the first words I heard him say. He was constantly, this Will, using the word *copious*, particularly if referring to 'copious amounts of alcohol' or 'copious amounts of sex', or, of course, 'copious amounts of money', none of which were relevant to my own circumstances. This word, 'copious', seemed the sign of membership for a certain category of Oxford student, all with similar voices, clothes, vocabulary. A password admitting one to this particular tribe. But I couldn't bring myself to use this password. It seemed like a betrayal. I was happy to adopt other words that had a literary or philosophical or classical provenance, but 'copious' seemed merely a group signal which I was unable, in good conscience, to speak. Even when I had made pages of notes in McGregor's lecture on literature and ideology, I couldn't bring myself to say 'copious notes' and was in fact asked by Will if I had made 'copious notes', to which I replied tersely, 'Hardly any'. And so, despite this word having respectable origins, etymologically speaking, and having presumably the same root as *cornucopia*, which I love, I cannot either hear or use this word innocently even now, and if I do hear it have to mutter 'copious piles of steaming shit' under my breath to defuse it.

When Margaret Thatcher resigned, in November of that first year, Will was plunged into anger and sadness, shouting 'perfidious traitors' from his arched stone window whilst I, unbeknown to him, danced and sang in the room two doors down.

The other, Ollie, was in appearance, or as I liked to think of him, a skinny spy with a cat called Aegeus that resided in Ollie's rooms 'unofficially'. He had hired a cleaner to tidy his room once a week, but also to complain about. 'Nature abhors a vacuum, and so does my cleaner,' he quipped. Within three years of leaving Oxford he had a job in the Cabinet Office. It was ludicrous to call these men my compatriots; they were for all intents and purposes foreign; they spoke with easy familiarity of 'townhouses' and 'housemasters'. Their language overlapped with mine, certainly and of course, but signified a world as distant as the Orient. There were words that I did not know the meaning of, such as 'concierge' and 'liturgy' and 'remiss', and shards of Latin such as '*in media res*' and 'apropos', which came easily to them and were used to communicate, as they said, '*inter nos*'. There were obscure words which, at the close of each day, I scribbled down in my notebook:

heuristic, fusillade, colophon, aplomb, aperçu, recidivist. I felt in fact like the man in Kafka's parable who, before he can even step into the street, must first of all make his own shoes, cut and sew his own shirt and trousers, and so on. He labours, this man, just to attain the starting point from which others set off, after having been dropped off by a driver.

For Ollie and Will, it was essential to wear your learning lightly, as if learning were effortless and free of labour, something they imbibed along with their mother's milk (unless of course they had a wet nurse). This is, I think, peculiar to the English. In England, everything is stained by class and bears its accent, and the way an individual 'wears' his or her learning is always also a sign of relative distinction and endowment. Or the lack thereof. Someone who wears their knowledge in too cumbersome a fashion, someone who betrays the fact that their knowledge was only won through hours at the workbench, and armed with a pile of dictionaries and encyclopaedias, will be viewed as a pitiful and comical figure. As, no doubt, was I. Everything in fact which shows signs of labour, of the sweaty origins of what is now taken for granted, the vials or barrels of sweat from which insouciant privilege grew and prospered: that must be hushed up, and it is hushed up by scorn and social embarrassment. An autodidact at an aristocrat's table might as well be exposing his belly or hairy arse. I wore my learning, such as it was, like a trench coat on a summer's day. While they peppered their conversation with casual Latin and French, or Shakespeare, I used words like 'adventitious', rescued from the obscurer pages of the thesaurus. But Ollie and Will found such lexical peculiarities endearing and a sign of 'English eccentricity', which was in any case marked as vaguely aristocratic and therefore familiar and recuperable.

I came to Oxford determined to reinvent myself and annul what I had been. I did not mind doing this, for I saw that I had been as riddled with error, a hive of error from which I had thankfully escaped due to an intuition, precisely, that I could be someone else. I desired only to be faithful to that intuition and to recreate myself in accordance with it, just as a writer seeks fidelity to a single insight or affect out of which a whole novel grows. But the mistake I made of course was at first to imitate these others, the Wills and Ollies, who spoke of things 'risible' and 'superlative'. And so I peppered my conversation with such Latinate words and Latin phrases. For it seemed that these words and phrases were themselves not only the signs of intelligence, but like small pastilles of an intelligence which could only be released by sucking on these words and ingesting them. But it was Julia who taught me what I already should have known and at some level already did: that many different idioms, vocabularies, dialects and accents can serve as conducting rods for the intellect, and that Ollie's mode of expression or Will's did not indicate a calibre of mind but only a grade of cultural capital. For my days at Oxford would doubtless have taken a predictable trajectory for someone of my background, a trajectory of imitation and rebuff, of overzealous imitation compensating for prior exclusion. Except in my case this trajectory was in fact intercepted by Julia.

I met Julia at MacGregor's Marxism and Literature seminar. Julia was a graduate at Linacre College, and introduced me to a number of other postgraduates, such as Carvell, Nicos and Alex the philosophers, Alice the Yeats specialist, Grainne the anthropologist and Raphael the economist. She helped me with the pronunciation of certain thinkers, such as Barthes, which I had always pronounced to rhyme with hearths, and Althusser, which

I rhymed with 'abuser'. Thus was I spared a hundred or more false steps by Julia... I had never, likewise, before meeting Julia, tasted, or even heard of, avocados. She once pointed to one in a bowl on her table: 'I've a spare avocado if you want it.' I stared at this dinosaur egg, wondering how I should cook it. It was at hers I first ate lentils and hummus too; nor in fact had I eaten pasta other than tinned spaghetti... When today I open the spices in the cupboard or the fridge I am often reminded of Julia, the smell of garlic, paprika, Italian herbs, fennel, Parmesan, thyme... I associate these smells with that house on Walton Street where I first smelled them, and they are in turn capsules filled with my emotions I felt back then, awe and wonderment, a sprinkle of infatuation, a dream called 'Oxford' clothing every contour and cranny of the real. Julia introduced me in fact to all these things, as well as to a number of philosophers and thinkers, such as the great Deleuze and the pudgy but cerebral Adorno. More importantly, she facilitated an introduction to myself and what she herself named my 'inner volcano'.

I remember with bright exactitude those long evenings and nights in Linacre College Common Room, me and Julia talking, and her listening to my wounds and thoughts with her infinite patience and the pale infinite vigilant blue of her eyes; a blue reliably there when the clouds and torrential rains had passed; and yes, we sat there talking and laughing, laughing and crying, till the morning sun told us it was time for bed.

To describe Julia, I have often used the phrase 'voluptuous pulchritude', rather than 'beauty'. Although I am drawn to androgyny, to androgyny as something that points beyond the institution of the heterosexual Couple, I do not necessarily or only mean physical androgyny, for as far as the physicality of women is concerned, I am happy to announce that I am attracted only to the buxom, the rounded, the proudly extruded and jutting, the protuberant, to arcs and curves. There are others, of course, the overwhelming majority in this particular cultural and historical province, drawn to the chiselled, the slender, the petite, the so-called 'trim' and 'toned' – all qualities and attributes which, historically, have not been marked and numbered as Female, have not been attached to the name of Woman. Only now, in our peculiar times, have these qualities been reassigned, just as those older and lovely attributes, celebrated in luminous colour, in oil and acrylic, up until the latter half of the twentieth century, have been marked as negative, and 'fat' is now coded as 'disgusting' and superfluous by an overarching cultural apparatus that most people salute and obey willy-nilly. This was true also of the women who worked in the office and their obsession with weight and diet. The office where, I repeat, I served and squandered ten years, and where parts of my soul were charred or destroyed. I remember those women who talked always of diets, who were so thin as to be X-rays of themselves. They would be blind, these women, to the milky abundance, topped with copper fire, of a Christina Hendricks, the remarkable Bellucci, the Amazonian prowess of an Anita Ekberg, who turned eternal Rome into a backdrop, or indeed any women of substance. But yes, 'voluptuous pulchritude'. 'Pulchritude', people often say, in so far as they are aware of the word, for most are not even aware of the word, and have to be made aware of it, is an odd term for beauty, for it sounds more like disgust, seeming to contain a covert belch, a bubble of rancid air, or at least to conceal, as in a dirty and hidden pocket, the word 'putrid' or even 'putrefaction'. But in any strong attraction there is always a countervailing repulsion, for the simple reason that attraction is always a precursor to transformation. A part of us, the more conservative part, realises that we will be altered, and part of us of course, a part moulded and shaped by habits and repetition, is loath to be transformed. Hence there is always a counterweight. This counterweight is the element of repulsion in attraction, and what we call attraction is in fact the uneasy tension of attraction and repulsion, which is why we are often confused and troubled by attraction where we might expect unidirectional pleasure. Instead, there is a complex and extended movement which illuminates contending parts of our already multiple soul, the conservative and the experimenter, and stirs up our guts and nerves as well. And so it was that part of me, in relation to Julia, was reluctant to cut my moorings, to cede the initiative to a something I could only begin to understand or predict. But I am glad I did, and the person I am now can never return to those moorings, nor do I have much in common with the ingenue I was then, when I started out at Oxford. The person I am now is not repulsed by that earlier self, only embarrassed and amused, impatient and frustrated with him, and altogether glad I left him on the island of late adolescence and sailed off elsewhere across extraordinary seas.

When I was at school, in the musical desert (excepting only The Pogues) of the 1980s, before I had any inkling of going to university, when I was ten or eleven or so, the boy named Tanner tried to befriend me. Tanner, the bully. This I found invasive and intolerable. I have no idea why Tanner tried to befriend me. It may be that he was impressed with my fight with the Lawrence boy on the first day of school. I cannot remember the provocation, but I think it was something about my father. Yes, my father had been seen scooping some horse dung off the road for his garden. 'Your dad shovels shit off the road,' he had announced with confrontational glee. The only legitimate response was to close in on the Lawrence boy demanding an apology, which of course he would refuse, for this was only the ritual overture to violence. A crowd gathered, baying and chanting. I punched Lawrence hard on the nose – a piledriver busting his nose – and he doubled over, covering his face. I have never understood why people bend forward when hit, for, even if they cover their face, it avails their opponent the opportunity of a series of heavy but swift uppercuts. This is what happened with the Lawrence boy, who after being pummelled in the face was soon on the floor in a ball. I could not bring myself to kick Lawrence, for this image, of a boy being kicked on the floor, is one which has always been very present in my mind ever since it happened to me.

In any case, the teacher Ledbury, respected only because he taught woodwork, arrived to break things up. So that might have been why. But anyway, this is what he tried to do, Tanner. He came knocking at the door, asking if I wanted to play out, or 'laik out', as we said then in Yorkshire, a word that I was surprised to find, years later, in *Gawain and the Green Knight*, meaning roughly the same thing. Or he would ask if I wanted to listen to an album he'd bought by Whitesnake, to show me that the tongue of the serpent on the album cover was meant to 'look like a fanny'. I didn't want to do these things or to take pleasure in these things. He showed me a lighter he'd obtained, a golden lighter, like contraband or a talisman of delinquency. I told my father, who asked where he'd got the lighter, what he was doing with it, why I was hanging round with him. I said I wanted nothing to do with him, but that he was a 'scary character', a phrase I'd overheard elsewhere. Tanner asked me if I'd 'go with Paula

Simpson' because she 'fancied me', but I had no interest in Paula Simpson, the world of which she was part, a world of gangs gathered in the damp air under the concrete bridge, spitting on the floor and smoking, of denim jackets embroidered with band names and smelling of patchouli oil, of mouths moving and clacking with chewing gum, of loitering by the 'chippy' and the off-licence, big plastic bottles of sweet cheap cider. Paula Simpson was in no sense separable from this world, she was in fact only a component of this world, one of the vessels through which it was expressed, as I then thought. I wanted nothing to do with any of this.

After his botched attempt to befriend me, Tanner pinched an ornament from our garden, and also threatened me thereafter until my father went round to his house with an old friend from the police, an intervention which perhaps saved me from suffering the same fate as a boy called Nigel Ruddley. Nigel Ruddley, with his blue eyes and pale skin; poor Ruddley with his slender awkward body and his brown curly hair, sat on a step reading Dickens. Tanner couldn't bear it. The sight of the book, the boy sat reading a book at playtime: he couldn't bear it. Like the glass of wine that I held in my hand on the lads' night out, an anomaly in the picture. It made the picture wobble and the viewer disorientated. There are people who instantly move, with open childlike hands, towards these anomalies, who on seeing these anomalies see also a window leading through to a different landscape entirely, who on seeing these anomalies extend their curiosity and sympathy outward. And there are those, like Tanner, who seek to restore the picture to its everyday banality. 'What you doing, reading a fucking book, Ruddley, it's break time, you daft cunt'. Ruddley would look down, trying to hide in *Oliver Twist*, fixing himself to the page, willing himself a Victorian urchin rather than being here among prefabricated classrooms in the late twentieth century. 'What are you reading?' 'It's Charles Dickens.' 'Charles Dickhead? Who the fuck's that?' 'He's a nineteenth-century novelist.' 'Well it's the twentieth century now, Ruddley. Thought you were supposed to be brainy.'

Tanner wanted nothing less than Ruddley's removal from the picture. But there he was: Slim, Milkybar-pale limbs, so delicate, as were the eyelashes, too, so long and bashful. The stammer made flesh. He seemed drawn with a pencil, like a sketch of some other boy, or a lanky girl, as I thought then. 'A lanky streak of piss,' said Tanner. Awkward and gangly, yes, like a gazelle, a foal, lines and angles bumping and collapsing. Until he started running. Because Ruddley was also the fastest cross-country runner in the school. A few seconds to kick in, the body collecting its long parts, then suddenly graceful and in his element. I am familiar with this; I learnt it much later. At some point you begin to glide. There is a kind of stillness, a stillness within motion, attained and maintained only though motion, and the runner runs to keep this stillness in place. Carrying not only this stillness, but also your solitude that no one could reach. That's what you do, you scoop up your solitude inside yourself and run with it, a precious numen, you take flight, use speed to exit *their* territory and enter your own. The landscape shakes and blurs and bumps but you *stay in place*, stay in place whilst moving. Ruddley was an albatross, flying over fields, beyond us. Tanner rubbery and flatulent at the back, smelling of half-cooked onions.

But in the changing room afterwards Ruddley was back on the deck of the ship. It was all about flaws and blemishes, penises and pubic hair. Initially those with pubic hair, myself included, were ridiculed, the early bloomers, then gradually of course the late exceptional baldies. Ruddley was in the latter category and so had to wait for his torment, the waiting itself a torment. At lunch, he was surrounded by Tanner and his pot-bellied salty mariners stinking of farts and tobacco and stale sweat.

One must understand what the lunchbox is and what it represents. It is the introduction into school-space of your home, a little Tupperware cube or cuboid of home, revealing the secrets of home, unsealed and exposed to view, to brusque and malicious judgement. Tanner would sit opposite Ruddley in the canteen, staring at him and repeating his name in a slow mocking voice: 'Rud-leeee, Nye-gel Rud-leeee'. Ruddley would turn hot with discomfort, looking down at the table, or sometimes murmur 'Please leave me alone', which was fatal of course: 'Leave you alone? That's not very nice when I've come to talk to you, is it? No need to be rude is there Rud-leee, or should we call you Rude-lee, Nigel Rude-lee. I'll see you under the bridge later and we can have a talk about manners.' Tanner would grab one of Ruddley's sandwiches and take a bite before spitting it out: 'Fucking hell, that is disgusting Ruddley. What's in there Ruddley, some of your dad's fucking knob cheese? Tell your mum her sandwiches are fucking rank.' And so on, drip drip on Ruddley's head, day after day. I was reminded of this years later, watching *Reservoir Dogs* and the torturing of the policeman, the torturer smiling and dancing, and the scene dragged out so long that, as a spectator, you just want someone to put a bullet through the torturer's head, which Tim Roth obligingly does. But Ruddley, back then, had no Tim Roth, and Tanner kept singing and cutting. Over years and years.

Of course, when you are at school, as a young child, it seems like this is the whole world and there is no exit, a world of total capture. This is not a result of the rules imposed by the headmaster and the staff. 'The Teacher', like 'The Police', is in any case a stock authority figure, and part of a pantomime image, a lazy and uncritical idea of what constitutes authority. People who want to show their arse to the Teacher and the Policeman are blind to the actual sources and forms of authority; to the multifarious ways in which authority and power secure our collaboration. The petit-totalitarian world of the schoolyard does not take the form of a law forbidding things, such as, for example, 'do not run in the corridor' and so on, laws which incite, almost mechanically, petty forms of disobedience. No, it is a petit-totalitarianism of the pupils. It urges and demands predictable enjoyments, copied and borrowed from the pack. At my school, anyone not wearing Doc Marten boots and high-waisted trousers was automatically suspect and would be interrogated about their clothing; similarly, people who did not like the designated bands, fashions, the latest gadgets, the latest games, certain new slang phrases, TV programmes; those who refused to hear in Ken Dodd's song 'Happiness' the words 'A penis' or denied that this was the 'real meaning' of the song; those who did not perform the agreed forms of disobedience – flicking rubber bands in class or smoking under the bridge. These laws, demanding enjoyment, and excommunicating those who refuse, are far more effective than the kind of laws signposted and enforced by the teacher. And it is no accident that Tanner's cronies, the petty rebels, the smokers under the bridge, have all grown up to be not the great creative rule breakers but the wife-and-two-kids, nine-to-five conformists, the money chasers who left school at sixteen.

My intuition, although I had no proof at this stage, nothing tangible, was that there had to be other worlds and different kinds of people. This was my thin hope, my pale light under the door. This intuition was in part due to Janet Bolton-Smith. Janet Bolton-Smith was the only girl, and in fact the only person, at my school with a double-barrelled name. She also had what, I would learn, was a London accent, even if the word 'London' meant something only very vague, a mere mist of associations. I had never heard such an accent before. What did it mean? Nobody knew. Bolton-Smith with her London accent and her double-barrelled name. Disturbing the equilibrium of what existed with a perverse difference. At some point I was told she 'fancied' me. The children used this word, 'fancied', without any clear idea of what it might entail or where it might lead. They used the word 'fancied' to tease and mock someone. They, we, were flirting with language. This is what children do of course. They first flirt with language before getting involved. She was skinny, Bolton-Smith, and one day came to school with a bleggy eye, which is to say she had a stye on her eye. At our school, this constituted an event. One of our friends arriving at school with a bleggy eye. A circle of children around her. It is so long since I have used that word, 'bleggy', or heard it. Perhaps when my dad came down to London to interview for a minor job at the Ministry of Defence's housing department. Arriving off the train with a bleggy eye. 'Just my luck,' he'd said. He didn't get the job.

That's by the by. All I want to say for the moment is something else. It is this. The existence of Bolton-Smith, with her name and her London accent, was perhaps the first time I became aware of other worlds, and not simply what, in simpler parlance, might be called other parts of the country. Let me explain. When I was a kid, a five-year-old kid, we'd make trips every so often into Town, by which was meant the centre of Bradford. We'd park in the C&A car park, and walk down through C&A onto Broadway, as it was called, the only Broadway in the world.

We'd go shopping, or I'd be taken along with those that shop, to Rawson Market, which no longer exists, for a 'nice bit of brisket'. But then there was a time when my father had to get some particular thing. I can't remember what it was. But it was unavailable in Bradford. Imagine!! This itself was a source of wonder. And so we had to drive to 'Huddersfield', and park somewhere in 'Huddersfield'. As we drove into Huddersfield, I realised suddenly that there was more than one Town. This was a total revelation. That there was another Town to ours. I don't know what I expected 'Huddersfield' to be, but certainly not another Town. Similar in so many ways to ours, but clearly also different. And only here could Dad purchase his whatever it was. Special hiking boots perhaps. The world of Bradford had been complete, it had no circumference, no outside. And then, out of nowhere, the fact of Huddersfield. How did I view Huddersfield? As a parallel world rather than simply outside Bradford, if that makes sense. As a kind of double, a doppelgänger. Something uncanny. But Bolton-Smith was a visitor from the proper Outside. With her name and her accent. For these things, names and accents, belonged to the world of the symbolic. A different language is above all the ambassador of a different, not merely a parallel, world. How lightly she wore it, how elegantly she carried it, this Other world.

And no, I did not 'fancy her', whatever that meant, but part of me desired the world she came out of, in so far as she came from the Outside, although where it was, how I might get to it and who would show me, I didn't know. I knew nothing, then, of the thunder over Amalfi, of tanned old booksellers on the banks of the Seine, of the beers of Prague sipped in secret taverns, of silent walks by the Cherwell at daybreak, nothing of the reassuring existence of Italy, of white clouds tumbling over the dark cliffs of Thira, of a skeletal Blanchot glimpsed in the Place des Vosges, of that late-night café on the Rue Mouffetard, its tables round and gold as planets, of the wild cats of Greece lying patiently under the table, the insect hum on the dry hillsides; I knew nothing, then, of mizzle and burning turf in quiet County Sligo; nothing of poetry or love, in fact, and nor did I have a pantheon of poets and writers to help me or converse with. I did not have a language in which to speak and write, thrown together out of books, blood and silence, part armour plating, part conducting rod for rage and beauty, this language with which I rendered extinct my earlier incarnations. I had instead, back then, only an artificial sky, an orange sky, starless, created by suburban street lamps, so that looking out of the window at night you would see only this orange sky like a great plastic sublunar shell above the estate; I had only rows of terraced houses, and the playing fields opposite the wool-combing mill, I had only a living room thick with cigarette smoke and the buzz of the constant TV, I had only Nescafé and Angel Delight, I had an estate populated by Tanners and Simpsons, but no one to guide me through it, no way out, no air, no escape. No escape.

It would have been consolation at this stage to know that Oxford and Julia awaited, with Julia as my guide. For I can say that we each need a Virgil to guide us not only through the ginnels and alleys of hell but also across the Elysian Fields, which is how I viewed Oxford. Oxford, which in my memory is always soaked in sunshine and basks in eternal summer, a place where that great 'unimaginable summer' comes to rest and stretch its limbs beneath weeping trees, has a serenity which is, in part, bought with privilege, exclusion and symbolic violence. Granted. But that is not unique to Oxford, and there is no part of our world not compromised by injustices and inequalities, handed down and made normal by custom and language, from generation to generation, along with the burden of collective guilt which can be appeased only by self-justifying ideologies. Beneath the lush and peaceful forest lies the vanquished village, abandoned too soon and forgotten. And while we might inhale the fresh and vegetal air, and listen to chirping birds, elsewhere the refugees linger and pine by the shore and long for their no-longer-home, until they die and rot unburied.

So, there are very few innocent pleasures. And the silent courtyards of Oxford, where stooping birdlike dons converse, where gilded undergraduates read or chatter, is a silence bought with exclusion. And I am perfectly aware that my image of Oxford is doubtless nine parts myth, an image made of stone, some magnificent statuary chiselled and then set singing by the incipient lights of the imagination. I cleave to it regardless, for it plays a necessary role in my mental life or the topography of my soul, as does the hell of Belsham, and the wet orange lights of Bradford, and other places besides, turned by time into mere markers and symbols of the part they played in one's evolution, for ultimately do we turn all we have lived and touched into symbols. And all the places we have loved are also the name of an idea and a desire to which we swear fidelity. The Idea called Oxford, the idea called Paris, the Idea called Rome. Each of these places, these cities, etch this idea in our minds, with our own loving connivance, of course; they deposit this Idea, this Desire in our minds, which we could not have done ourselves, and we must always remain true to these Ideas which are also places, and they in turn will help to orientate us at times of loss or times of despair.

Cahun was always on his phone. 'We need a digital transformation manager.' Fuck off, fuck off, I muttered, you can't have one, now shit the fuck off. 'It would be great if you could get back to Google today to fix the cross-domain tracking...' It would be great if you could get back to your fucking office, you fucking tedious twat. He was a businessman of that particular sort, the sort that talks about 'concepts', even though what he talked about had nothing to do with concepts at all, only with dressing things up in such a way that they could be marketed, or 'monetised' as he also put it. This is an abuse of the word 'concept' and its philosophical pedigree, an attempt to requisition the vocabulary of philosophy, to borrow its nimbus of rigour and seriousness, but then turn it towards a different and nefarious purpose. This is what he talked about, various 'concepts' and 'propositions', once he had finished blathering about travel. Of course, I only ever heard his side of the conversation, which was, nonetheless, probably about 80% of it. One day I politely asked him to keep the volume down. He frowned, then turned his back towards me and hunched his shoulders, like a petulant hedgehog. 'Sorry mate, some guy's on my case,' he whispered into the phone. When he finished his call, he barely acknowledged my presence. People assume, in all kind of casual and ostensibly innocuous ways, that they can treat other people like nobodies, that other people who are not part of their gang or caste can be dismissed or are invisible. We might call these incidents microhumiliations. And the more the perpetrators escape punishment, the worse they become.

I am, I admit, and I have always been, susceptible to injury. Not physical injury, and in fact I have a perdurable toughness and have never suffered significant injury, with the exception of a smashed elbow when I fell from my bicycle in Oxford, and minor contusions inflicted by my father. As for the Oxford incident, a syringe was stuck in my elbow to drain the blood, and the acute pain — almost pleasurable in its sheer extremity — was masked with alcohol. As for my father, nothing was ever visible really. But in any case, I am talking about those other kind of injury, emotional and psychological, which are not 'merely metaphorical', caused by lack of courtesy and active contempt. The graze or puncture wounds caused by speech rather than objects or objective violence, when one person addresses another as a thing of no worth. There are a small number of such incidents over the years which have affected me and which have lodged firmly in my mind and formed lesions or scars which can easily be opened again and freshly bleed.

I remember very clearly one time I was travelling back from Oxford to Bradford on the train. I had a heavy cold and was sniffing and sniffling, full of phlegm. Across the aisle was a man not much older than me, in an expensive suit, with papers spread out before him. He kept trying to buttonhole me with a bold stare, some sort of high-velocity fuckstare that he was, doubtless, accustomed to firing at people who annoyed him. 'Excuse me,' he barked. 'You're making some disgusting noises. Why don't you get a tissue?' I was very taken aback of course. You don't expect to be addressed in this way on public transport. 'Thanks for pointing that out,' I replied, with the faintest smack of sarcasm. But of course, he wasn't just 'pointing something out'. He was very far from 'pointing something out', just as most acts of 'pointing something out' are also acts of another sort entirely. He wished to *posit* me as an object of disgust. Words are always also the channels for certain forces; they are never quite innocent. In this case, his words were the *expression* of a desire to humiliate. He was obliged, in attempting to realise or execute this desire, to use socially acceptable language. He did not quite succeed in this of course, in that the word 'disgusting' was too strong, and like a fumarole giving egress to his supercilious rage, which was a class-rage, that had passed through the collective class intestine before exiting his mouth in all its poisonous and smelly arrogance.

All, or almost all human exchange, is of this kind, whereby the ostensible meaning is the outward face of a force or power which has to do with positioning and positing. People are too busy with such positing and counter-positing to actually say anything. Only when we speak to each other as human beings of equal worth will we actually communicate. This is why we have poetry; this is why we have literature. Poetry accommodates and shelters the frail human being, the being who creates and suffers. This being finds refuge within the den made of language as she does not in the callous world. Poetry therefore always has a political function, insisting on this fragile human being (who we all in fact are) against the forgetting of that being, the corrosion of the frail and suffering being by politics, by money, by institutional and symbolic violence. People who feel assailed and battered by the world, its stupidities, hatreds and injustices, go, instinctively and unarmed, to poetry, knowing they will find there love, justice and wisdom. And political regimes of a despotic sort always want to crush poets, because poems insist on a corner of flesh that can't be reached by power, the grain of sand that Satan cannot find. All poetry and all literature are political merely by existing, for they posit nothing but this common humanity. But what people fear, above all, is an unfortified encounter with another human being, face to face, without symbolic support or guarantor. They would rather shit themselves, just like this man on the train.

In this case, the man, to whom I assigned the name Roberts, or rather to whom I *now* assign the name Roberts, in telling this story, wished to posit me as the source object of his disgust. It is clear, and commonly agreed, that 'disgusting' objects are of a certain category: things that are excremental, various forms of discharge and disjecta, things that have irreversibly exited the body – the guts of a squashed bird, a steaming pile of faeces, or the clot of cold blood I saw one morning in a public urinal near Beak Street. This is what the man was invoking in speaking to me, grouping me with such things, treating me, very precisely, as a piece of shit. What is more, of course, he was asking me to go along with this, as when someone says 'Pick up the litter, vermin', where to respond by merely picking up the litter is, by that exact same stroke, to posit oneself as vermin. In my case, to respond with 'Sorry, yes, I'll get a tissue', would, of course, be to accept my status as an object of disgust, to define myself as such. This was, in fact, one of those microsadisms that people get away with, or assume they can get away with: forcing people to collude in their own humiliation. Any such person, a person who posits another as an object of disgust, is the very worst kind of person, and the fact that he (it often is he) operates within the law only makes worse his crimes. For the worst crimes are those committed *within* the law. The law is a high perimeter fence, beyond which there are acts of murder and theft, fraud, embezzlement and vandalism. The fence has many policemen, guards, sentinels, wardens, beadles, bureaucrats, judges and so forth. It's no surprise that few people venture beyond the fence. They are threatened and penned in. But inside the boundary of 'What is Permitted', people can do as they please. There is no law against laughing at the beggar who asks for money, ignoring the calls of the friend in mental distress, meeting someone's evident pain with cold logic or polite condescension. These are the true crimes, and such a criminal was this Roberts fuckdog on the train.

After my brief reply, I blushed and blew my nose, but the barb was still in my side, and after his words had bubbled in my belly for a while, my anger rose and reddened, my skin blushed and tingled, to the extent that I could no longer stay seated, and I rose and left the carriage. Of course, it was not possible to kick him in the goolies or break his nose. I walked instead to the buffet car. I ordered a black coffee: 'Extra hot please, extra large.' And, as I returned to my seat, I tripped – or 'tripped', I should say, I took a tumble, and the scalding coffee darkened his belly, his papers, his crotch. He squealed like one of Circe's pigs, his face a blazon of pain against the rushing light. Then, such a furore of shouting ensued, with 'You fucking arsehole, for fuck's sake, you idiot' and so on, all in his clipped posh voice. I rolled out the expected apologies, offered to call for assistance, a few clockwork phrases to serve as an alibi. I was tempted to use the word 'copious' for a laugh. He continued shouting and bawling, something about suing me and so forth. Just a wall of sound really; I wasn't listening. He took with him his Mulberry bag to the toilet and returned in tracksuit bottoms and a T-Shirt, stripped now of his symbolic integument, defeathered, ashamed to be merely human. He asked for my address, which was an act of laughable imposture, as if he were the official registering the event, as if it had to be listed by him before it existed, before its meaning solidified. Anyway, I gave him the address of my doctor in Broad Street. When he rang the number, and heard the receptionist, there would be a dawning realisation of the wool pulled over his eyes, which would also be, at the same time, a subtle adumbration of my smiling face looking down on his, as Ali looked down on Liston.

My actions in this anecdote might be thought 'extreme', but I had only caused temporary anger and pain. I had scalded his skin, ruined his paperwork and parboiled his bollocks, whereas he had asked that I deny my humanity. The two things are not comparable. When he left the train, I knocked on the window and he turned to see me laughing, as one might laugh with a friend, reminiscing about the old days. I will always remember that train journey, in great detail, and will always be able to unspool it, frame by frame in my mind, but not only because of this small victory against rudeness. No, I had been called to Bradford to repair, my mother perhaps thought, my father's mind.

The aetiology of my father's breakdown was ultimately a political as much as a medical one. My father had worked at the council for several years, after leaving the police. He loved working at the council. 'There was never a day,' he told me, 'never a day when I thought "oh no, it's work this morning".' But then, at the council, my father was put in charge of the latest round of 'Compulsory Competitive Tendering', even though he privately stood opposed to it. Like his father, he was a socialist, and thus had no interest in introducing CCT, which, he said, albeit in different words, was a Trojan horse for the creeping privatisation of the country's assets, a view which was of course afterwards vindicated, as also demonstrated by the catastrophic deregulation of the bus services.

Whereas my father had loved working for the council under previous administrations and was celebrated as a character of a kind that no longer exists, henceforth he hated work and was forced to implement, or help implement, policies which he detested. The introduction of numerous regulations and directives would, in the end, drive out all such characters, for such people can only thrive when not stifled by rules and procedures, and where there is a corresponding trust in people's good sense. But such trust no longer exists, and I am certain also that no such characters now work for the council, which has doubtless been repopulated with officious bureaucrats and middlemen. This has of course happened at every level of society, most obviously in politics, where nobodies, phrase-makers and intellectual eunuchs such as David Cameron have superseded the likes of Denis Healey and Keith Joseph – an intellectual heavyweight and a borderline nutcase respectively.

I have no idea why my father was put in charge of Compulsory Capitalistic Tendering – as I prefer to call it – by his bosses, but these bosses must in part bear responsibility for what happened, and when years later, but not enough years later, they appeared at my father's funeral, I spoke to them with cold politeness. One of them said to me that my father had the reputation within the housing department of being a shrewd enforcer and a 'maverick' who, by hook or by crook, would 'deliver results', with limited resources. They perhaps imagined that these qualities could simply be transferred to another kind of task entirely, as businessmen are supposed to lend their expertise variously to a mining company or a restaurant chain, without any particular interest in coal or food. But my father's gifts were bound up in the particular world of housing like the proverbial fish in water, which is not a bad thing and in fact a good thing, and his bosses thoughtlessly removed him from the medium in which he moved and breathed. He was of course aware of his reputation and, like too many men, fatally attached to it, no doubt, so that this reputation cannot be taken away without also taking with it a pound of flesh and nerve.

He was removed from his office in Keighley and relocated to a 'fancy office' in Forster Square. The workload was disagreeable and too great, he explained when he visited me in Oxford, unaccompanied, five months into my doctorate, in March 1994. This was an alarming development in itself, I thought at the time, for he had always come down with my mother and at my mother's suggestion. But I had a phone call late one night, telling me he was travelling down for a conference (which was, I think in retrospect, made up) and could we meet for a beer. In fact, we went to the old Indian restaurant on Walton Street, where we had the place mostly to ourselves except, oddly, for the Russian agronomist from college, eating alone by the window. Over dinner my father tried to explain his predicament and showed me a pile of documents written in an idiom 'Dry as old boots', as he put it, as indeed it was. No one with a living soul could read them without undergoing a slow and painful exsiccation. I think he was, without asking explicitly, wanting my help, which I was unable to give him, or at least in the form he wanted.

My father's breakdown, his 'crack-up' (as he once put it), was the kind where everything seizes up. The body and mind, in order to protect themselves, return the bill of demands addressed to them, or 'shut up shop' as my father later put it to me, albeit when talking about something completely different. I remember quite clearly how it started, which was also the start of a distinct period in our lives, mine and my father's, as also of course my mother's. My mother asked me to return home from Oxford because my father was unwell, but she'd explain when I got there, she said. I found a man transformed, sat in a chair on the floor of the ocean. We gently asked him questions, suggested he call in sick. But these gentle questions were doubtless to him like missiles or instruments of torture. 'Nobody, nobody, nobody understands,' he said, breathless. 'Nobody understands.' I can still hear these words, like an incantation, a drum, a heartbeat, a flow of blood. I can still plug into these words very easily and will always be able to plug into these words and to hear these words from my father, which connect immediately with my own heart and revive immediately my father as he was at that moment, unreachably distressed and lost and on the edge of his breakdown. 'I feel like I've been through a washing machine,' he told me. Suddenly I was his confidant, who had never been his confidant. Suddenly I was entrusted with the piece of himself he feared he was losing, a pebble, a small irrevocable pebble in a tobacco tin.

He found himself, like his mother before him, at Highwood mental hospital, which only compounded his illness, having to return to the brutal ground of his mother's incarceration, which was also the antechamber of her death. Shortly after exiting Highwood, she was admitted to hospital and died. Highwood had removed her from life then shunted her to the hospital to die. Highwood, in its antiseptic silence, a silence which is that of a cloth stuffed in the mouth, was for my father an augur of death, a place where – removed from the stream of life and placed in a stagnant backwater – you wait for death to come and from where, it seems, there is no route back. 'Promise you'll get me out of this bloody gulag,' he said. I promised. At the hospital, we found out that he had contemplated ending his own life by driving into oncoming traffic. Only the thought of his family saved him. He told all this to the nurse, with me and my mother present, but looking only at the nurse and speaking only to her. On the way to Highwood he had handed me his car keys, with great earnestness and care, and asked me to look after them.

With my father, the idea had taken hold, many years previously, that there was on his mother's side of the family a 'faulty gene', which had resulted in his mother's breakdown and had now triggered his own. His faulty gene had been activated, he said, and he was 'going crackers' just as his mother had. I could not remove this idea from his head, nor stop his consequent surrender to Fate. Perhaps this was a good thing, whereby he allowed himself to 'go crackers' and ran through the open door and away from the world into childhood. For immediately after the onset of his breakdown, his childhood was suddenly present and the present itself disappeared. He sat in the conservatory and divulged to me many things about his childhood, including the mysterious Blabsy woman, who had looked after him at various times when his mother's mind shut down. The mother would be in the bedroom and Blabsy would step in. This must have been very early on in his life, for my grandfather was then away at war, and subsequently in Palestine. Thus was my grandmother alone with her child and frequently unable to cope so that Blabsy was forced to intercede. Blabsy took him to Peel Park and to Shipley Glen. Meanwhile his mother was in bed. He spoke fondly of Blabsy, who he had never before mentioned, and told me also about his mother's terrible childhood, spent inside silence.

I remember her, that grandmother, only in the stations of her decline. She sat in the chair smoking Woodbines, the ashtray a boneyard of stubs. She liked watching the snooker. That was the only reason they bought a colour TV, my grandparents, so she could watch the snooker. Her hair was white as sea foam. Yet she must have only been in her late fifties then. And only sixty-five when she died of 'complications' following a pitiless sequence of strokes, for our bodies are double agents who betray us to death in the finish. Her father, after the First World War, back in the twenties, inherited some money – 'A lot of money in them days,' my father told me, also after his breakdown – but gave up working and went on the drink. He squandered it all on drink. Her mother, who'd come over on the boat from West Belfast, an Irish Catholic, swore never to speak to him, and kept her promise. She would write notes, passed through her daughter. 'Tea on the table', 'We need some more milk', 'I'm off to bed'. A go-between in a phantom marriage. Silence like deep water pressure filling each room and portal. And she carried within her, I thought, a mutation of that same silence.

I have always thought that my father inherited not a faulty gene but this silence, and that I had as well, like some bubble in the soul, or like an heirloom that grows stranger and more stubborn as it's passed down. I remember, also, the silence inside our house. The light bulb shattering silence. I must have been five or six. We were having tea. Tea, as we say in the north, is dinner, or supper. Although typically earlier than supper. Around 5.30 in our case, when my dad got home from work. But anyway, we were sat around the table having tea. It was a cold dark day in December, not long before Christmas. We were eating sausages; I remember that much. Their glistening greasy skins. And mashed potatoes with brown sauce. Then the light bulb exploded. We had to pick the bits of glass out of our food and carry on eating. I always wondered if I might have swallowed a shard of glass. If that might have damaged my intestines. On a permanent or ongoing basis. In any case, this is one of the very few memories of my early childhood. Weeing myself on a tiny plastic tricycle. And then the light bulb. I can't remember how old I was. I only remembered this because of Julia's child, William, anyhow. Sat in Café Amato, I thought of it poetically, that is to say, as an image of the silence exploding.

The exploding bulb was implicit in the silence. The silence in which we mostly sat at teatime. As if it was some uneasy truce. Or as if each of us, my mother and me, had been fastened in place by my father's presence. My father brought a new smell into the house when he arrived home. He smelled of 'outside', outside and cigarettes. And this smell was like a chemical agent added to an otherwise innocuous solution. It changed the composition of the room. It created a new volatility. Silence was the best container for this volatility. The air thick with the steam of boiling vegetables. Condensation. The gas fire. All these things more present because of the long stretches of silence. And what few words were spoken by one never crossed into the soul of the other, never reached the inside.

But I do not regret that silence. It incubated monsters, it incubated stories in my head. I populated it with fictions, with imaginary beings of all kinds, and with characters like Bezerk McFraudy, as I called him, with an overhanging front lip, a few tiny hairs, and eyes goggling out of his head. Later, I committed these characters, these monsters, these shapes and shadows to that other silence, the page. As drawings first, and later as writing. And at school, at Shawcross, what I liked most was writing stories. Of course, they fell on deaf ears and sightless eyes. At the end of one story, the Hayes teacher simply wrote 'Is this your own work?' It was a story about a man who travelled to a remote place to get away from the world. He pitched his tent among the bracken. And he was a businessman, I've just remembered, called Stuart Goddard, which was the real name of the pop star Adam Ant of course. So even then I disliked businessmen! But anyway, as he slept, a knife ripped through the side of the tent and a madman chased him over the moors till dawn. Perhaps the madman was modelled on Bezerk McFraudy. 'Is this your own work?' was all she had to say. When I had eagerly awaited her comments. I must say that these words confronted me like a sentence, I mean a judicial sentence. A verdict. And also a nasty graffito defacing my work. I should have been flattered of course; I suppose. But instead, I felt deflated. Instead of excitement or interest only this accusation. This verdict. When a child offers forth a piece of himself and meets only with a judgement. This is a form of cruelty. To another child, less robust, this might have crushed their spirit. But I had always been suspicious of adult verdicts arriving like maledictions to intercept a child's vitality.

Of course, one cannot literally inherit a silence; there is no molecule or gene carrying silence, I know that. Nonetheless, it happened, and it will always be there, like the drifting snow inside the abandoned house. There have been rooms and bedsits too that have been filled with this same airless hush, as for example my last room in Oxford, in the converted public house overlooking the canal in Jericho. A kettle, some bits and bobs in the fridge. The books I could no longer be bothered to read. My desk by the window. The back of the building, facing other backs of buildings. In the dead of night, there was nothing, nothing but the soft music to steer me to sleep and forgetting. Emer, the fragile lunatic, came round that once with a bottle of wine she'd found in a cupboard and a copy of Sylvia Plath. She noted the silence, she was arrested, and perhaps alarmed, by the silence of the room. She inspected my palm criss-crossed with fractures, and this too alarmed her. In any case, in order to populate this silence, I would put on music. Occasionally Satie, for example. A path of notes you can follow, in the dead of night, when the lights in the neighbouring houses have been switched off, one by one, until you are left with something lonely, insistent, gentle, myopic... and in fact mad. A man in a tattered suit, trying to tie his shoelaces in the rain beneath a vast indifferent sky.

That was near what I would call the centre of my illness. For illnesses are often like territories which we enter and cannot then find the way out. In that architect's house in Jericho. The German student next door and his reams of toilet roll. The drunken old man upstairs in the attic, who worked at Ruskin and cooked fatty meats each night downstairs. Every evening the vapours of frying fat, the tiny globules of airborne fat, would reach my room and make me retch, me who was then meat-free, me eating tofu and spinach, me eating miso and grains.

But yes, I had to have the music on, at the edge of audibility, as if the notes were barely afloat on the water of a great calm lake. Often, it had to be Beethoven's late string quartets. Let me say as an aside that I first encountered these extraordinary pieces, written with imagined notes by a deaf man, as a teenager, when I determined to acquaint myself with the great composers, in alphabetical order, as autodidacts typically do. I did not get very far, of course, and even today I listen almost exclusively to Bach, Bartok and Beethoven, although my interest in the letter K led me also to Kurtág and Kodály, and my obsession with Gould, via Bach, also introduced me to Mozart. So, in order to slip into sleep, I would listen to String Quartet no. 132, with that long sonorous introduction, that note neither hope nor despair but a luminous thread that implicates both, a thread that the mind follows, down the fading ladder into the underworld. And every night I would follow it and wake up, at daybreak, abandoned on the sheet, having followed the violin to that same house, and its French doors open onto the lawn. Or I would dream of that silent grandmother, the first of the old ones to die. She appeared as she did in life, sat in the chair smoking Woodbines, the minutes smouldering slowly away. Watching the snooker and drinking tea, except in the dream she was blind. For the dead are always subtly different from the living. And also, the living, sometimes, in the lead-up to death are also subtly different. As for example my father.

Just before he died, my father stopped having Weetabix for breakfast and developed a taste for grapefruit. There was a funny taste in his Weetabix, he said. At first, he tried a different packet, but it was still there, it had been infected with a new taste he found disgusting. It made him switch to grapefruit, which he'd never eaten before or liked. Suddenly he liked grapefruit, after fifty years of Weetabix. This is how death announces itself, in tiny changes, little pin-sized holes in the ordinary fabric, until suddenly one day the whole thing disintegrates. The last time I saw my father alive I addressed him as 'mate'. We were at the train station in Bradford. We'd arrived with moments to spare. There was no time to say goodbye on the platform. We had to say goodbye in the car – before I made a dash for it. And for some reason, when my father said 'Goodbye son', I replied with 'Goodbye mate'. For a long time, it irked me that I said this, for no reason, having never called him 'mate', and that this inexplicable farewell was the last memory of interacting with my father. But it strikes me now that this was perhaps one of those anomalies, those glitches, like the funny taste in his Weetabix. In any case, back then I worked at that shithouse telesales office,

Belsham, and ached with regret at having left Oxford, and longed, even, for the days of my illness, when I worked at that antique and rare bookshop on the High Street, next to Queen's College. Hardly anyone entered. A few old dons would sit in the corner for hours and fill the room with their musty and cloacal breath. That's where I went that night, in my slippers and baseball cap, and read Celan until three in the morning. That's where I went on that marvellous irreplaceable night.

I had started writing a monograph about my father, at Julia's suggestion in fact, when Cahun started appearing at the café more or less every morning. It was crucial to begin this monograph, I felt, after Julia's visit last year, in March, not long before Cameron's second election victory, with her five-year-old child, William. I had forgotten or disavowed childhood, my own in particular and the fact and magic of childhood in general, as we all do. But I was utterly taken aback and almost redeemed by Julia's child, William, and by the rediscovery of childhood, by the force of joy and creativity that childhood *is* before it's colonised. And it was William who was responsible for a very personal revelation. If I, or Julia, said to William 'You're a brilliant little fella' or 'Aren't you clever', he would reply 'No, I'm not a brilliant fella, I am William!!' and 'No, I am not clever, I am William!!' At once I understood this completely. The refusal of the epithets foisted on you by adults. In this refusal of epithets, which I admired, in his stubborn adherence to his own proper name and nothing else, something dawned on me, or some disavowed rivulet rose through the earth, it was this:

Julia, before she left Oxford, in the last days of August 1994, just before my illness, said that I was 'blossoming'. Even as I was flattered, I took this as a kind of command – blossom! – to blossom, a pressure, a directive, and it's true that I did have and do have still a propensity to experience things as directives, orders and judgements. And so, because Julia had spoken of my blossoming, the next time she saw me she would also expect to see the blooms, the flowers, the calyxes and stamens, and yellow powder of pollen, she would expect the arc of that blossoming to arrive in its expected place; and anyway I certainly didn't like it. It has always been the case that if someone says, for example, I am *handsome* or *articulate*, or *radiant*, I experience discomfort, annoyance even, and want to shrug them off, these word-encrustations, for they are unwelcome demands imposed by some alien intelligence which is not just the intelligence of the person issuing the compliment but the whole of Society, society that first of all *owns* these words and uses these words to *recognise* people, where *recognition* is in this sense an act of symbolic violence. It is not that I cannot 'take a compliment' but that I cannot take it *as* a compliment precisely. I experience these words, applied to me, any words that are applied to me, as a foreign substance entering my soul, and my impulse is to hibernate or to rebel.

Of course, this is very childlike. When a child hears a word used to describe her or him, there is always a share of that word owned by the grown-ups. I remember this very well, the grown-ups confiscating part of me and hammering it into a new shape, the shape of *their* grown-up words, the child's image caught in a mirror that is nonetheless turned towards the adults and which the child never sees. You are outside yourself in the word *cute* or *pretty* or *bonny* or *cute* or *cheeky*. All of your experience – which you thought yours – is *in reality* 'cuteness', something the adults know more than the child. This is why children make up nonsense words, to disturb and deny these generalities by which they are seized, in which they scarcely recognise themselves. A child might say that I am not *blossoming* but *blomising*, for example, and I might say the same. This is how children see it, but peculiarly, my blessing and curse, is that I have retained this attitude into adulthood. I could not bear to blossom, it was, so to speak, 'asking too much', and instead I wanted to intercept this blossoming and engender some sort of monster blossom or canker blossom; that was my impulse, to *refuse* blossoming, rather than be eaten up and defined by it. This is how I thought, back then, and I have not completely banished it even today, this strain of thought, and all this crossed my mind after William and Julia went, as well as the thought that perhaps I could not bear to blossom specifically whilst my father broke down; these after all seemed like countervailing movements. And so did I choose, as Julia put it, to bend towards my father. But somehow I now smelt the blossom once more, after William and Julia came.

Everything seemed to hinge on beginning my monograph, without knowing what 'everything' was. Starting the monograph would also begin something new. I didn't know what, of course, because if I did it wouldn't be *properly* new. It would pitch me, this monograph, head first into something new. To write I needed a blank page, a page like newly laid snow, a page that was the external representation of my mind, receptive but full of appetency (a word undeservedly sunk these days). Instead, only two months after starting, the page was soiled with noise and anti-language.

'You take retail,' Cahun was saying. 'Fundamental, fundamental changes in the way people shop. Bricks-and-mortar retail stocks are at rock-bottom... Whole world of retail fundamentally disrupted... It's a competition between online and in-person shopping. But there's only one winner, right. Over in the US, Walmart launched Walmart Labs, it's a whole tech arm... I mean, that whole distinction between technology and non-technology companies is becoming meaningless, right?... Right, right... Think about traditional toy companies, we're working with one at the moment. I mean, you've got toddlers with their parents' iPads and phones... you know, less and less time putting jigsaws together, playing with coloured bricks or dolls and Action Men... What place do analogue toys have today... I mean, these kids have expectations created by tech... so the cutting-edge firms are having to introduce tech into all areas of the business... It's not even a choice, right, if they want to survive... But it's also about marketing, no point in shelling out millions on TV ads when these kids aren't watching TV. My brother's kids... they wouldn't sit down and watch TV... They might have three conversations on the go... they might be watching something on YouTube... These kids aren't even dual-screening, they're multi-screening, let them do the marketing and create the hashtags!... We're in an era of unprecedented innovation... smartphones, apps, cryptocurrency, driverless cars, internet of things, QR codes... Ten years ago most of these things didn't exist, most of the jobs millennials want didn't exist ten years ago, and in ten years' time there'll be jobs that don't exist now... The most important job in any company is going to be CDO, chief digital officer... Look at Uber, look at Amazon, look at Laughing Kangaroo... revolutionised their respective fields...'

This Cahun fellow was, and doubtless by his own confession, an avatar of the digital age and what he called, in one of his Skype conversations, 'the digital revolution', which was, he said, comparable to the Industrial Revolution in its repercussions for the way we think and work and live. Anyone who was unaware of, or not prepared to accede to, the digital revolution, he said, would go under. 40% of the Fortune 500 will sink by 2020, he said, that's just five years away, because they are unable fully to come to terms with the impact of digital on all aspects of their business. Those unable to breathe the spirit of the age will suffocate, he said, albeit in totally different words (especially as the phrase 'spirit of the age' is precisely at odds with the current spirit of the age). 'Look at Nokia,' he burbled, 'massive company, total complacency about smartphones, failed to recognise the increasing importance of software.'

The digitalisation of reality was of course, according to Cahun, irresistible, and our only option was to swim with it or sink and drown. Cahun ran a company called Jabberwock, which I also looked up on 'the internet' (as I still like to call it, holding on to that fogeyish expression): a newly formed, or newly merged, digital consultancy and marketing company. It warned of 'the effect of digital disruption on long established business models', and 'that no company along the whole spectrum of commerce is exempt'. Jabberwock would offer 'innovative and bespoke solutions across your whole digital ecosystem: websites, apps, social media'. The Jabberwock website spoke of 'adding real value' and 'tangible deliverables', of 'transforming strategy into practical execution', of helping people 'navigate today's ever more agile and complex business landscape', of 'geo-targeting' and 'brand awareness', and 'visual identity'. It, Jabberwock, or 'Jabberwank' as I chose to call it, had an 'inhouse specialist team' of 'creatives, digital developers, digital rockstars', various 'specialists who will deliver "Actionable" marketing campaigns...' These individuals, Jabberwock's website said, would help 'increase traffic and engagement rates' and 'deliver innovative solutions'... as well as 'next-generation information and analytics'.

Afterwards I looked up some of these rebarbative terms, such as 'actionable' and so forth, but found only more vacuous jargon. Each jargon term is glossed only by other jargon terms until we return to the first, a kind of lexical 'circle jerk', as they say. In the popular imagination, jargon is associated with academics such as myself, who are thought of as deliberate obscurantists. Well, each tribe, each profession has its terms of art, but as far as jargon goes, the world of business, or so-called business, is the worst offender. Jargon is always an attempt to remove the history and connotation attached to a word. In removing from words their penumbra of connotation, their history, jargon also removes from words their capacity to express, to serve as vehicles for our affects. Jargon always purges affect from the world and as such is always inhuman and a preparation for brutality. Jargon is also almost always an attempt to dress up some highly partisan or alternatively completely banal behaviour in the appurtenance of science and technology, where these are seen as both neutral and inevitable. Developments in science and technology are always accepted as facts of nature. How will we adjust to this new technological development, how will it transform our way of life? Well, how about we just ignore it, how about we choose not to pursue it and direct our energies elsewhere? Let's spend the money on feeding the starving instead. You'll never hear this suggested. That's because both science and technology are seen as beyond discussion and so too is the world of business, whereas the world of business is shit and its terms are shit also. Not only is business jargon shit, but the businessmen who trade and converse in this jargon are also shit, shitheads like this specimen here in the café. Not entirely of course, but once again it *pleases* me to say it.

As for Cahun, it was obvious that his mind had been colonised by business jargon to such an extent that he was now an *ontological businessman*, as I call it. What does it mean? It means that in all spheres, not just the world of business, they see things in business terms and employ business categories, that they see life as a business, and 'business' is the virus infecting their whole experience, like jaundice. This Cahun weasel, for example, I hear him on the phone. He's arranging a get-together for someone's birthday. 'I'll reach out to Scott,' he intones, 'see if he's got a window.' 'I'll push you out of the fucking window,' I whisper, clenching my fist. But yes, this is the problem of course. We increasingly live in a society where all things – whether nubbly or smooth, tall or chubby, leisurely, intemperate, euphoric or catatonic, whether something climbs slowly towards ecstasy or speeds to a splattered denouement – are measured by this single yardstick of business, where the only questions asked are whether something is good for business, imitates business, is compatible with new business, whether the world of business will like it. Everyone, whether they are an academic or a council worker or a theatre director, is asked not only to wear a business hat but to grow a business head in addition to their own, or to have a small business gremlin on their shoulders supervising their activity, monitoring their efficiency, checking whether it's time-efficient to read a book whilst having a shit, so that eventually all of us will be required to carry around with us this tedious apparatchik, all of us will start speaking of 'reaching out' to our friends and referring to our own personalities in terms of 'brands' and USPs, and the world will disintegrate as the fearless racket of business stupidity advances unopposed, as it has already advanced into education.

I spoke to the vice chancellor at Carvell's university, who talked about 'learning outcomes' and told me that the university was very effective in reaching its 'end user'. 'End user?' I asked. It turned out he meant the students. Imagine: the students had been knocked out, gutted and turned into 'end users'. It's beyond all reason and belief. You smile politely of course, in such situations, but in reality there is no end user because there is no 'product', no one who simply 'transmits' this 'product' and, finally, no one who 'consumes' or 'uses' this non-existent product, so that, at every level, the term 'end user' reveals a fundamental failure of understanding and a rodent ulcer of stupidity in the mind of the speaker. If I were a giant, I'd pick him up by the ankles and smash him against a tree, intoning, with each crack of the head, 'Who's the end user? Who's the end user?' until, still with a twinkle of life left in him, he'd weakly croak, 'No one, there's no such thing.' And then I would exit in triumph.

Regarding Cahun, it was certainly true that my animosity also derived from the fact that Cahun summoned the spectre of McCann, the boss of the telesales office where I spent my decade in hell, where I too was a pedlar of meaningless business jargon. McCann, like Cahun, I had turned into the designated Enemy, and it is true that I always seem to discover or elect, in any given situation, a designated enemy. My therapist suggested that

McCann, the Enemy, was also a father figure, a ludicrous suggestion of course, if entirely reflective of the prison house of ideas within which the therapist lives. Everyone and everything is a 'figure' for something and not the thing itself. Even one's own father is in some sense also – or indeed – only a 'father figure'. McCann was simply a dickhead figure, as well as an actual dickhead. An exact marriage of literal and figurative, perfectly illustrating Coleridge's definition of the Symbol in that respect. This individual, McCann, regardless of only being fifteen years my senior, was the very opposite of my father in every respect and particular. A self-important windbag, a 'natty dresser' and so forth, and, like Cahun, an unabashed capitalist, a businessman, indentured and compromised in every pocket of his existence by the world of business, albeit one who had tried to sink his claws into the world of culture. I saw both of them – McCann and Cahun – only as 'businessmen', for after a while it is seldom that we see people in themselves but according to a typology based on our own experience and history. So, for example, if we know three businessmen, we accumulate by degrees an Idea of 'the businessman', so that the fourth businessman we see seems little more than an instance of this Idea. Any features that stand out do so only against the background of this Idea, as anomalous to the Idea, as for example was Cahun's extraordinary delicacy and androgyny – demolished at once by this speech. In the case of McCann, however, there was not one scrap of sweating flesh resistant to the Idea of the Businessman, and this made it easy to hate him.

'Now, I don't know if you like money?' McCann the indigent dog had burbled at my interview for Belsham, back in 1997. 'Nobody's saying it's an end in itself. But frankly I love money. I know you can't say that these days.' Of course, as soon as someone says 'You can't say that these days' you're alerted to the fact that they are some kind of reactionary fuckwit. What they mean is that you can't say it without being challenged. Merely being challenged on their dickhead opinion is to them equivalent to some sort of totalitarian PC interrogation scenario, the brittle-minded morons. Anyway, he continued: 'More importantly, I love the lifestyle it gives me. I don't know whether you're the kind of person who likes Michelin-starred restaurants, fine wines, flying business class, holidays in Tuscany or the Alps... but what you should realise is that this job can get you such a lifestyle... Where did you go for your holiday this year?' 'Cornwall.' 'Cornwall,' he repeated scornfully, ruefully. 'I want to hear Capri, I want to hear St Moritz...' And he started talking about his skiing holiday, occasionally pausing his peroration to shake his head and repeat 'Cornwall!'

Forget the name 'Cornwall', which is all he'd heard, and ranked it accordingly in keeping with some hierarchy of names, wherein 'Cornwall' had less value than 'Tuscany', for example. Walking close to the sea, to the cliff, you are sprayed not by 'Cornwall' but by the cold salty water, one touches not 'Cornwall' but the algae on the wet rock, and one is dazzled not by 'Cornwall' but by the big blue luminous sky or by the great grey ladders of rain falling from on high, the concentric circles of light moving across the waters, the swell and crash of implacable waves, none of which this dummy could hear or comprehend. McCann was in fact someone who never touches actual things but only their monetary tag.

I remember he showed me a Samuel Beckett manuscript he'd bought at Christie's. He thought I'd be impressed. He told me he'd bought it as an investment. He would sell it a decade down the line when it had 'accrued value'. It existed for him only as a promise of money. The smell, the touch, the specificity of inscription, the snail trail left by an extraordinary mind, the odour and watermark of history... these meant nothing. Only sometime later would I explain some of this to him, at my disciplinary hearing for a different matter entirely, the scene also of my sudden resignation. 'You see things only in terms of money,' I would explain, 'and assume that money – not nouveau riche money but a supposedly more "discerning" money – always wears certain clothes, namely the skiing holiday, the vintage wine, the first edition, whereas in reality,' I would explain to him, 'there is nothing to separate you, McCann, from the youth spending a packet on a pair of trainers fashioned in third-world degradation, not of course to do any running, but only to signify money, to walk around with £200 strapped to his feet. Such people, who see things only in terms of money,' I would explain to him coldly, 'present company of course included, are ripe for the assassin's bullet, the peremptory ambush of quick bony fists, the massy and spiked hammer of Justice coming down hard on the crown of the head.'

It was also the case that McCann's wife was on the books at Belsham and received a salary despite having never set foot in the office. McCann's wife was nominally an HR administrator, but of course did no administration of any kind, and her 'employment' was a ruse to pay less tax on McCann's part, a ruse used by many businessmen of course, employing their wives and daughters and sons and husbands in purely nominal roles in order to pay less tax, to ensure that less money is made available for kidney machines or social housing, for example, to withhold money from the homeless or ill and give instead to a spouse or indigent offspring.

Businessmen are always trying to avoid tax and lower labour costs, and can no more stop doing this – to return a Larkin quotation to its proper object – than a rat with electrodes attached to its brain can stop giving itself an orgasm, even preferring this to food. Businessmen, such as this McCann, are of course always threatening to leave the country if taxes or labour costs go up, businesses are always invoking this trivial and childish blackmail of 'relocating'. As soon as the election campaign starts, they start packing their bags, packing their undies and shirts, their suit collection, ready to scuttle off, ready to phone the estate agent, so they can sell up and move out. Some of course already have, such as the manufacturer of turbocharged sewing machines or whatever the fuck it is he makes, various rocket-propelled domestic appliances supposedly created through 'science' and selling themselves as representatives thereof, whereas in fact no one needs a rocket-propelled 1000 cc kettle or whatever it is this man manufactures, or rather his near-slaves manufacture, whilst he sits laughing and drinking champagne. This man has relocated so as to exploit the cheap labour available overseas. As they all do. These so-called great businessmen upon whom the whole country depends, supposedly, as we are repetitively told, our collective fate in their hands, have in fact no allegiance to this country but only to whichever country provides them with the cheapest labour, irrespective of course of the cost in terms of human degradation and misery. But I invite you to feel how cathartic it is, in response to business's provocations and childish threats, to say simply 'Fine, fuck off and leave. Pack your bags and fuck off to Malaysia.'

He was always badgering me, this McCann cretin, to go to the theatre. 'Do you fancy a night at the theatre? We should do a night at the theatre' and so on. I resisted these invitations for as long as it was possible to resist. Eventually I capitulated. I took him to see *Endgame* at the Donmar Warehouse. I *inflicted Endgame* on him. The 2004 production, with the great Gambon playing Hamm and some other man, a bandy and lithe comedian, playing Clov. When the play ended the audience was silenced. I had never witnessed, nor have I since, an audience so reduced to silence after a performance, and I imagined, with good reason, that the imposition of silence on this audience was exactly what Beckett would have wanted, as if the whole of *Endgame* was simply a machine to shut these people up and rob them off their waffle.

McCann too of course was briefly silenced, but once outside he resumed bloviating, like the proverbial fish returning to water. He wanted to 'talk about the play', or rather he wished to engage in the activity 'talking about the play', the middle-class signature activity known as 'talking about the play', just like 'having a night at the theatre' and other such middle-class signature activities, whereby one is merely signalling that one is middle class. They shit themselves, the middle classes, in case they might emerge from the theatre with nothing to say about the play, and waste much of their time in the theatre thinking of things to say so that, afterwards, they can replace the play with their jejune middle-class summary. Had McCann any genuine interest in the play, or any real sympathy with the play, he would, out of respect, and to allow it to sink in, have simply shut the fuck up. The only valid and serious response to this play, the only real 'interpretation', would have been to preserve that unbroken arc of silence extending from the last note of the play to the initial notes of sleep.

He said, McCann, that this was a 'fairly punishing night at the theatre', a stock phrase of course but exactly right in this instance. For it was designed to punish people like him, to inflict upon him something akin to what was inflicted on Hamm and Clov. 'I don't like Beckett's view of the world,' he whined. 'I don't accept Beckett's view of existence, you know, that life is joyless and without purpose.' I told him that Hamm and Clov were not simply mailmen delivering Beckett's 'view of the world', Beckett's so-called message that the world is a desolate place. Not only are they not simply Beckett's postmen, I said to McCann, but they – Hamm and Clov and all the rest – have no existence beyond the stage. They are, Hamm and Clov, and Vladimir and Estragon, not aware even of their transient existence as creatures of the stage, of their fictional and partial existence. But no, there is no 'world view', no 'message', for meaning adheres non-transferably to these 'spirits', brought to brief life by Gambon and the Comedian, granted a life blown into them, golems trapped on the stage, before an audience, an audience of the bourgeoisie who expect to smile and nod in agreement with Beckett, sharing his jokes, whereas this nodding and smiling is precisely what Beckett makes impossible.

I had rarely if ever used the word 'bloviate' prior to meeting McCann, but the word was already written on his forehead, so to speak, like stigmata, and so it was impossible to look at McCann without also looking at the word 'bloviate' and thinking about the idea of bloviation. McCann's only contribution to the English language in fact was to revive the word 'bloviator', being the person to whom this word was most aptly applied. The word 'bloviator' had fallen into desuetude – nobody really used it, or 'bloviate' for that matter – but when McCann came along, the potential of these words was rediscovered, reactivated. 'Bloviate' was the dominant verb that defined all his behaviour and speech. When he was for example *reminiscing* about his lost loves, or *expressing* his opinion, or *arguing* or *bewailing*, these were only subordinate verbs in so far as he was, above all, *bloviating*. It is also true to say that, if someone were to write a biography of McCann (a book which would never get made unless McCann committed some horrendous crime, which he is lamentably incapable of), the trick, the difficulty would be to describe the life of a bloviator without also sliding into bloviation.

Of course, I have subsequently looked him up on the internet, McCann — as we all do, let's face it, in order to confirm to our own satisfaction someone's eventual demise — but there was no trace of him. These days of course this is highly unusual, almost suspicious. Not that we should judge someone by the footprint they leave on the cloud, as it's called, for this cloud is no more permanent or impermanent than anything else, given the fact that the earth will one day burn and expire like the sulphurous head of a match. But in any case, it struck me that it is perhaps the fate of bloviators to be with their own wind burst open, their atoms borne by chill winds to outer space. This is perhaps what happened to McCann.

Having said all this, it's true that in no small part my animosity towards businessmen, and to 'business' in general, is hereditary, as it were, and inveterate, and to this part I have added a purely personal supplement, which I both need and enjoy. My grandfather was a welder before the Second World War. He served in the war as a private. They talked about Marx, he told me, and socialism. This is perhaps the great untold story of the Second World War, although the historians instead fixated on the aristocrat Churchill, Churchill who, as a very young man, bears a passing resemblance to the comedian Johnny Vegas of course. Anyway, imagine the privates, fighting fascism, with their copies of the Communist Manifesto, the German ideology. I learned my politics from him. 'When they talk about bureaucracy it's always to attack socialism. But what are banks but the bureaucracy of capitalism?' My grandad would counter every lazy thought that fell from a politician's mouth. He should have been up on stage addressing them directly, were it not for the ongoing evil of social injustice. Sometimes we need our grandparents to pull us out of the present, to laugh at various modern stupidities we take for granted. I should have asked him more of course, about the war, about Palestine, where he was shot by both sides. I should have recorded his voice. There is a local newspaper article from 1923. My grandfather kept it. A six-year-old boy from Shipley fell out of a tree and was admitted to hospital. He was recovering and expected to be fine. This boy was my grandad. A reality fragment from a different age. I remember visiting him when he had dementia. His smile remembered me, but his mind had forgotten. When I told him I was his grandson he laughed. I still have his welding goggles and his copy of *Das Kapital*, and the story of the boy in the tree. He retained his socialism and passed it down to my father and me. My father thought that, in working for the council, he had entered the enclave of what used to be called municipal socialism, but sadly he was wrong, as the council was itself subject to ideological business imperatives.

So yes, I am irritated by businessmen, but inordinately by that subset of businessmen who convene conference calls and invent 'concepts' which are nothing of the sort. Such a one was this 'Cahun' who had occupied my café.

It was in that café, in the interval between William and Julia's visit and the introduction of Cahun into my precious space, that I had written an academic paper for the conference, 'Transgression and Crime in Modern Literature'. My paper, I had decided, was on a single sentence from Adorno: *Every work of art is an uncommitted crime*. It's a stand-alone sentence in his book of exile, *Minima Moralia*. There are paragraphs above and below it, but they have nothing to do with it. It could easily be a situationist graffito on the side of a bank. There are few such sentences in the book, held between two slim fingers of white space. I imagine it was one of those 'lightning thoughts' which is intelligible only as it happens. A moment later it's a hieroglyph. Many have said that the meaning of this sentence is obvious. Art is a substitute crime, a crime that stops halfway, a criminal impulse detained, so to speak, in the house of art. This may even have been how Adorno would gloss it. But thoughts are not owned by their thinkers. And I would argue, I would urge, and do in fact urge to my students, a different interpretation, or rather two interpretations. Firstly, that there is a desire to transgress so strong, so powerful, that its only exits are crime or art. Both exits have equal force. We have discussed, my students and I, those artists who were also actual criminals, most obviously Genet and Caravaggio, in both cases brilliant artists and not dissimilar aesthetically, redeemers of the reputedly vile and abject, who have doubtless exchanged, across the centuries, a mouthful of sweet wine. And I have introduced also into the discussion the paintings of Francis Bacon, which to my mind are often like crime scenes, the dark energy still in the room, and the paintings are themselves rooms wherein a violation has taken place, except it's not the violation of a person but a violation of reality. Reality itself has been dishevelled and undone, for a force has broken through and, like many forces, is only visible, only visible in what it destroys.

Now perhaps I am engaging in sophistry when I also offer a second and slightly different interpretation. Granted, most obviously, the phrase *uncommitted crime* means a non-crime, i.e. an intention to crime which was never realised, through lack of will, courage, or, conversely, the stronger force of conscience. But I say it is an actual crime, which has, as one of its properties, the quality of being uncommitted, just as it might have the property of being appalling or sordid. Works of art are crimes which, not having happened, are not corrupted by time, and retain their potency.

What I also suggested to my students is that the great crimes, the true crimes, or transgressions, are certainly not committed by criminals. Criminals, members of the criminal community, we might call it, are obliged to act in accordance with certain laws and prohibitions. The prohibition on being a 'snitch' or a 'grass', most obviously for example, elevated to a kind of Abrahamic law. They, the habitual criminals, abide by the rules of the criminal community. The true crimes, by contrast, are the sudden accountable acts of those who otherwise live within the law. The motion photographer Eadweard Muybridge, for example, who shot his wife's paramour. Whereas the criminal finds in crime only a confirmation of what he already is, the true crime will shock its perpetrator; he cannot recognise himself in what he has done and is an accessory to his own crime, as it were. The true crime transforms its bearer, for his so-called identity is cracked open like an egg and a new self is born. We must every now and then attempt such an action; if not an actual crime according to the letter of the law, then at least something which cracks us open, something that we cannot account for, something which creates a new self that cannot but appear monstrous at first glance.

Adorno himself was by many accounts a repellent individual, as I doubtless was during my illness, without being in any way evil. I have always been interested in this question of repulsion. The question of what is it about some people that repels others. I would have liked to have written an *Anatomy of Repulsion*, just as some have written anatomies of disgust or melancholy. What attracts us, I thought at the time, is invariably autonomy and confidence, whereas what repels us is not simply meekness and dependency. Repulsion may not really therefore be the opposite of attraction. We are certainly also attracted to what repels us and repelled by what attracts us, as I have elsewhere suggested. In fact, I am sceptical as to the very idea of opposites, for various sound philosophical reasons. I recall, most laughably, being told as a child that cat was the opposite of dog. Laughable, and yet most of what are called opposites are not so removed from this ridiculous example. Sour and sweet for example. As far as repulsion goes, Kafka certainly thought of himself as repellent, and this repulsion, he imagined, resided in being outside the human community. He was always in the position of an ape or an insect who was yet to be human, or had once been human or was forced to plead before a packed jury of humans. But Adorno, I feel, was repellent because of his cold aloofness. His Oxford colleagues, during his brief sojourn in that gilded city, found him a comical figure given to dandiacal display, his outward aspect cold and mannered, the carapace of a stylish suit and hat, a stiff demeanour which at once attracts and deflects gaze *tôn pollôn*. He was one of those who reach for adulthood too soon, who throw their doll on the floor and demand to sit at the dinner table with the adults, talking politics and ideas. At the age of thirteen, he was reading Kant and composing music. Having not allowed himself full room to be a child, he blocked his route to adulthood. For there is no road to adulthood except through the monstrous and embarrassing follies of adolescence and, before that, the dirt track through the sunlit fields of infancy.

In any case, the conference was a waste of time. Mine was a small perineural intervention between two others of roughly equivalent drivel. The first of these was, ostensibly, a paper on the philosopher Jacques Derrida, a man who, despite his prolix brilliance and bursts of originality, resides, nonetheless, in the Academy of the Overrated, along with the likes of the late Wittgenstein, the novelist-hairstylist Amy Martins, who places different stylistic wigs on the same blank mannequin, and of course Jane Austen. I say 'ostensibly', in so far as these Derrida papers were less about Mr Derrida than exercises in stylistic imitation, it being de rigueur to speak 'in the style of the master'. But so many had done this already, there had been so many imitations and embellishments, that Mr Derrida himself had long since disappeared behind a millefeuille of simulacra. 'Dare we deride Derrida?' the speaker asked, twinkling with self-delight and pointless mischief. 'Who are we, the reader, to deride Derrida? Does he, Derrida, not deride us also, and can we, the reader, be rid of derision or be rid of error?' Equally, dear readers, what might be a 'dear reading' of Derrida? Is there a 'dear reading' which rids itself of deriding? Dare we write 'dear Derrida'? And to whom is this addressed? And so on. Now, French and Italian philosophers write with elan and make surprising conceptual and linguistic departures, but when the English try and do something similar it's an unreadable or unlistenable traffic jam of jargon and false starts. Nothing is more embarrassing and boring at once than attending a conference where English academics attempt to ape continental philosophers and only fall to joyless and clumsy imitation: pathetic flightless birds flapping at the lectern, earnest parrots with copied thoughts squawking at their own image.

I was already, at this point, strategising an exit, the sudden light of the back yard into which one jumps from the kitchen window, then out through the gate and down the silent alley to the unexpected pastures, and nature uncorrupted by concepts.

The third paper, the one after mine, was by a man called Andrew Mellon, whose talk, 'Unnameable Women', concerned the 'absence of women' in various texts by Beckett, a paper which had no relevance to the conference title. To give him credit, he was taking a risk in criticising Beckett, who was generally beyond reproach, a kind of literary saint with an ethically impeccable war record, and Irish to boot. Anyway, 'I'm angry that there are no women in these texts,' he declared as his coda, suddenly rubicund, his lip quivering. But as Beckett knew, there are neither men nor women in the text, only creatures of language, incomplete and asexual, sans genitalia, often bodiless — voices as flickering and intermittent as a radio signal in a remote dwelling, a point I put to Mellon after his paper, but he was, so he said, too angry to answer.

My paper was received with initial politeness, and only a very few questions. The Derrida man, Rob, said that he wanted gently to 'pull and tug' at the word 'committed', just as he wanted to pull and tug at everything. He was interested in the difference in meaning between, for example, 'I've committed a sin' versus 'I'm committed to upholding the statutes of the University'. 'I'd like to ask,' he said, 'how "committed" is somehow both "to have carried out" and "to pledge" respectively? I'd like to ask,' he said, 'how committed to art is the artist in *not* committing a crime?' I'd like to ask whether we might take Adorno's "uncommitted" to mean not unexecuted but "uninterested"?' 'I'd like to ask "where's your fucking ball sack?",' I muttered softly. But they were clearly wetting themselves, the audience, and chirping with rapture at these superficial and in fact bogus conundrums. How clever they found it, these cunning punsters, how reassuring that things were this delectably ambivalent. But I answered that this double meaning did not exist in German, and that my principal concern was whether, in some sense, Adorno's apophthegm was *true*. This was of course a rude violation of academic protocol, and various flappings and furrowings could be heard and seen at various points in the room. Rob had stopped pulling and tugging.

This violation of protocol was doubtless a threat to their community and its incestuous language game. Each language game or aggregate of games creates a spectral 'We', and the continuation of the game is a way of maintaining this 'We', with its several backs turned outward, a kind of creature with a hard exoskeleton and multiple heads and multiple bottoms. Every genuinely creative person, when she or he meets with these language games, these games whose function is to fortify the We, to institute a zone of inclusion and a line of exclusion, must seek to destroy it through creative infiltration. You do not use balloons filled with water or crude incendiaries, civil or uncivil disobedience, dirty protests and so on. No, you make the game wobble or judder very slightly, you tinker and bend and remain poker-faced. You put sugar in their sandwiches and ground glass in their tea. You try and escape the game from inside. Eventually it collapses. Or if it doesn't, we flee. And so eventually I slipped out through a fire door and down the stairs, without telling anyone, naturally, and got a train back in to central London. The carriage was nearly empty, and as we passed the deserted docklands, the sun lazing undisturbed in the post-industrial waters, the pure balm of quiet entered the carriage and the blather receded like mist at daybreak.

On leaving the conference I had passed by Mellon's open briefcase. There was a book poking out, *The Pleasure of the Text* by Roland Barthes. I already had a copy of this book, but I took it nonetheless. There was no reason to steal it. Now and then, it is good to do something unaccountable. Not just that others are unable to account for but even oneself. It makes a cut in the fabric of everyday life, which also then allows the air in. At home, I used it as toilet paper. This caused me minor inconvenience, since I could not flush it down the toilet and had to place the stiff soiled pages in a small bin, as they do in Greece. I found it amusing to contemplate the gap between Mellon's speculations as to what might have happened to the book – left at the conference or on the train etc – and its actual destination, wiping a colleague's arse, which was entirely beyond his power to imagine or comprehend. It amused me also to apply the phrase 'A violation of academic protocol' to my act of theft and defilement. Because of course it was entirely beyond what might be considered a 'violation of academic protocol'. Violations of academic protocol are still within the ballpark of academic protocol, so to speak. Giving a student a few strong hints as to exam answers and so on. That is a breach of protocol. But again, it is good, occasionally, to place yourself entirely outside this ballpark. And to look at it from the tree house, drinking wine and laughing, a handful of stars in your pocket.

The only page I didn't use was one which contained a kind of luminous quotation, a quotation which I ripped out and stuck on the bathroom wall above the mirror: *The pleasure of the text is that moment when my body pursues its own ideas — for my body does not have the same ideas as I do.* So, my actions in fact displayed more fidelity to the text than Mellon's anal marginalia. The body pursuing its own ideas exactly. The body escaping its mind and not, as commonly imagined, the other way around. A pianist would understand, a painter would understand. Even a writer maybe. Remember Lawrence: *I write with my hand.*

I have always been attracted to forms of exit and escape. I'm not talking simply or mainly about escaping through vents, portholes or skylights, or from cells or cellars, or from attics or through apertures. I mean exiting certain oppressive or airless situations. I mean fleeing the weight of custom and of symbolic obligation. I mean engineering some space beyond or behind or above.

Sometimes my escapes are orchestrated and also seemingly trivial. The office party for example, which I was obliged to attend at Claridge's my first year at Belsham. The words 'Office Party' are already a cage, inside which the actual office party, also a cage, is enclosed. The 'Office Party' has also to be seen as a living genre. A generic mould that people are either prepared to squeeze themselves into or not. The Office Party is not in fact the office party, which is to say it is fully part and parcel of work and the culture of work, it does not escape work, it does not place work in parenthesis. Absolutely not, and on the contrary, anyone not attending the Office Party is marked as suspect precisely as a colleague and an employee. An extension of work but masquerading as its Outside. Laughable. Letting their hair down, dressing up, emerging from their everyday self into a drunken butterfly, or conversely demoted into a slurring beast. All part of the same senseless machine. Fuck off. So, for much of the office party at Claridge's I sat in the toilet cubicle reading. It was a nice large cubicle with beautiful wallpaper, anthropomorphic crescent moons such as might adorn a child's bedroom. And warm. I had a tiny copy of Rilke's poems. Rilke, who Auden described as the Santa Claus of solitude or some such. This amused me. Me having found an isolation cupboard removed from the Christmas melee and reading the Santa Claus of solitude. Rilke with the 'Pride of Lucifer' as someone else said, insisting on his cold apartness but also unique feral openness to the world. A perfect combination. Downstairs they were 'getting pissed', drinking expensive wine or drinking *through* the wine to their Pissed destination, crashing through red lights in order to arrive at the Pissed terminus. Office Banter had been let off its leash, rubbing its muzzle against everyone's legs, urinating on the carpet. The party was full of people saying either 'Mate, I'm shit-faced', or alternatively 'Mate, you're shit-faced', licking or polishing this word 'shit-faced', as well as 'wasted', even 'wankered', words that they would then roll out the following morning at the office post-mortem. 'Let's drink the fucking bar dry,' exclaimed the manager, Nicholson, but he was simply ventriloquising the transpersonal voice of the Office Party, for 'the Office Party' is not only a cage, not only a genre, but simultaneously the bearer of an obsessive shouty voice ordering you to 'Enjoy yourself' and unable to tolerate anyone reading Rilke in the toilet, for example. Everyone there, drinks in hand, experiences a squirt of selfless ecstasy as they submit to this idiot injunction: 'Enjoy yourself'. It's just like school. Granted, I did speak to a few people at the party, but I was, even whilst speaking to them, thinking of how long I could legitimately spend in the toilet, and also the earliest legitimate time I could leave. I calculated this end time with mathematical precision: 11.05 p.m. I left by a side door and escaped from this charade into the welcome reality of crisp fresh air. The entire party charade on the one scale, the single moment of genuine air on the other, and the latter had infinitely more weight.

It is always an escape into a *different quality or intensity of existence*. At home, as a child, I had ways of escaping whilst staying inside the house, retreating into my intestine for example, or the intrauterine cave made by the pillows and blankets.

When I was a kid, my father caught a hedgehog and put it in a cardboard box for me to look at in the morning when I woke up. But by the morning, my father told me, 'it had torn the box to bloody shreds' and was gone.

And I too felt the rage of the hedgehog. I too wished only to tear up the box.

If you smelled my father's fingers, they smelled of ash, but also a hint of musty sweetness. I smelled his fingers when he pinned me down and tried to squeeze blackheads from my cheek or nose. But long before that I was aware of this smell on his fingers and on his breath. I smelled his breath when he gave me a 'chin pie', which is when he rubbed his stubbly chin on my face and laughed.

This smell was the smell of the world of Men. It was not simply a human smell but a smell of dirt, matter, compost, smoke, metal as well. Men in general and my father in particular are characterised by their commerce with such things. Harsh substances, I might call them. Men have ingested or besmeared themselves with such harsh substances in order to harden themselves. To ally themselves with what is harsh. They themselves become amalgams, partly made from tobacco smoke, wood shavings, nails, oil and so forth. As they ingest more, as they smoke more, hammer more, as they place nails or tacks in their mouth whilst fitting a cupboard, or chew a match, so do they assume more and more the carapace of harshness. As grey-blue smoke exits their mouth and nostrils, as they scrub the dried paint off their arms, as the movements of chiselling and shovelling – brute, precise, relentless – become second nature, so are their bodies remade. So do they advertise their alliance with matter and poison. You must understand that each of these gestures has an affective lining, as I call it. A low-level brutal enjoyment, an indifferent violence, in hammering a nail, in splitting the earth with a spade, even if the earth or the wood are not sentient of course. There is still a cold pleasure in subduing, splitting, compressing, which potentially can be carried over onto flesh, so that these actions are always preparations for brutality.

All of this was true of my father. One thing I do remember though is the smell of tobacco in the tobacco tin, dark and soft and loamy and almost edible, a smell that bore no resemblance to the smell of a cigarette, a smell that I would steal every now and then when he wasn't looking even though he wouldn't have minded perhaps. My father placed maggots under his tongue to warm them up before using them as bait. Or I remember him placing a brandling worm on a fishhook and the worm writhing as yellow fluid came out of its side. Then he invited me to do it. I pricked my finger and it bled. 'Never mind that.' This is how it's passed on. Your body becomes a body capable of such gestures, and the indifference to pain, one's own or the pain of others. A kind of discipline whereby the boy's body with its softness and sensitivities is subdued and silenced and remade as an instrument, an accessory to hammers and chisels and spanners, honed to bone and muscle. It is true I have refused all these things and more: cigarettes, nails, paint and plaster, fishhooks and WD-40, pint glasses and greenhouses, beading and spirit levels. I have refused DIY and car engines, nor do I have a dank hut at the garden's end full of tools and rust and an ashtray full of butts. I stay with my glass of wine. I stay with the aroma of coffee that forever quells and suppresses the smell of strong tea and the sight of wet teabags and tab ends. But I have in my pocket his unremarkable silver lighter. Which I always carry with me. And which I cannot throw away. There are still a few orange sparks left in it. It is the sole surviving remnant of it. The hard, metal, implacable remnant. And I cannot throw it away because it is, this hard thing, inoperably, part of my soul.

Once or twice, he took me to a football match. Leeds United at Elland Road. It was when there were still standing areas. We stood in the 'Cop'. Acres of men shouting and pointing. 'You're gonna get your fucking head kicked in' is what they shouted, pointing at the away fans. That's what they used to shout, back then. The match seemed incidental. We moved and bobbed around like a boat at sea. I was excited but also appalled. Excited at the possibility of injury, of getting lost, of drowning. Appalled at Men.

Everything has come to me through women, said the eminent Althusser, albeit shortly before strangling his wife to death.

Nonetheless, the same is true of me. Friendships with women have been journeys of the most revelatory sort, whereas male friendships, with the possible exception of Carvell, are mere games of wit and logic, refined over years, the evolution of a set of rules known and practised only by the friends themselves. They are typically, in my case, largely academic affairs, dialogues about philosophy and literature only, from which the life of the speakers has been surgically removed or is present only in some invisible ink that becomes legible by the lights of retrospect when the friendship itself has died. Friendships with women, on the other hand, take place directly in the stream of life, the intellect swimming in the stream of life, each one of us with an oar, rowing together and inter-reliant while the male–male friendship watches from the bank drinking beer and talking about football.

I have never assumed for myself the name Man, or wanted anything to do with this name in so far as it means anything over and above bare biology. Julia once said to me, as we sat outside the Bar San Calisto, the early-morning sun feeling its way over the cobbles, that I combined, in equal measure, the best of those things called 'Male' and 'Female'. This I took to be the highest compliment, which of course it was. All of us, of course – those made with a penis and those made with a vulva – come in various such combinations of the things called 'Male' and 'Female'. But there is a cultural system, we might call it, which insists we nail ourselves to 'Male' and 'Female' and see these not as characteristics we contain but as containers for everything else. All of us are naturally androgynous in this sense, only most suppress and veto the Female or Male characteristics under the duress of Culture. In Plato's great myth, you might recall, there are first of all androgynous human beings, perfectly round, with four arms and four legs. But these creatures were too unruly and potent for Zeus, who split them in half, so that each half became a creature in itself yet incomplete, forever seeking its demi-body. We are still such incomplete creatures, but what of course cuts us in two is not Zeus but Culture, the symbolic cuts and partitions we impose on unruly nature, nature teeming with eager chaos, nature polymorphous and perverse. For of course the great founding cultural gesture has been to organise society around the distinction between two 'genders', and to split apart the originary androgyny with curious arbitrary colour schemes, clothing schemes, toy schemes. But it has always seemed to me that the addition of a penis to the basic human template, as Shakespeare imagined precisely in his most intriguing sonnet, and subsequent science proved, is neither here nor there, and barely important to a neutral eye. But what that bare difference has been made to signify, the cultural infrastructure built up on that meagre base, the differing symbols and habits of expectation, the pinks and blues, the dolls and Action Men, the regulation of hair growth and hysterical commands concerning trousers, the fixing and truncation of Nature in the service of power, all this is, to that same impartial eye, a joke, astonishing and stupid, and what we now call Men and Women are the monstrous and lost progeny of this fatal founding gesture.

At this moment, the moment of writing, it strikes me that I myself was most androgynous, physically speaking, when I was most ill. Back in Oxford. A beautiful, unisex angel, my shoulder-length hair and shining eyes. Granted, I was way too thin, eight stone if you must know, if I must know, even as the head stayed big, as if balanced on the body, the body that kept on stalling, and thick raven-black hair shielding my shoulders, the eyes enlarged and the pupils seeming to fill the whole eye. The rising of the bones, I called it, as the flesh thins out and the bones advance and walk towards me through the occult mirror. I was invisible and too visible at once. Good. Fuck off. That's how I was. But desperate as I was to return to myself, I liked him, to be honest, me I mean, this thin androgynous creature, this otherworldly soul. The bone and its milky sleeve of spirit. Staring eyes and bat-like ears. Renunciation, sainthood, dedication. It fits as well with the blank page, the empty room with a table and the halo of a desk lamp. The body an elegant object, like a racing bicycle or a walking stick. And in the mezzanine of the Taylorian library, looking across at Balliol, I was a lone rook in the rafters; walking home, a bent shadow blown against a wall. Perhaps I saw in the thin and elegant Cahun not only a repetition of the telesales bossdog and bloviator McCann but a ghost light of that former self.

This was one thing about Cahun, I remember thinking on one occasion, when he was sat in front of his laptop, one thing in his favour I mean, is that he was not in any obvious way a Man, a 'lad' or 'bloke', and did not speak, in his long and noisy phone conversations, of laddish or blokeish things. Of course, he was immersed in the world of 'tech' and enjoyed discussing and talking about 'tech' and a whole range of irrefutable new facts about tech and its implications and possibilities. For it is one of the tedious things about men that they must 'know things' and enjoy the unanswerability of facts and data, and will try and refer to facts and data as soon as possible in order to shut down debate and close the space in which interpretation might thrive. I have always prided myself, by contrast, on knowing very little. In his appearance too, as I think I have noted already, Cahun was strikingly androgynous and angular. He also had a very slight squint, which to my mind always suggests depths of intelligence, as if the gaze has been bent or deflected by a weight and bias of inner concentration. But Cahun's squint had no corresponding deep intelligence. I was drawn to Cahun in so far as I have always been drawn to androgyny, which is not, however, quite the right word, for it suggests something vague, blurred, neutered, a 'neither–nor' rather than a 'both at once', and this both at once is what I'm talking about. The 'both at once' power which Zeus, and Culture, could not stand.

In the company of Men, and in particular little claques of Men gathered in pub corners, or on football terraces, or huddled together outside buildings exclaiming 'Ah, mate!' for no good reason, I have always been in enemy territory. I have always been present only as a witness and observer, or as a secret agent, not on behalf of Women, whatever that means, but humanity. I have always been happy to betray Male confidences and secrets, by which I do not mean, of course, the mawkish and predictable intimacies told me by Men concerning, say, their childhood (before they were bashed and brutalised into being men), or marriage, their infidelities or the criminal activities they may have engaged in or flirted with. Not at all. I am talking about those confidences you are assumed to share as a Man, the handshakes and winks implicit in conversations about the 'Missus' or 'the game' and other bullshit wherein you are asked to join the chorus, the clucking company or risk some churlish censure or ostracism. When they speak about the 'Missus', they are not speaking about their actual wife or girlfriend, for they *dare not* speak of her in her blessed particularity, of the foibles in which love nestles, but only this shared archetype, the Missus, to which all wives and girlfriends are assimilated. They are instructed to joke about how much control this 'Missus' has over them, and what she will or won't 'let them do'. And the pleasure of saying 'the Missus'll give me a load of earache' is the pleasure of dissolving themselves blissfully in the collectivity of Men. Generally, they speak of women in the most disgusting fashion, and this is not different to how it was at school. Everything that degrades women to the status of matter is applauded, this is one of the rules of the game, thus expressions like 'Beef curtains' or observations such as 'Her box won't be the same after she's popped one out, it'll be like a clown's pocket' are directives to laugh which cannot be countermanded or refused. 'The Missus says she's bored,' jokes the Liam cretin. 'I said the washing machine's working, the cooker's working, the tumble dryer's working. How can you be bored?' Jabbed by the poker of this 'joke', they all laugh. None dare disobey the peremptory orders of the Male game, because they cannot tolerate the isolation they imagine lies outside it. This is what I am happy to divulge to women: the cowardice of men, men who are not brave enough even to simply remain silent, even to keep their faces straight.

Belsham Media, that telesales office, blagging shop, gashouse, where I charred and burned whole areas of my soul, was in fact populated by Men of the basest sort, self-styled Lads and Blokes who performed their Blokeishness or Laddishness to each other, an endless charade, performed in the office or of course in the pub, the place par excellence of blokish familiarity and round common sense. The social function of the pub, which of course always changes over time, this function, so there is almost nothing in common between an Elizabethan tavern of the kind in which Marlowe was murdered and a contemporary gastropub, is to serve as a space in which people can opine that 'It's all bollocks.' Their job, politics, existence... 'It's all bollocks at the end of the day,' they announce, before sobering up and getting on with their lives the next day. But this admission, this recognition that it is all bollocks, in no way makes any difference to their practical existence, the existence that is 'all bollocks'. Or rather, it makes a crucial difference, for the inebriate and rueful admission, once a week, or perhaps even once a night in some cases, or however frequently it is made, serves as a kind of valve which, in releasing pressure, allows the mechanism to go on functioning normally. 'It's all bollocks but we do it anyway' is also the essence of English humour in a nutshell.

Anyway, every evening they trundled off to the pub, these Blokes and Lads. I remember very clearly those initial trips to the pub, from which after a few weeks I excused myself and was thereon marginalised. In fact, I had been shunned and ostracised before that, simply for drinking wine. My glass of wine was a brute fact and an affront they were unable to digest. 'What are you at, a wedding reception?' they would bark, the glass of wine ruining the whole picture, a disagreeable object which they tried to attack with jokes, trying to lasso it with jokes and mockery and thereby remove it from the table, this mote in their eye. It did not budge. Inside they wobbled and flapped, seeing this glass of wine in my hand, willing it not to exist, clutching their pints all the more firmly, moving from side to side as if squaring up for a fight, all because of this mere object, a glass of wine, acting upon them like a living thing and affecting directly, no doubt, their temperature and heart rate, synapses firing in their angry heads. It would take a Sartre to do justice to the clammy facticity of this glass of wine as it appeared to the Men. A burnt hole in the fabric of their stupidity. 'Drink it,' I imagined saying to a chair-bound Liam, removing the wet rag from his mouth. 'Drink it!' I would say, in a gruff cockney whisper, holding it to his lips. 'Drink this lovely Austrian wine, you whingeing wankseed.'

As a man, a biological entity of a certain sort, you are pressured into going to the pub and enjoying pub life just as, at school, you are pressured into being disobedient, smoking, saluting and consuming certain musical and sartorial fads. Refusing to go to the pub is a shortcut to ostracisation, to stand accused, silently, of being joyless and less than a Man, as is the refusal of football. Men's relation to football is what I have always found most laughable, and few things, in fact, are more ludicrous than the pronouns men use when talking about football teams, than hearing a claque of men talking about how 'we' have signed such and such a player, 'we' have sold such another, 'we' hammered 'you' on Saturday, 'we' lost last night, and so on, when in fact they have bought nobody, sold nobody, won or lost nothing. 'You gave us a good hiding at the weekend,' Nicholson would say, except the man he is speaking to, the wizened goblin Reg, had given no one a good hiding, he had only sat on his sofa watching television, or popped to IKEA to look at some bathrooms, just as the speaker, Nicholson, had in no way been the recipient of a 'good hiding' but only visited his in-laws and taken the kids go-karting. They are in fact referring to what some other people have done, people who they do not know and whose behaviour they are impotent to influence. If the club wins a cup, they think they have themselves triumphed, even as they have only continued in their monotonous failure and done nothing out of the ordinary.

I am more than uneasy in such company, it is no exaggeration to say (and even if it was, that's no bad thing, for exaggerations are only a magnifying glass through which we see the micrological structure of the truth) that I am in a pocket of hell, filled with cigarette smoke and noise and bravado. And it is not difficult actually to draw a brief vignette of this hell, for I am cursed in that certain episodes from my past are perpetually available to my memory, as if playing over and again in some inner auditorium, a private screening which most of the time nobody watches. But occasionally I stumble by accident through the door of the theatre and it's there, intact, the entire scenario. I remember very clearly the first night I went with them, these Lads and Blokes. Following some inane debate as to who would win in a fight between a gorilla and a bear, they began to pass between them the names of the office women and speculate as to how and where and if they would 'fuck' them, turning these names into tokens to be passed round for commentary. Sue, Jane, Anne-Marie, Tracy… 'You'd have to do her from behind…' '…yeah, with a bag on her head,' 'No, two bags in case the first fell off…' 'Yeah, but after ten pints…' 'No, I reckon seven pints with a blindfold…' And so on. 'I'd do her on the photocopier,' offered Gavin, a wizened sixty-year-old creature with a red shiny beak and beetroot cheeks, then Reg: '… You'd better watch out mate, don't want to leave any evidence. Your fucking skinny arse on a sheet of A4…' 'What you on about mate, I'd be on top, it'd be her fat arse on the photocopier…' 'You'd need two fucking sheets of paper for that mate…' And so on. Each burst of so-called banter is answered by a round of red-faced, cackling laughter.

Liam was the worst of the lot, an obsessive onanist and addictive consumer of the vilest pornography. When their chatter veered — or was steered by a robotic hand — from women to pornography, Gavin told us that Liam 'likes the hard stuff, I mean the really hard stuff: choking, slapping…' and so he went on, with details which cannot be repeated only because description always collaborates with its object. There is no reason why one cannot simply say 'scenes of the most appalling degradation and violence'. Beyond that, to specify, to picture and delineate, always involves a prurient but illicit enjoyment of what one purports merely to describe, a sly and faint repetition of the original evil. But in any case, Liam's enjoyment of the 'hard stuff' met with delighted mock disapproval, 'you filthy bastard' and so forth, but this only as the prelude to bringing him back more closely into the fold and strengthening the dirty complicity that binds them – and Men in general – together.

Liam was regarded as a 'good bloke' in the office, a 'good laugh', despite spending much of his nocturnal time in this fashion, doubtless: crouched in front of the LED screen, the retina drugged with toxic light, spectres of humiliation and torture slipping through his optic nerve, his face like a face at a seance, hand going ten to the dozen, the wife and kids sleeping upstairs, a sad ill-lit orgasm, a tissue of wasted seed, and then limping back to bed like a criminal. I heard him once in the work toilet, not that he knew. I'd arrived at work very early. Behind the cubicle door I could hear him under his breath. 'You're made out of rubber,' he was saying. 'You bitch, you fucking rubber bitch, you're made out of fucking rubber.' He repeated this until I heard a noise not dissimilar to the noise that, in certain B-movies, dogs make when shot by an ominous intruder. This is what passes as the behaviour of a 'good bloke', this is what meets with whoops of delight from the little nest of colleagues. Any Man, any husband, boyfriend, is not a thousand miles away from Liam. He's not even round the corner. You just need to fold the Man inside out and there Liam, in all his slimy unpleasantness, will stand.

Liam, this one-headed dog from hell, was in fact regarded as a quintessential 'geezer', and in any company of men there is typically one who is asked to wear this mantle. Men actually measure each other against the Ideal Geezer... 'Geez, geez!' they ejaculate when the designated Man does something suitably 'geezerish' and coincides, however briefly, with the Ideal Geezer... 'He had a two-pint lunch then comes in and closes a deal...' 'Fucking Geez! Put it there, Geez,' they gibber and squeak, jubilant as a toddler before the mirror. And so a special corner of hell is reserved for this Liam, who, slung on some cold shelf or in an empty shop's window, would serve as the chosen visual spur for a host of glopping demons and be given a day off only to serve as a gimp at Satan's wedding.

I would do almost anything and be almost anywhere rather than go for a 'night out with the lads down the pub', and in fact I have not been 'out with the lads' since my late adolescence. Me and some others – including the grandson of the man who bangs the gong at the start of Rank films – would go on a pub crawl in Pudsey. I remember coming back late at night, very late, and how I would bump into my father, one eye shut tight, in his underpants, on his way to the loo. And incidentally, now that I sometimes get up in the night to wee or on the back of some invasive dream, I can see the sense in that one shut eye: it's so that you retain, through the brief intermission of cold white light, a toehold in the world of sleep. We were both deep-sea sleepers, my father and I, we both could never remember our dreams. Of course, towards the end, he would fall asleep in the daytime, my father. One time I called for my weekly chat. There was a longer than usual silence. 'Dad, Dad?' I said, but then my mother's voice replied, 'Hi love, sorry, he's fallen asleep.' Anyway, that image of him in his underpants, the one eye peering at me, is all that the dredge net of memory has brought back from the countless 'nights out with the lads', the only luminous permanent thing.

———

When Julia and William were here, I was reminded, one time as I was marking some papers whilst Julia played with William in my flat and knelt on the floor to be at his level and earnestly spoke about the monsters and machines confected by his still limitless mind, as William and Julia laughed and played, and shared their knowledge, and exchanged daisies, and blew raspberries, that this relationship, the mother–child relationship, is, or is often rather in fact one of friendship. As the great Sartre says, 'those sweet friendships that come into being far away from men and against them.' Far from Men, exactly. Against Men, exactly. The father typically wants to induct the child into the world of Men. He complains that the mother is 'soft' on the child, but she is not 'soft' on the child as a parent, she has discovered a companion. She wears the mask of parent when the father is there, but conducts this almost clandestine friendship. The mother is aware of its transience, this friendship; the child imagines it lasts forever. Across this misunderstanding – and in defiance of it – they hold hands. I remember my mother chatting to me on the bus, I remember her reading to me *Treasure Island*, that revelation of darkness, when I was too young perhaps to understand fully what its pages contained but delighted that she could, through her gentle enchantment, turn those tiny black marks into sounds and words and stories, which in turn would paint articulate pictures in my head and light unfamiliar emotions in my body. The mysterious figure of Blind Pew, and the black spot, the ominous black spot, which in my child's mind was a kind of rodent mole burrowing into the skin, charged with cold terror and magic, for words to the child have an intensity and independent life that adults can only imagine; they lodge like hard green thorns in the skin, they grow and blister like a red infection, they open cupboards and doors where sleeping creatures come back to life and take up home in our dreams. My mother loquacious, reading, talking. My father silent, encouraging silence by his presence. And me an amalgam, but the silence first, always the silence first.

I remember that March visit, with Julia and the child, William, as an interlude of great happiness, interpolated almost from another life. I think he was four years old. They stayed only for a couple of days before travelling to Europe. She had divorced the stockbroker and married a hedge fund manager called Max, who we'd both in fact known at Oxford when he was a vegan anarchist with dreadlocks. He introduced me to patra leaves, which I've eaten ever since. We took William on a riverboat, and to the Tate gallery to see the Blakes. He shrieked and giggled at *Ghost of a Flea*, a reaction which represents aesthetic experience at its purest, a nerve running directly from the object to the soul of the perceiver. From there we meandered through Battersea Park and finally to the church where Blake was married. Julia talked about her marriage to the hedge fund manager, who owned the largest hedge fund in Asia. He was always working, she said, always in his office before his computer. William called it 'Daddy's lair'.

William would talk about his father, and had a whole arsenal of insults he used to refer to him, such as *Infernal bottom worm*; *Rusty rotting poo pipe*; and, despite the fact that the father, judging by his photo, had a good head of hair, *Shiny slaphead fool*. Of course all of this amused me, partly because of the target of these wonderful coinages, but more than that was the relentless joy of the coinages themselves and the ability to unlock and recombine words and invent new rules, endlessly, as only children can do. The child takes the 'osaurus' suffix and adds it to a mouse, a dad, lump of cheese, in each case creating new monsters, a dogosaurus, a slugosaurus, a bugosaurus, and the world seems as friable and pliable as language itself. It is this untrammelled inventive abundance which Joyce and Carroll detected, of course, that surplus vitality which I once had, if only I could revive within me that boundless infant jazz, genius of course being the reanimation of childhood, as Rimbaud, little more than a child, reminds us: genius is the unconcealment of childhood, the unquenchable vitality, needing material but never exhausted by it. Rimbaud, who described the Thames as *wide as an arm of the sea*, which is exactly how a child would see and think, a child would ask its mother or father, 'Is a river an arm of the sea, and how many arms has the sea, Daddy?' I quoted this line in fact to William as we walked by the great wide river at dusk. And earlier, when we walked through Battersea Park, it was very windy, the Thames was choppy, and the trees were dramatically swaying and bending. 'The trees are panicking,' said William casually, and what a beautiful image this was, what a revelation of language and the world this was, the instant poetry of childhood, unmindful of how words ought to be ordered, as fine as anything in Rimbaud. To be in the company of children is to be in the company of such liberated words, and therefore to rediscover not simply the world, but the vital appetites long disavowed which bring that world to life.

What will you do when you see Daddy? I asked him. *I'll throw rainbows at him. I'll send him to sleep with an evil lullaby and make him sleepwalk into the sea.*

And what does he look like, your daddy? I asked.

Well, he's got mechanical eyes, and a rather strange-looking wand that's also a snake, and one time he waved his wand and a red laser beam came out and it hurt a poor innocent lizard and it started floating in the air uncontrollably.

And are you the lizard? I asked William.

No, I'm an innocent little piglet.

Once upon a time, William told me, *once upon a time there was a little innocent piglet with a very strong stupid-looking owner. The owner was ugly, thin and had a very spiky nose, and a fart that was the most disgusting fart you have ever smelled. Also the piglet, when he wouldn't eat the hay the owner made for him, he got shooted on the tail by a bullet, and eventually got knocked out. But he came back, he came back because he was a strong one, and his owner tried to shoot bullets at him again, but, before he shooted, the piglet bited his face and trotted its hooves right on his foot, until he was well knocked over and couldn't come back, but instead he went to that doomed city guarded by a three-headed dog. The owner lived sad and the piglet lived free, happily ever after.*

What a beautiful story, I said to William, what a beautiful story it was, for almost everything a child says is a veiled allegory of Vitality in the face of the powers ranged against it, the innocent pigs against the owners and the slaughterers. We must always be on their side, we must always let them invade us, we must try, without ever being a child, to *become* one. We must leave our departure point, adulthood, and, without arriving at childhood, fall into *becoming* a child. For ranged against you on the other side is much of the general adult population who hate children.

On a gravel track outside the Blake church William stamped and scuffed his feet on the gravel to make a noise. 'This is a designated cycle path,' mumbled a middle-aged man on a bike with pent rage. 'And you're a designated dickhead,' I shouted after him, immediately apologising to William. Similarly, in a restaurant later, irritated diners shot stares in our direction and spoke under their breath. In this country, too many people hate children and scowl and tut and shake their heads, they grow tense or start to panic or are beset with rigor mortis. You only have to travel to Greece or Italy or Spain, where the baby or toddler in a restaurant or other public place is the star of the show, a VIP, an entertainer applauded and feted by all. You only have to witness the delight of the waiters and shop workers, suddenly lit up and animated by the prodigal presence of the child, and who always meet the baby halfway, as it were, and become babies themselves, to realise that by contrast my ostensible compatriots resent and are embarrassed by children and wish them invisible, inaudible or unborn. Of course, their hatred wears the mask of concern, or the muzzle of concern, as in 'That baby should be asleep really', or 'They shouldn't be letting it behave like that...' and so on. What you see on their faces is not one simple thing but a kind of compromise between the underlying hatred and this muzzle of concern, where the wearing of the muzzle is dictated by the social code but the hatred it stifles is primary. They 'blame the parents' where nothing is blameworthy but life itself, and they can be heard sniping at the parents from adjoining tables, barely audible of course, for most of their cancerous bile is rerouted inward where, with other pale monsters, it festers and mutates. They cannot admit to themselves their hatred of children, for that would amount to confessing a hatred of life. But this is exactly what they do hate, the exuberance and uncompromised delight of the wobbling baby, the toddler circling in gleeful triumph around the listless, ironic adults, who sit decomposing on the sofa.

When we enter this state of becoming a child, of course, how can we not meet again our own childhood coming towards us, how can we not have it again, the gift of our own childhood too, from the child we play with, the child who speaks to us.

You are growing down, Henry, you are growing down to be a baby not growing up, and when I grow up you can be one of my childs and I can look after you so that you won't die.

Don't worry, little William, I'll be OK. Is there anything else you're worried about?

I'm worried about the trees being poorly, I'm worried about the alphabet falling over, and edible stars falling onto the floor, and the snow falling through the window. I'm worried about the light breaking. It goes on and off and goes off and on and goes on and off and it breaks.

The light will not break, I promise, little man, the light will not break.

I brought them both to Café Amato. I have a photo of them there in the cosy green corner where Cahun later squatted. 'Now is the time to write the tale of your father, your father and you,'

Julia said. 'I will,' I said, and I told her a number of stories from my childhood, including the stubdog, 'but there is one thing that cannot be written and only vocalised,' I said. 'In pronouncing it,' I said to her, 'I am forced to own it as mine, to *assume* it. I have never been able to say it, as if keeping it in the realm of the virtual. But now I'm ready to speak it. It is this: I regret not telling my father I loved him. There, I've said it and it is now the case. And although my other regrets are mostly minor, inconsequential things, like not going to a certain café when I had the chance, this other regret is a rock rising up from the sea, minatory and unmoving, and unavoidable in a storm. For love unexpressed is not the same thing,' I said to Julia. 'It is a lesser and impoverished love, denied light and air and flesh. All it had to do was make that short transit from mouth to ear. To cross an arm's length of accustomed silence. But it didn't. And so now it rages with guilt and regret.'

Anyway, I could not write, nor cross that arm's length of silence, with Cahun encamped here with his phone and laptop and sloppy latte. It was impossible to think when Cahun was present. He diverted, Cahun, my thoughts into other things. He had nothing to do with any of these things, necessarily, Cahun. No, he was a kind of wall against which my thoughts rebounded, or were redirected along various overgrown lanes and through sleeping rusty gates, away from everything he represented.

No doubt I had elevated Cahun to the status of The Obstacle, and in particular the principal obstacle to writing my father monograph. This is something we all do. Our flourishing is blocked by a variety of knots and stoppers, internal and external. The internal ones are tenebrous and elusive. But what we typically do is find something convenient which stands in for these various things. Very recently, for example, I had a drink with Carvell, heavy with incomprehension he was, inert with baffled sadness. His wife had coolly asked him for a divorce, laying out her reasons rationally and without emotion. They'd been in Ireland at the time. She'd told him that he was *blocking her evolution*, holding her back, that he had ceased to be someone who *empowered* her and become a bar to her progress. He, he alone, it seemed to Carvell, was the blockage, the *obstacle* in her life. And although I was in part trying to cheer Carvell up, I suggested that she had in fact elevated him to the status of The Obstacle, which is to say she had amalgamated all the disparate internal and external problems, usually internal actually, various emotional inertias and blind spots, and projected them onto a single external source. This source becomes the bearer of and shorthand for all these various impediments. However, I said to Carvell, and here's the twist, the person so persuades themselves that this is the case, that there is a single external rather than a variety of internal blockages, that the removal of the obstacle, the *so-called* obstacle, creates such a sense of intoxicating freedom that it allows the person, perhaps only temporarily, to flourish. And yes, this, I wondered, might be what I had done with Cahun. Not that I really cared.

'We're defined by our data,' Cahun was saying to some invisible interlocutor...

> ...biometric data, official data. Usage patterns, likes/dislikes, favourite destinations... Everything we do can be broken down into data... That online quiz you do on the way to work, that's

data... the data you share defines who you are... a unique data footprint... that's your identity... All this is trackable... from a marketing point of view this is the Holy Grail... the absolute golden age for marketing... massive opportunity for businesses... they can create individual customer profiles. They know their customers better than they know themselves... A company like Amazon is going to know you inside out... This is where you can now install yourself as a marketing person: right in people's data profile, right alongside their likes and dislikes... we can use emotional audience data to totally change engagement rates... I mean, they've shown that every time you get a 'like' or a 'retweet' you get an endorphin release... that's what we need to exploit... It's Pavlovian. The bell rings, a chemical drops into the bloodstream... This is where marketing people need to be, right there... Marketing is psy-ops... it's gonna change everything... Take passports... It's goodbye to passports. They're finished, like hard currency is finished... What can the face tell you compared to a quick retinal scan?... One day it'll be a straightforward retinal scan, pop, and all the data will come up... Just like *Minority Report*!

Identity, Cahun said, had for centuries been fastened to the face, but that was about to be undone, identity henceforth would have little or nothing to do with the face and everything to do with data. Our faces would dissolve in the field of data. And the algorithms that could make sense of the data would also make marketing gold dust.

I relayed all this to my American students, for I was in the habit of using anecdote and example, not just for pedagogical purposes but also because I believe that Ideas are little more than a constellation of examples. 'There is a sense in which Cahun is right, no doubt,' I announced to the students, without using his name, which wasn't Cahun in any case, of course, 'but a greater sense in which everything of value resides outside data, in those grains of our soul which Cahun and his robotic watchfucks cannot find.' This also I said to the students, who were impressed at least by my vehemence. One can smuggle any content into the students' heads using the Trojan horse of vehemence and also humour.

And so I told my students, first of all, and in order to illustrate my peculiar form of life, about the time just before I left Oxford, in late 1995, when I ate at the Indian restaurant in the interzone. I called it the interzone: 'As you approach London from Oxford, on the A40, there is a sector of dual carriageways, large roundabouts, office blocks for rent, warehouses and industrial estates, a narrow remnant of council flats facing the railway. An expanse of demolition and construction, untidy, without any kind of overview or planning. And there is a peculiar type of house which in fact can be found all along the periphery of London, whether west of Shepherd's Bush or north of Finchley, serving almost to mark the very outer limit of the city, its disorganised and disintegrating periphery. Terraces and semi-detached. I think they were built in the thirties. Their square bay windows, upstairs and downstairs, their triangular gables at the front, the black and white Tudor pastiche beneath the roof. Unremarkable, ugly. Almost all are tatty, neglected, thick with dirt.' The students, doubtless, wondered where the fuck I was heading with this. 'They've fallen between the cracks, these houses, the cracks of where one century ends and another begins, encircled by wasteland, warehouses, too close to the relentless road, the front gardens foreshortened by compulsory order when the carriageway was built, brutally ignored by what surrounds them, technically within London but severed from the city itself. Nor are they quite suburban. They are no place in particular, only on the way to somewhere else. They fascinated me,' I declared to the students, pinching this fascination between my fingers like a glowing yet malleable transparent bead, trying to imagine who lived there. 'I pictured little coteries of criminals, or perhaps just wheeler-dealers, seventies wallpaper, cold teabags and endless background TV. And just past these, as you approach White City, there's a straggle of shops. A launderette, a DIY store, a video shop, and the curry house, the Star of India. As the coach stopped at the lights, I would briefly come face to face with the Star of India, its name in white plastic letters on a purple background. "Time Out 1988" in the window. The interior dingy and red. There was never anyone in there. Utterly soulless, I thought. And for this reason, I wanted to go there. To this desolate restaurant in the interzone near the rows of half-abandoned houses. I wanted to feel this soullessness, neglect, anonymity, sink into my body and mind. To dip my toe, my calves, my knee, in its waters. This to me was a more interesting prospect than going to India itself,' I confessed to the students, 'which would be doubtless full of things, whereas what I wanted to experience was their absence. As it turns out it was a passable curry. A fiery jalfrezi, with some okra and bhajis. A Kingfisher beer. I watched two or three coaches to Oxford go past in the time I ate. The place that I'd seen was now the place I was looking from. A childlike delight in that simple exchange. I was initially disappointed that someone else was in there, but they were merely waiting for a takeaway. It felt like the edge of the world, and maybe the end of time. Such experiences are gloriously pointless,' I emphasised to my captive audience. 'They serve no function, they involve needless expenditure, inconvenience. You would be unable to explain in the practical language of everyday life why they happened. And that is why it is always important to carry out such secret operations, as I call them, or secret escapes, perhaps. They are secrets, but without any *need* for secrecy, which precisely reinforces the secret, carves it forever in memory. After such an experience it was, needless to say, impossible, in terms of the logic – or rather illogic – of the event, to get the coach back to Oxford. Of course, there were still coaches running at that late hour, for the Oxford Tube, as the coach was called, ran all night. And I could easily have got a bus to Marble Arch and then boarded the coach, and sat gazing out of the window, passing once more that lone restaurant. But no, only a taxi would do it. On the coach one is too aware of other people. In a taxi, if one is spared a conversationalist, one sits in the cell of oneself. A bubble. This bubble is the perfect vessel in which to carry the aftertaste, the distillation, of what one has experienced, the flavour of the experience but divorced now from its material paraphernalia, from the tables and red napkins, the worn red carpet. You wear the mask of a fugitive. Speeding away in the cab, having stolen your own experience, holding it with you like a cache. Then there is the ridiculous and needless expenditure of the taxi back to Oxford, without any conceivable justification, unaccountable and mad. I had to go to Blackwell's the following day and sell some books to recoup the money. Well, this mad expenditure was continuous with the event itself. The naked mad freedom of slinging aside all rhyme and reason. This mad expenditure is life itself. It is difficult of course fully to convey the magic of what happened, for finally there is always this: *the loneliness and rapture of your own peculiar form of life, your own madness.*'

And abruptly and with equal vehemence, I continued to tell them, to advise them, no doubt fruitlessly, that 'the only injunction you need obey, as René Char said, is to develop precisely this "legitimate oddness". When I fetch a glass of water,' I told them, leaning on the lectern and suddenly smiling and relaxed, as if I'd arrived home, 'I pour only an inch or so into the glass and leave the rest empty. I wait until I've drunk the inch and then go back and pour another. This irritates people, or rather it did, in the past, when I lived with people. But anyway, this is the kind of detail I am speaking about. The freedom to part-fill your glass, against all "sense", against all "prudence", to "waste time" doing such things, whereas time is there for the wasting. This is what I am talking about in so far as these stupid details are the sign language of your single immutable soul. They are, of course, ostensibly unremarkable – to others – things, irrational – to others – things, and yet without them you evaporate into everyone else, as of course most of us do, or else your legitimate strangeness is confined to a sort of allotment or shed where it becomes harmlessly eccentric, like a pet griffin, or like the huge tethered owl I saw recently at a fair, subdued and surrounded by a crowd of snapping cameras behind which passive faces stared. I say there is nothing else but this strangeness, and there is a constant territorial battle, a continual war, by various social and religious and marketing agencies to eliminate this strangeness, to colonise it, to replace it with the merely generic, as if all pronouns flow into They, the anonymous They. Do not try and defend it before the court of reason, your strangeness, to someone armed with a questionnaire or a spreadsheet or – God forbid – the *Diagnostic and Statistical Manual of Mental Disorders*, or a self-help book, a bureaucrat or marketeer. Because your only defence can be to say "Sorry, this is who I am", like the composer who, when he was asked to explain the meaning of a piece of his music, simply sat down and played it again. That's what you have to do, you see: keep playing it again, your strange irrefutable music, again and again and again and again and again and again.'

Of course, it was not possible to hear my own irrefutable music because of Cahun and his constant blather. Cahun was an invader, or occupier, not just of this physical space in which he was obviously out of place but also the more intimate space of my Desire which, having wilfully capitalised, I will explain. I remember when I first had an espresso. I was with Julia in a café in Oxford. The one on St Giles, the Italian greasy spoon where posh boys 'slummed it' and liked to pretend – trying to sink their port-stained hangovers – they were enjoying a proletarian breakfast. But it was the only, or one of the few, places back then in Oxford with decent coffee. The first time I went there with Julia, believe it or not, I had only ever drunk instant coffee. At home, in Bradford, we only ever drank instant coffee, such that for me, instant coffee simply *was* coffee. But suddenly I was presented with a number of options which Julia talked me through. 'Which is better,' I asked her, 'cappuccino or espresso?' 'Well, cappuccino is nicer, I think, but espresso is cooler.' Of course, I chose espresso; I wanted to don the mantle of 'cooler', however briefly. So, firstly, it tasted repugnant, a mouthful of ash. This is what growing up involves. Ingesting things that one initially finds repugnant. Beer, whisky, cigarettes, olives. You overcome it, this initial revulsion, you overcome and metabolise it, and feel augmented, fortified. There's no way back. And each cigarette or whisky or espresso you have, over many years, contains – however faintly or implicitly – the memory of this overcoming. Julia told me about espressos. Julia who was herself a part of the world of which espressos were another part. Café tables and philosophical discussions, but also shots of pungent fuel drunk at the bar by workers and industrialists alike. Julia whose mother had lived in Paris, whose parents went annually to Rome. It is difficult to communicate what it meant for me, that small white porcelain cup, with the crown of crema and the quick dark punch beneath. It was a tiny perfect escape hole, and through that hole I would exit England. When I looked into that small white cup, I saw the portal through which I would travel into Europe, or *the idea of Europe*, for my desire for an espresso was also the desire for this idea, for a shelf of Les Éditions de Minuit, for a Gauloises cigarette smouldering in an ashtray like a white existential stick of time, for wine decanted into those small Duralex glasses served in a local bar, for gold-rimmed tables advancing into the boulevard, a small shot drunk at the bar with a sweet pastry, the passionate energy of conversation making the world light and pliable. And each of these things was, and is, linked to yet more, each one is the part of a whole which is never complete. For Desire is not simply for the single thing, but for the world of which the thing is part, and Desire amplifies itself through all of these plural components with gradually growing elation. (Of course, in reply to all this, there will be a chorus of English voices crying 'Pretentious', that much is obvious and as it should be, for if you can hear those cries then you're already on the plane, and the *apparent* cries of 'Pretentious' are in fact simply the transient ringing in your ears, caused by the difference in pressure, as you ascend up into the new blue sky.)

I thought this Desire had landed and nested, here on Berwick Street, with Café Amato, I thought I had discovered, here in Soho, my little bit of Europe and Italy in particular of course,

Amato with its extraterritorial status. And in fact, before Cahun started appearing, as he did regularly over the coming months, the only person I saw in that café was an old Italian man in a pale-blue tailored suit and matching fedora; a man who doubtless 'cut a dash' in his day, a man on the wrong side of retirement, which is to say the right side of retirement, blossoming as only the retired can do, knowing that work is behind them, enjoying the new vistas of earned freedom and drawing each day with a free virtuosic hand. He had a slight look of my father, this old man, although my father was always a 'scruffbag' as my mother put it, and also Irish, or half-Irish, rather than Italian. And I was reminded how my father had, after his retirement, undergone a kind of renaissance. Anyway, the old Italian man was a fireball of croaks and gesticulations, gimlet eyes and knocking joints. He'd sit at the bar, sipping espresso slowly as if to summon the Old Country, like Tiresias in the underworld drinking the blood, and chat to the baristas, this old fella, about football and food. I could only catch half of it. I was learning Italian, or making gentle and respectful forays into Italian, which I had always thought the most musical language, for in each phrase there is a quiet rapture, a slow and rising ecstasy, or, alternately, a note of plaint, of maternal lamentation.

This is, for illustrative purposes, in every respect, phonetically and rhythmically, the exact opposite of the Birmingham accent, wherein one hears only the murmur of diurnal disappointment and which, defined by bathos and anticlimax, is quintessentially English. I had occasion to visit Birmingham to deliver my Adorno paper. There was a woman on the bus reading a newspaper. Apropos some article in the *Birmingham Mail*, she turned to her neighbour and said, 'You can tell they're a murderer by their eyes,' where in that final word, 'eyes', such a sad misshapen diphthong, which rhymed almost with 'toys', you could hear not only all the air escaping from the end of the sentence, as from a punctured tyre, but also the soul escaping from the body, and, finally, hope taking leave of the world. And someone unfamiliar with English would infer from the cadence alone that the speaker was irreversibly crestfallen and defeated. And these words, so flat, so despondent, would stay with me for the rest of the afternoon, tracing through my insides their falling arch, again and again, so that by evening I was appreciably sadder. If there was a child who grew up half in Birmingham, half in Italy, with a Birmingham parent and an Italian parent, the result would be a monster, a living contradiction, confused by its own existence and barely able to speak. A bum note would stop every rapture, 'Buongiorno' would skid and sink on the second syllable. The truly gormless fact that Birmingham has more miles of canal than Venice (a fact that must immediately cede to parenthetical laughter) can only remind us that Birmingham is not so much the opposite as the active negation of Venice, an attempt, point by point, to invert and destroy the impulses and principles that built St Mark's Square and the Doge's Palace.

In any case, in my efforts to learn Italian, I'd meet, sometimes in Amato, with Faustina from the university; we'd have lunch and work on an Ungaretti poem. His great, great 'Natale': *Sto/ con le quattro/ capriole/ di fumo/ del focolare.* She was an administrator, Faustina, but had a better understanding of poetry than most of the faculty, which isn't saying much. Poetry can be taught to an extent – the techniques, the metrics and forms. You can measure the distance from ordinary language, or the rediscovery of ordinary language via a different route. But to be a poet is to have a certain kind of soul, and only those with a similarly disposed soul can truly understand you. Poetry, the faculty members fail to see, is not just a form of words but a form of life, a form of life which, if it blossoms, must blossom in words. It would not surprise me if the old man, wizened but twinkling with life, had such a soul. Such souls cannot be easily put out. As I say, he was the only presence in that café in the early hours, in the pause before day gets started. Until Cahun started coming. Then the old man left. I saw him a few times in Bar Italia. Cahun had driven him out. No doubt this expulsion represented for me the expulsion of old Europe by modern digital commerce, to put it in cartoon abbreviation, and nor was this merely imposed symbolism, for people are indeed the bearers and agents of history, even if only Retrospect can see this.

Almost every day of the week he was there in the café, Cahun, almost every day on his phone talking about concepts and deliverables, that which was 'actionable' and that which was not. There is no difference at all between Cahun imposing on me a jumble of business jargon, I thought, chipping away at my auditory circumference with his shiny terminology, and me standing up and delivering to him a lecture on Wittgenstein. In both cases the one person inducts the other into his world, willy-nilly. And the only reason I did not do this was out of consideration for the barista and the cook.

But I did in fact prepare a brief peroration on Wittgenstein, which I considered serving to Cahun whilst he was mid-blather. 'The English have an anti-philosophical disposition,' I would have begun, 'which is why they so readily accommodated the anti-philosopher Wittgenstein, who knew practically nothing about the history of philosophy and was like someone who, having read hardly any novels, and caring little for the great novelists, nonetheless declares that he has written the novel to end all novels, and that henceforth all novels are stillborn on account of his own modest innovations. Wittgenstein thought that philosophical problems could be "fixed", as one might fix a leak, or repair a creaking door with a shot of WD-40, or perhaps install a new door in a more ergonomic part of the room, or rather knock down the through wall and dispense with the need for a door altogether. Wittgenstein, like many English philosophers, thought that if we took apart the plumbing of ordinary language our philosophical problems would either be resolved or simply disintegrate like limescale. Wittgenstein used to hit children round the head, and is lauded for his ethical purity because, years later, bothered and scratched by guilt's contusions, he went back to apologise, humbling himself, making the pilgrim's journey of supplication and self-abasement, the philosophical prince walking naked and ashamed through the eye of a needle. Wittgenstein is of course everyone's cut-and-paste "genius", all intense stares and ascetic discipline. "Raisins are the best part of a cake," he opines, "but a bag of raisins is not better than a cake." An interesting piece of whimsy any of us might think of whilst gazing out of a bus window. But of course Wittgenstein's cake is elevated to gnomic brilliance because countersigned by Wittgenstein's head, balancing precariously on his neck and fronted by his craggy, staring face. People are mesmerised by Wittgenstein's face, and no other philosopher's face has graced more young students' walls, hanging above their desks like a destination and a guardian. People who say they like Wittgenstein are often merely held captive by the image of his face staring absently at nothing.' Anyway, I did not do this, after deciding on another course of action, based upon observation of Cahun's morning routine and movements and also upon my needs and fantasies.

My fantasy began as a dream, a recurrent dream. In this dream, Cahun was living in my flat as a lodger. I had the room on the ground floor and he was in the room above me, although in reality of course I have a one-floor flat. He was always trying to ingratiate himself with me, smarmy and unpleasant, asking me about my books, my music, my food, my coffee. He was, in the dream, a sycophant, one who covets, crouches, chuckles, and with his presumptuous intimacy attempts to pierce my too-private world. In my dream, I hear him enter the premises around midnight. The light in the hall goes on, then footsteps. I crouch down at the keyhole of my room and see his face very near the door. Of course, he is unaware of being observed. It looks like the face of a criminal. An ugly, worried expression, the eyes sightless and dull. No longer plugged into his phone, the muscles slacken and reveal the resting evil underneath. I get out of bed and without warning strike him with an iron pole. The bones in his head crack. He is astonished that I, so ostensibly quiet, can rise to such anger and force. But it's easy. He buckles quickly. He curls in a ball on the floor, his face wrinkled and red. I make him stand and repeat, through his tears, his usual sycophantic banter, but it's choked beyond recognition. 'Ooh, that looks yummy mate, I wish I hadn't just eaten!' Say it again, I instruct him. Like the scene in the Greenaway film where they make him eat his own books. His head shakes; his voice burps then jumps like a wounded rabbit. I make as if to hit him again and his hands try to cover his face. He is so reduced. This phrase, 'He is so reduced', enters the dream in shining letters. Anyway, it isn't enough to see him hurt and bewildered. I push on. I drag him to the woods. He lies on the edge of the pond, cold among the reeds, with tiny red blinking eyes. Worse for wear but alive. His brittle voice still repeating the lines I'd fed him. Shrivelled, naked, blue around the gills. I stand on his neck; I kick him in the mouth. 'Don't you enter the house again,' I say, 'don't you slither and grin in the kitchen. Don't defile my gentle music.' His soul knocks and buzzes against the panes of his eyes. I instruct him to go back to the flat and pack his bags. He crawls back to Soho on his hands and knees. The dream ends accompanied by Bowie's crepuscular 'Diamond Dogs'. 'You'll catch your death in the cold'. Or is it the fog?

I wrote it down, this dream, in more elaborate form, so as to try and dissipate my anger, to get rid of it by writing it out, those wriggling black thoughts now dry and external, calcified, turned to matter, insects pressed between cream-coloured pages. But the act of writing it out also transformed it into a fantasy. When I had written it out, late one night, I lay down and snugly slept.

But the next morning I realised there was an unquiet remainder. It was important I felt to make contact with this fantasy. What I wanted to do, without fulfilling this fantasy, which is the last thing we want from our fantasies, actually to complete them, was nonetheless to make contact with it, to brush against it, kiss it on the cheek, or, in other words, do a fist bump with it. Yes, that is the perfect image: a mere fist bump. It was also important, as well as making contact with this fantasy, to make more literal contact with Cahun himself, but anonymously of course. For Cahun had presented himself in two forms: as an image, almost sculptural (when off the phone), and then as a voice, as an auditory assault (when on it). Whilst the former was pleasant but nonetheless a mere semblance, the latter was invasive – and more than invasive since the voice, being immaterial, is in some sense like another soul entering your head. It is immaterial in the sense that you cannot ask 'how high is a voice, how much does it weigh?' – just as the same is true of a thought or indeed any mental event. It was important therefore that my contact with Cahun should be counter-invasive, should, as it were, redeem and reverse the invasions I had suffered. It should also, and simultaneously, puncture the image of Cahun as well, in so far as that image was false but also insistent, like a lure, right from when I first saw him in his 'marmoreal isolation', as I described it as the time, such that 'marmoreal isolation' has itself become a component of the image, the verbal stencil within which the image was drawn and tinted.

I made this 'fist bump' decision shortly after Cahun had conducted a Skype conversation with someone in New Zealand, a man called 'Si'. 'Investment in UK digital tech is more than twice any other European country,' he was saying. I tried to ignore him but was rudely brought to consciousness by his raised voice asking Si about 'the value proposition'. 'What's the value proposition, Si?' he demanded, and kept reiterating this phrase throughout the conversation. Si tried to explain what the value proposition was. No point of course, as the phrase is meaningless. Both of them, Si and Cahun, spoke in a language infected and in fact colonised by business jargon and so-called 'business concepts' which, as I have said, are laughably remote from anything that might with dignity be called a concept. 'Value proposition.' Fuck off. 'Value' as some sort of quantifiable add-on unit. Fuck off again. I imagined – a kind of daydream following on from the night dream – Cahun standing in front of manifold lovely and costless things, stupidly repeating his demand for a value proposition. He's on the Rue Mouffetard at a café terrace. There are two old ladies drinking a bottle of wine and laughing; they've been there for hours. But what's the value proposition? Or he's in the Buttes-Chaumont. There is a group of old fellas playing boules under a tree. They were born in the war, they're talking about the 1950s, about austerity and about De Gaulle. Cahun's watching them, puzzled. 'What's the value proposition?' he intones to himself. He has no idea. He's reading Genet's essay on Giacometti, where Genet says that these thin and selfless gifts are presented to the Dead not the Living. 'But what's the value proposition?' asks Cahun. He doesn't know. Now he's back in London; someone's helping a blind man cross the road. Cahun walks on. There's a busker playing Django Reinhardt. No one's stopped to listen, but the busker is smiling. Cahun stands closer to him… 'What's the value proposition?' he asks him in a Stephen Hawking voice. The busker can't hear him of course. Fucking robotic bullshit is not on his radar. The noise from Cahun's mouth has less meaning than gravel or wind, and none of the zest. His voice grows slowly insistent, like a Dalek. Unable now to see value propositions anywhere, his brain short-circuits and implodes. He lies on the ground, his arm jerking up and down, his eyes white and sightless, the voice reduced to a loop of 'what's the value, what's the value, what's the value'. Eventually, he's towed away by the council.

Cahun, Cahun the business goon, crawls back home by the light of the moon. Cahun, Cahun, lying in a swoon, jerked into life by a spastic tune.

It was no accident that not only did Cahun remind me of McCann, the telesales dog, the jackanapes, who was a spectre from hell — a hell of my own part-devising — but that in retreat from both of these business goons, and their respective wordshit, I had mental recourse — through a seraphic gauze of nostalgia – to Oxford. Oxford, whose inception predates capitalism, was and is, I always fancied, a space at one remove from the present, or at least contains such spaces. An enclave, inward and circumscribed, a place which, by nature, resists the noisy imperatives of the age. The willpower to be at odds with the present, to sit on the knoll apart, is something that only a few can summon, for it yields almost no financial reward. It is something which, when explained to the average punter, will meet with 'What are you going to do with that?' I'm studying marginalia in ancient Irish manuscripts, the child-raising habits of the Maasai, the founding principles of mathematics. 'What are you going to do with that? What are you going to do with that?' they ask, with angry insistence. The only answers they recognise are Money and Success. I'm always tempted to reply, in Pinteresque staccato: 'Your arse, I'm going to ram it up your arse. Up your fucking arse.' Everything about Oxford, as I remember it, the architecture and the space it defines and arranges, is geared to contemplation. The quad of Worcester College (for example) is an exact frame for contemplation, perfectly designed for thoughts of the highest quality. Behind each facade in Oxford is a revelation of space. Each college has a taciturn frontage, continuous and linear with the street. But to pass through this facade, this portal, is to step through a looking glass. Suddenly, a roomy courtyard with its calm geometry. A courtyard, sequestered from street noise; and then, through the narrowest arch, a sudden expanse of countryside, a long lake hung with trees, where I often walked with Julia. Behind the surface, concertinas of space, compartments and vistas.

And the libraries of Oxford are vast aggregate collections of a silence which the occasional shuffle of papers, a cough, a whispered enquiry, only serve to reinforce. If you sit in the Radcliffe

Camera, the halo of a desk lamp beside you, there is above your head a great dome filled with silence, stacked with silence, so to speak, and with stillness. This dome is as big as any thought you might have, curved and shaped perfectly like a concept. The Radcliffe Camera is simply among the world's most magnificent and inviolable thought sanctuaries, although I haven't been back for years. They might have got rid of the desk lamps, there might be the humming of laptops, the insect click of keys, each screen a hole in the fabric of contemplation, an artificial light shining through the slit. It is too awful to think about. If the Radcliffe has fallen then civilisation has fallen, *its great battle lost*, as Yeats put it. Shut the door of the Pope's Chapel, keep those fuckwits out.

I had retained in my London flat a number of objects, relics, from Oxford, one of which I still wore – the baseball cap that belonged to my friend Alex, the philosopher, who had left it with me when he returned to Chicago. Julia introduced me to him at Linacre College. He owned very few books, and I never saw him in the library. This was because he was doing a PhD in Logic and all he had to do was think, as he told me, just sit and think and write. His desk and papers were in his head and he carried them with him to, for example, the side of that lush green canal, overlooked by the sun-dappled walls of the old factory. Where I might see only a buzzing busyness of midges, he would be like Blake's Newton, his calipers of rules and reasons, blind to the variegated whole of nature and to his own vital corporeal life. This was, in some sense, an enviable position to be in, I always thought. He could do this anywhere, unhooked from books or ladders or footnotes, sat by the quiet canal with his laptop, working through the logical structure of sentences and scribbling notes, wearing his cap.

I'd join him there and we'd analyse a film we'd seen, such as *A Heart in Winter*, or we'd talk about a woman he was pursuing. It was always a question of uncovering the implicit rules and following them. 'So I was in the toilet today at college, and I heard this great fart like a trombone, I mean just like a trombone, from inside the cubicle. So when the door opens it's Radson, my supervisor. We have a really good relationship. I mean he's a friend. But I'm like "can I make a joke about the fart?" because if he does it in front of you, that's fine, right. But does the cubicle constitute private space? Even though it's audible of course. But anyway, it's an interesting question. There's like a rule that anything you hear from inside a cubicle you don't mention, right.'

'Why does garlic smell so good on the fingers but so rank on the breath,' he queried another time. 'Even disgust has its rules, right?' And so on. I always thought that this view of things, of a world structured according to manifold rules and laws, *expressed* more about Alex than anything else. It suited him, and pleased him, to think of the world in this way, as if all the surface confusions, the plurality of textures and sounds, was underwritten by a clean blueprint of permutations. No doubt he would say that the world really is like this, it really is structured by rules and laws, and his view simply reflected this fact, just as Leibniz might say the world is really composed of monads. But just as Leibniz's system is now thought of primarily as a fantastic imaginative construct, almost a work of art like Joyce's *Wake*, so Alex's picture of the world as a web of rules can likewise be seen as, in fact, the web spun from his own imagination, and as an elaborate and implicit autobiography, a geometric sketch of his inmost desire.

'Of all the people I know in Oxford,' Alex told me, 'you're the guy I'll keep in touch with.' This sentence is always there under my tongue, kept artificially alive by saliva and regret. That was before they all started to fall away, my friends at Oxford. After I became ill, they all fell away, and I can't blame them. Alex or Grainne, Nicos or Raphael. I don't attribute any blame. For we are not attracted to persons but to their traits and tics. A dimple, a tone, a laugh, an expression of glee, the shape and texture of the voice. A 'person' *is* only an assemblage of traits and tics. We pretend we are attracted to the whole person, but no one can say what the 'whole person' consists of without simply listing these traits. It's the same as in a novel, as I tell my students. A novelist presents us with a constellation of tics and traits and we infer a person supporting these, but in fact they rest on nothing. It is a depth-illusion, no more, just as in real life. Yes, there is certainly less difference between real and fictional characters than we allow, one difference being that imaginary beings always have a sadness – a share of sadness that we cannot grasp – concerning the fact that they do not exist.

A French writer once said that he *fell in love very unexpectedly, perhaps because of a beautiful, bitter smile*. This is how it is. The great film stars, to use a slightly different example, are in fact only the bearers of stubborn traits to which we are repeatedly attracted, which we desire to see again and again in slightly different guises and situations. De Niro has an amused but manic glint which is not only the signature of Travis Bickle but will reappear in Rupert Pupkin and numerous other roles. The traits persist and the characters fade. Eastwood, who is not a great actor, nonetheless has an enraged astonishment which persists through each of his incarnations – the anonymous nomad of the spaghetti western, the Maverick Cop and the various other dark angels of American justice, a watermark repeated but differently time after time, for difference is only the handmaid of repetition. It is true, also, of Brando, a mad inwardness only half visible, and Bogart, a hardness melting round the edges or from the centre.

In my case, for example, just to give you an example, Alex would remark on the 'speculative glee' in my eyes, and in my voice, when I advanced some contrarian opinion (as he thought), some 'devil's advocate' (so he thought) position. And although he and Alice, the Yeats specialist, were doubtless interested in the substance of what I said, they were nonetheless drawn not to that but this speculative glee and desired only to see and hear this glee in its various modulations, for this was my 'amused but manic glint'. They loved, in fact, this 'twinkling audacious joy' (Alice's words) which defied and inverted what they had just argued, this delight that introduced what I said and would, in advance, colour what I said, or serve as a kind of melodic line vibrating through all my words.

I can say, with certainty, that their affection died when this glee died, although they doubtless failed to see this. They, the friends, became busier, more polite, as they finished their research and left the city. I suggested, to Alex, some weeks before he left for New York, that he come round and pick up his baseball cap. We used to joke about him wearing it back to front like a teenager. He said he'd pop round if he had time, but of course he never had time and he never popped round. I was left behind by all of them: Alex and Alice, Grainne, Nicos the philosopher and Rafael the economist. I can still see them, before it all happened, sat round the table on my birthday, at the Lebanese restaurant on Nelson Street. Last time I looked it was still there. I made a point of walking into Jericho to see it. Anyway, it affected me at the time, this exodus. But now I don't blame them. I can't blame them. I can't, without being inconsistent, blame them. So that is how I still have this baseball cap that once belonged to Alex and is, technically, I suppose, still his.

It is always difficult to say when an illness starts, for the outbreak, the rash on the skin, the sudden paralysis of a hand, the weeping sore, the hacking cough, the freezing feet in summer, the tightness in the chest, the nocturnal trips to the toilet, all of these things are eventual filtrations into light and sense of what has long remained hidden, a hidden headless network of roots ready to poke above skin. But the moment of emergence – a victory flag waved by the illness – I remember very clearly.

A month or so after my father's breakdown and Julia's abrupt, as I experienced it, departure, which charred my heart and made the ground give way, I travelled down to London to visit Emer, the fey bourgeois, with her antique dictionary and rigmarole of manners, whose parents owned that tiny house on Tottenham Mews in Fitzrovia. I had eaten nothing all day and by evening hunger had still not arrived. We went for a curry, and as I ate the food, I felt it was merely piling gradually up into my oesophagus and mouth, that there was even some insidious and corrosive reflux up into my brain, and that my head was, incrementally over the course of the meal, becoming detached from the torso and fuzzy. As we ate more, so did my body thicken and my nerves were numbed so that zones of my body were one by one subtracted. I remember Emer for some reason talking about the Irish Civil War, but the words 'Irish Civil War' meant nothing and were no more than stiff sounds which I greeted with panic, as in some sudden exam. I tried to reply but she looked puzzled and said I was confusing it with the 'revolutionary war', but I could not recall what this was, the revolutionary war. There

I was, sat inside my body, eating a madras, listening to words I did not understand. This was a truly appalling evening, in actual fact, which inflicted irreversible damage on me as a person and marked, as I now see it, the onset of my illness, which had doubtless been planning its attack for months. I apologised to Emer and said I would get the coach back to Oxford. She insisted that I stay, which I did, but I left at 3 a.m., substituting for myself a yellow Post-It note and a scribbled apology.

On the coach back to Oxford it struck me, although my head was full of enemy dust, that everything I'd learnt, I'd learnt in the previous five years. When I did my A levels, I was also reading Pound and Joyce and Eliot, in order to prepare for the Oxbridge entrance exam. And when I got to Oxford, I went to all the lectures I could: to MacGregor on Marx, modernism and money; to Connor on the early, middle, late and terminal Yeats; the lectures of Ron Harris, the elderly but nimble white-haired chimp with his great telescopic view of science and philosophy, his vaunted 'synoptic sweep'; the eminent Frost, his bowel-emptying bass voice expostulating on Irish history. And all the while gorging on new language, and learning about ratatouille, wine and avocados, and forgetting about Angel Delight and boiled mince and cornflakes. I'd crammed it all into five years, but now it was all leaking out, I felt, leaking out of my nose and ears, the slow liquefaction of my knowledge, little drops of knowledge on my upper lip, dripping and dribbling away onto the orange and black seat of the coach from London to Oxford, Oxford where the skies turned grey and rain came down and never stopped, as I stayed in my room and did nothing.

It struck me, then on the coach but more and more in the coming weeks, that I had assimilated it all too quickly and too soon, the language of literature, the language of academics, so removed from my own, that I had borrowed the garb not only of other people's speech but of other people's thinking, the mimetic zeal of the excluded as Adorno calls it, and that perhaps I had only been an imitator. I was convinced, over those same weeks, that I had succeeded only *as* an imitator, that I owed my modest achievements to this fact. At Oxford, it is true, I achieved one of the best degrees in my year, but I was certain that my success was due to my facility, my flair, as an imitator not in imitating, verbatim or in paraphrasis, other people's work or ideas, but in adopting and reproducing their style of thought. Certainly, I had always found this a very easy thing to do, to imitate not the thoughts but the style of thinking, both the tone and the direction, the expected or unexpected turns, the characteristic rhythm. I was able to reproduce their styles almost in my sleep, as some musicians are instantly able to compose something *in the style of* such and such a composer. I was able to do this without slipping into parody or pastiche. I was able to stop just before this point, as it were, to exercise a certain discipline even in imitation. And this was the key to my success, I decided on the coach.

But I saw as well that I have been involved in this imitation all my life. I remember, for example, how I would imitate the facial expressions of my parents in order to uncover the emotion underneath, to *be* the emotion underneath, to see what it felt like to make such a facial expression and thus to gain access to the angry or loving soul behind it. My mother, for example: there was a smile she sometimes did, but a smile that seemed to hold in its curved hand a bundle of sadness. In my room I would keep doing this smile and try to catch the feeling that went along with it. I could feel it for a second, then it slipped away. But I think in the end I managed to get to it; I think it was what I'd now call compassion – she looked at me with compassion, an awareness of vulnerability and innocence, of a child's unreachable vulnerability, for the place from which a small child looks at an adult is finally an unreachable place. So this new thing, compassion, flickered through me when I did the face.

Anyway, time and again I have only unpicked the soul though imitating the surface. I have gained access to the supple soul only through the rebus of the surface. I had always been only a copyist, I told myself, on the coach and over the precipitous weeks that followed, and was convinced also that this, this insight, confiscated from me nearly everything I had achieved, and left me with a residuum of nothing, or next to nothing.

As I looked out of the coach window, at the rows of tatty shops, the Magical Wok and the Star of India, as we moved slowly through Acton the walls of my world gave way, as we sped through the land in the cold dead of night, I could hear and see only the collapse of masonry, all the double-locked wooden doors and windows now smashed and left by the roadside exposing the night of the world outside, which seemed only a cold revelation – this night of the world – of the selfsame thing within. The stage sets of my learning collapsed, my speech and my gestures as well, the backdrops and dei ex machinis, revealing the mere night underneath and behind and inside. For no doubt this collapsing masonry, and the revelation of Night, of bottomless depth, or bottomless height, was only a representation of what had already happened, seen now retrospectively on the coach and in the rear-view mirror as it were. It was in response to this woozy revelation of nothing – that scooped me out and exposed me as an imitator, a fraud – that I retreated into the gut, with all the disastrous corollaries.

It was ostensibly an illness of the stomach. This was my error. Thinking of it only as an illness of the stomach. This, this thinking, was itself part of the illness, a kind of outgrowth of the illness. But it is hardly surprising I imagined it to be a stomach illness, because the stomach had jammed up completely, it became *chaste and withered* (as I wrote then); the whole digestive apparatus was jammed and broken; I was *full of masticated food-filth* (as I also wrote then), and my organs, it felt, were distended with filth, and rotten, and sluggish and morbid; the stomach and all its appetites dead, the stomach, the *seat* of appetite dead, and hunger no more than a glimmer or word, a sound losing touch with its meaning. When I ate there were immediately noises to the left of the stomach like nothing that I'd ever heard, and movements like I'd never felt. But the doctors were deaf and set themselves against me, agents of cold mockery. In the face of medical deafness, of course, you are forced back on your own resources. Just as I had been forced to educate myself at the moronic and nominal 'school', Shawcross, yes, just as I was forced to educate myself and be my own master, so and in a similar fashion was I driven to try and cure myself as it were, with psyllium, peppermint, slippery elm; cardamom, cumin and dill; miso and tofu, organic wild rice, cereal soaked in weak nettle tea, ginger, dandelion capsules, dried banana in hot soya milk. A pitcher of rosemary tea in the fridge. My stomach became my object and my Enemy, and would sometimes stuff the mutinous gut with – crap – buttery and rich pastries from Maison Noir, for example, eating myself into a coma. Needless to say, my brain had also stopped, given that the two things, the stomach and the brain, are now recognised to be cut from the same cloth and in constant dialogue, so to speak, and fields of serotonin receptors like wheat, in the intestine, and subtle mutations in gut microbiota triggering thought vibrations in the mind. If only I had found the door to the stomach, the hidden director, the overseer, and answered his obscure demands. I fed him with all kinds of magical potions, this hidden and hungerless godling. I offered him all kinds of herbs. He refused them all, the stomach demon. He was spiteful and silent. Spiteful and silent, celebrating his triumphs. I punched him and swore at him, swore at him hard and punched him harder, and everything or almost everything that happened in my mind I regarded as the refluxes and repercussions of what went on down there, my stomach the origin and patent holder of the matter and timbre of thought.

Everything about this illness is recorded in the 1994–5 notebook, one of the few relics I have from this period. Only recently I found it sorting through stuff for the monograph. It was a gift from Julia, before she headed back home to Manhattan. I don't know where she got it. Its marbled binding and cream-coloured paper. Here it is to my left as I write, torn slightly and stained with the bottom of that porcelain espresso cup I used to drink out of then. Wall after wall of writing. Tiny, tiny microscopic script. Half close your eyes and it blurs to black. Each day for a year I wrote out all that I'd eaten, all that I'd drunk, every rise and fall in mood. The highlight of the day was to sit and to write in this book, the destination of the book, waiting at the end of the day, the light on the cream-coloured page, the day shrunk to that circle of light from the desk lamp and the ink briefly shining then dried by the heat. Accompanied always with coffee, that small Lavazza cup, that I still have somewhere like the ritual paraphernalia of an extinct tribe, a chalice from the museum of experience. I wish I could reach out to him, that earlier me, who had only the page to share his obsessions, only the page as his asylum, who lived and breathed in paper and ink.

And yet even now, when the belated owl of self-knowledge has landed on my shoulder, even now, by which I mean this very moment, I enjoy discussing my illness and am still attached to the stubborn crusts and dried strings of my illness that still linger, unflushed, as if the detailed description of the illness is actually an extension or afterlife *of the thing it describes*, and in fact it is not possible for me to resurrect this illness, descriptively, without living it, without it, as it were, summoning to life the invalid I was, lethargic and thin and defeated.

As I withdrew further into this illness, as I nestled within it and added to the nest, the chatter of others stopped like animals before a storm. I had entered an enclave so hermetic I lost the outside, the air, the voice of the outside. I entered a space of asphyxiation, so to speak, and just as some people experience intense and terrible pleasure at the point of literal asphyxiation and deliberately seek out and engineer such experiences, sometimes with fatal collateral effects — that obscure Tory MP for example — so in this airless (and, I sometimes imagined, terminal) place, I often experienced an inexplicable joy. Being invisible, the light simply passed through me. I was, at such moments, sat at my desk, with the nimbus of a desk light my only illumination, transformed. If I met with a friend, I would describe in minute detail the behaviour of my stomach and intestines. Bring people too close, and the distance suddenly opens. For it is obvious that people in fact require concealment. Whatever they might say, it is the case that for other human beings there is always a 'too much' which must be held back. Illness, abjection, wretchedness, madness. People don't want to touch it. Each of us contains a disgusting part. The social contract, that is to say, the successful operation of our relations with others, asks that this share is concealed, so that the social contract is a charade, a contractual denial of mutual disgust. And yet in the finish, in the last hour, when the lights have been turned off everywhere else, there is a sweetness and grace in being alone in this substrate, there is a heavenly luminosity in resting content with this abject and disgusting portion of yourself, in being unreachable and closed.

There are two individuals I think of when I think of my days of illness in Oxford, two individuals who I would always see in the library. Firstly, the cripple. He was only my age but pale and sickly, hobbling with a stick, an untidy clump of straw-coloured hair. His last years furnished and waiting, I thought, all heavy curtains and evening light, old clocks and embers and sherry. In the Upper Reading Room he read Byron and Keats, in brown leather volumes called up from the vaults, where albino librarians labour and blink under blank neon lights. His eyes, the cripple, were blue and kind. The pale face. The dry dusty smell in the Upper Reading Room, the light through the great leaded windows, the creaking silence, like that of a great ship resting. As well as the cripple another. A bent man in a tattered gown, with NHS glasses and greasy comb-over. The illegitimate son of F.R. Leavis, people said. But that was perhaps only a metaphor that time had dried out into fact. He'd enter by the corner door, glancing about like an intruder. He'd take down a reference book, a different book each time, frantically flicking through pages. Then stop to sit and look, only the finger in motion, like a metal detector looking for buried sense. Was he searching for sleeping secrets or was it an empty rigmarole, habit's relentless machine? I don't know. The book would slam shut and he'd steal away. A library bird picking at scraps, the limp gown flapping. The cripple and the madman, like gargoyles in the margins of medieval illustrations. Figures of what I feared I might become. Frayed and insane, a faint light flickering in a corner window. But I did not become either of these fixed allegorical figures, I did not.

There was a mysterious sympathy, during the first year of my illness, between my father and me. My father had returned to work after his breakdown, after his terrible interregnum. Perhaps too soon, for by January 1995 he was back at his desk. But he said nothing was the same. He complained that people no longer listened to him in meetings, people no longer took his ideas seriously. They, the others, were doubtless infected with the knowledge of my father's breakdown, and so perceived him differently. Previously, my father said, people hung on his every word and he spoke and steered the meeting, whereas now, he announced, they ignored or sped past his contributions. He was in some way marked and tarnished by his breakdown, his illness. He too had exposed his vulnerable and therefore disgusting part. He felt invisible, he told me, and people, when they addressed him, did so with a patronising politeness, just as they did with me. And like my father with his meetings, so it was with me and my seminars. My contributions, such as they existed, for they were muted and infrequent, went unanswered or were met with embarrassment and shuffling papers.

All my life I had found it difficult to share anything with my father, who I always considered an agent of the law, the law with its mantra 'Because I said so', deaf to entreaty. But with his breakdown my father and I, I and my father, came into an alignment. I never discussed this alignment with my father of course, because it only became obvious *post factum*, or post-mortem, as it were. It is obvious that our respective planets, which had for so long been in different orbits, now came into alignment and formed a new constellation entirely. He returned to work, my father, only for a year or two, I think. It was no longer the same. He was a 'spare part' and the office was no longer a congenial place. And so he took early retirement, my father, and at the same time I left Oxford, for still our stars were oddly linked. My father's departure from his work in the housing department, which he had always loved, and mine from my beloved Oxford, were parallel lines, drawn by some occult hand. At the time I made no connection between these two things of course, and imagined that the motive force for leaving Oxford was to escape a stultifying and enclosed world, whereas it was, in many ways, the voluntary descent into hell.

My father, in the slow autumn splendour after his retirement in 1997, did not immediately pursue his hobbies, his gardening, his allotment, his books about the Russian army in the Second World War, his obsessive watching of spaghetti westerns. No, he took a job at Hallowgill Cemetery, that great necropolis where the Victorian and subsequent dead of Bradford are laid to rest. This included his own father, who had died just after my father retired and who left my father the bungalow which they built together in the early 1960s. My father went to live with the dead and learnt their stories and language, under the stewardship of the cemetery's director. But this great city of the dead, comparable to Père Lachaise, is not located deep under the earth, in the airless bowels and snickets of the underworld. No, Hallowgill is elevated on a great hill above the entire town and supervises and monitors the living city beneath it: Olympus rather than Hades. From Hallowgill you are granted a god's eye view of Bradford and its satellites, and this elevation, the city on the hill, is to me a more realistic picture of the relation between the living and dead, for the dead are not benighted and concealed but congregate on the peak apart and are given the great panoptic vision denied to those on the ground. They are no longer bound in practicalities but see things almost aesthetically, for what they see has no longer any use to them, and, liberated from use, things stand revealed in the glorious fatness and lustre of existence. In this sense the dead are closer to existence than the living. The only way to approach the Dead, to be like the Dead, is, firstly, to be a tramp, a genuine lifelong tramp, or, secondly, like my father, to live with the Dead on the top of the world. To enter the world again by removing yourself from it. There are also a couple of ways in which one becomes a kind of honorary affiliate member of the Dead. To have narrowly missed death, like Dostoevsky before the firing squad, some great reprieve which allows you a posthumous life, or, perhaps, in certain instances, to have killed someone, to have committed a crime so terrible that you are exiled from the living human community, even if no one knows.

My father kept, albeit mentally, a kind of register of the dead, and was able to regale me, and my mother, with many facts and dates concerning the men and women and no few children who were buried on that incontestable hill. And when we went walking, me and my mother and father, he would stop at every commemorative bench to clock the dates and instantly declare the age of the deceased. He was like someone trying to calculate the lottery numbers by examining all previous combinations. The 'winning numbers' however were in this case the moment of his own fatal exit. It was only after some months that I learned the name of the cemetery director, and discovered it to be a boy, now a man, from my former school, Nigel Ruddley.

I told my father that I had been to school with this boy, and my father mentioned it to Ruddley, who spoke to my father about his school days and how he was relentlessly attacked by Tanner. 'Some bloody toerag made his life a misery,' my father said, whereupon I told him it was the toerag Tommy Tanner, who once pinched an ornament from our verdant garden and whose father was a crook. 'You went round to his house,' I said to my father, 'and he never bothered me again.' What upset my father in particular was the incident that became, at my school, notorious, a cause célèbre: Tanner forced Ruddley to eat some dog shit. 'It wasn't fresh dog shit,' a girl called Caroline Peel explained, 'it was some of that hard white dog shit, probably been there ages,' as if this were a mitigating factor, or as if they were slightly disappointed the shit wasn't softer, browner. Ruddley's name was then synonymous with eating dog shit, and anyone who touched him would declare they had 'Ruddley germs' and try to pass them on to someone else as soon as possible. I hadn't been there but could only imagine him knelt on the pavement by the grass verge, Tanner and his cronies craning over him, stupidly swaggering, spitting and leering, smoking and laughing, offering freedom if only he'd eat the dog shit, and of course 'tell no one' or he'd have his 'head kicked in'. The mindset of the schoolyard is such that Ruddley was always spurned as the boy who had eaten dog shit whilst Tanner was never spurned as the boy who'd forced someone to eat dog shit. Actually, this is not simply the law of the schoolyard; it is the way of the world. People like Tanner are everywhere, walking free and regarded as normal human beings. To treat the supposedly weak and defenceless as rubbish, this is what is called Evil. And it is not enough to claim that he was only a child. Tanner knew what he was doing and enjoyed it.

Ruddley communicated all of this to my father, who passed it back to me. He told me all about this over the phone, for I was living in London of course at the time, and, as he did, I heard his voice wobble.

In hearing these words of my father, Ruddley was present to me like a hologram. His way of speaking, his walk, his square Tupperware lunchbox with neatly cut ham sandwiches, the edges stained with mustard, the satsuma and the Penguin McVitie's milk chocolate biscuits in various flavours. I could very clearly see his long thin legs and the navy-blue trousers at half mast and other marks of poverty, and can actually again see them now as I write these words – for writing is often a form of sorcery – Ruddley sitting down in the corner of the canteen, the orange Formica tables with blue metal legs, the smell of boiled vegetables from the kitchen. I see it clearly unfold, like a well-rehearsed scene: Ruddley taking from the Tupperware box a thin square of sandwich, looking down at the table, trying to mind his own business as Tanner and his asinine gang sit opposite him. It was true that for many years I had neglected to think of this quiet serious boy, and it upset me afresh how this boy Ruddley, who was so quiet and so thoughtful, had been treated by Tanner and the systematic nature of the cruelty meted out by Tanner, the fuckshitter, which went unopposed, including of course by myself. I felt also, on hearing my father's words, something else, rising like sap. A rage. Or rather, the blush of guilt mixed with the rage for justice. Guilt, because I realised that Ruddley was an image of what I ought to have been had I been true to myself, an image of refusal, a refusal – courageous and lonely, so terribly lonely – of the world into which one is thrown. The courage, simply, to sit reading Dickens, the courage to not laugh at farts, the courage to wear his old-fashioned trousers to school every day, to abstain from the cruel obedience of the games of boys. What incredible strength he had, what fidelity and nobility... I should have been that, I should have done that, and at least been his friend. But I didn't, and I wasn't.

My father was audibly moved by Ruddley's story and was moved by many other things at this stage of his life, when he was flooded and augmented actually by an excess of compassion and love, as when for example some youths killed a hedgehog by throwing it at his car. It hit his windscreen and he slammed on the brakes. It still had a glimmer of life in it when he picked it up and put it on the back seat of the car resting on a newspaper. By the time he reached home it was dead. He buried it in his garden, his beloved garden.

I have thought frequently of Tanner, of course, and his bullying of the poor Ruddley boy, and my father working with Ruddley at the eminent cemetery beneath the cold grey welkin, and Ruddley telling him everything, and how he, my teary father, was 'right upset by it', a phrase he used only rarely, as when they threw the hedgehog at his car and it died. The needless cruelty of it, the grievous disappointment in his fellow human beings. And thinking of this poor hedgehog, and of poor Ruddley, I have fantasised about seeking out Tanner, on behalf of my father and on behalf of Ruddley of course. It would after all be easy to bump into him. He still lives in the vicinity. Of course he fucking does. I had a lucid idea of what I might say. I'd go for a walk by the river and see him stood under a tree. Thinned red hair and a great big belly. I'd cross the bridge and walk very closely past him. I'd reproach myself for not saying something. I'd pause and remember everything he'd told my dad. My rage would rise, and so I would circle back. I'd ask without preamble if he remembered Nigel Ruddley. 'Do you know what he's doing now?' I'd ask. 'Do you know where he is now?' 'No fucking idea mate,' Tanner would respond. I'd tell him that Ruddley was in Hallowgill Cemetery. He'd ask what I meant. 'What do you think I *mean*,' I'd retort, livid and laughing in equal measure. 'He's dead. He died two years ago.' I'd say this for no reason other than to confound Tanner. 'What did he die of?' Tanner would ask, springing the trap. 'As far as Nigel Ruddley is concerned,' I'd say, 'he died of eating dog shit. You, you fucking despicable cunt, fed him some dog shit, and the consequent poison entered his veins and also worked its way up into his brain,' I'd say. 'You, a cretin, a bag of skinless gibbering shit,' I'd say, 'made him eat dog shit, if you can imagine, forced him to kneel on the grass by the road in some tatty suburb of Bradford, so that he was made to walk back home with shit in his mouth and speak also to his mother, or his father, with shit in his teeth and gums, telling no one, not his father or mother it seems, about this, and keeping this cankerous humiliation within, where it percolated and festered and eventually overwhelmed him and he died.' Tanner would walk apprehensively backward as I pressed forward, violating his soft penumbra, until he fell back into the water and drowned.

And in my imaginary speech to the corpse I had continued: 'But long before that, long before Ruddley had died, he had retreated into his intestine; he became a creature with long eyelashes, burrowed in his own bowel, like an animal in its den, and trapped, therefore, in his own body. Nor could it be coaxed into daylight, but hid like a blind and brilliant creature,' I said to the pale, vacant body. 'Perhaps only at the point of death did it escape,' I said, 'this bashful creature lodged inside him. At the moment of death it emerged blinking into daylight and ran off through the graveyard into the yellow fields. It looks at you now from the opposite bank, waiting to trap your flatulent soul...'

But I realised, once again after the visit of Julia and William, I realised that although Ruddley may well have recoiled into his airless bowel and remained there inside a cold shell of sweat for some years, in reality this was me, it was me, yes, of course. It was just as I was about to blossom, but I feared it, feared it as well, so I locked myself in my stomach, I padlocked myself in my stomach, and that I too, ever since Oxford, and in fact for a year before, had become a creature lodged in my intestine. It, or I, whatever you want to call it, had burrowed to the left of the stomach, lodged in the lower bowel like an animal, stuck, undernourished. I had heard it many times over the years, I had heard my vital self, transformed into an animal, and cooing, faint bubbles of sound, which I perhaps mistook for external noises, such as a sleepy bird. It was me, in fact, it was me, it was me all along, it was me in fact, I had blocked it from living, from thriving, from breathing, and realising this I was suddenly enlarged by the fierce creature I always was.

Within months of Julia's departure, Oxford had become haunted, and I could no longer live with or in its absences. Everywhere had something missing. The St Giles café was missing Julia, Alex was missing from the canal bank, and the sibilant silence of grass and the plop of occasional fish in the water were *only* the absence of his Brooklyn drawl. Julia's departure had sounded a chord, which distributed its sad and rueful vibration over the vacant things of a once enjoyed world: Linacre College Common Room, the Taylorian, Broad Street, Blackwell's, the Covered Market, Port Meadow, Walton Street, the Jericho Café, the University Parks, the Gatekeeper's House, Peppers Burger Place, the Lucy factory, that pub near Leckford Road, and Jericho itself with its tiny terraced houses, made tinier by the imposing presence of the Oxford University Press building.

Carvell was similarly disaffected, although for different reasons. And so we abruptly left Oxford for London late in 1995, prompted by two untimely suicides, superficially connected but utterly dissimilar. At Oxford, Carvell had been working on the militant and philosopher Guy Debord. Carvell 'identified' with Debord, which is to say he made him into a kind of Double, whose successes and failures he somehow shared. This of course is not peculiar to Carvell, in so far as we all have our doubles, surrogates and proxies, who live on our behalf whilst we exist mechanically inside the wheels of routine. This is certainly true of academics. For Carvell, Debord was the name of a map, of how to live in an 'alienated world', as Carvell called it, wherein 'everyday life is opaque and unbreathable' (as he said to me once on Broad Street, overtired and smelling faintly of urine). Debord, Carvell told me, was a man who never worked and somehow lived by writing and by other activities forever covert, all of which was, for a time, true of Carvell. And yet Debord,

Carvell's idol, was also a proud alcoholic, forever chasing the 'last drink', the door into darkness, who only managed to squeeze out a single book of note, albeit one which, according to Carvell, names, with exactitude and justice, the historical epoch in which we live as no other book has: an epoch of spectatorship, a life lived in the shadow of signs and symbols but never quite touching the thing itself. Conquered by drink, the later Debord resembled nothing so much as the later Behan, a crestfallen sac emptied of its former eloquence, baffled by existence and sunk in wordless nostalgia. This image, of ruin and self-sabotage, I suspected, was the secret attraction of Debord for Carvell. For I always thought that Carvell would end up similarly capsized. In fact, utterly to my surprise and disappointment, he married, some ten years after leaving Oxford. This was, for me, a major blow. But I am sure that he would have remained single were it not for what happened in 1994, one afternoon in November.

Carvell called me on 1 December from a phone box somewhere in London, for he made frequent visits there – using a stolen bus pass – to see films at the ICA. I was in the common room drinking a cup of coffee from the big vat they placed near the door after lunch. Disgusting stuff, actually, and I'm not sure why I drank it. A call came through and the Russian agronomist picked up, summoning me over. I had no idea who it might be, and was very surprised to hear Carvell's voice. 'Have you heard the news?' he asked, in a tone that suggested the outbreak of war. 'Debord has killed himself. He shot himself in the chest.' In his remote house in Champot, in a blizzard, utterly estranged from all the world, he'd taken his own life. Carvell was stunned, stopped in his tracks. His double had died, and just as some children, when a parent commits suicide, interpret this as a message addressed to them, so did Carvell seem to take this very personally, stumbling through the winter streets let down and unloved. It is fair to say that the death of Debord was an event not just in the remote village of Champot where the suicide took place, but also in the remotest provinces of Carvell's body and mind, wherein some crystal of light and faith was shattered and a treasured portion of soul escaped through the broken glass of his eyes.

It was a remarkable coincidence that less than a year later, in 1995, my own beloved philosopher, Gilles Deleuze, would also end his own life, although for very different reasons, I think. My thesis draft had included a very substantial chapter on Deleuze and literary language, his contention that chaos is not the opposite of creation but its ally; that the opposite of creation is in fact cliché, opinion, calcified habits, thoughts made into commodities, inherited frameworks masquerading as fresh perceptions; that the writer or artist begins not with a blank page or a blank canvas but a world already there, an assemblage of stereotypes, a world of seeming facts, opinions and habits that have to be rubbed out and destroyed; that once he or she has cut into, or punched holes in, this canvas of clichés, this page of preconceptions, something else is let in, something behind or above or underneath it – air, chaos, *a breath of fresh air from the chaos that brings us vision*; that this act of destruction is the first creative act; and that literary language is both the destruction of received language *and* an escape, a continuous and innervating escape from the weight and numbness of consuetude, from a world crowded with the already-fabricated.

It was about eighteen months into my doctorate, and six months into the illness, that I read in *Le Monde* of his death. Needless to say, it was front-page news in France, a country where 'intellectual' is not exclusively a term of derision or immediately prefaced by the prefix 'pseudo', as in England, which is above all others the anti-intellectual country. He jumped from the window of his apartment onto the pavement beneath, dying of lesions, internal haemorrhaging and broken bones, I read.

There is a word, defenestration, to refer to the act of throwing someone, yourself, out of a window, but apart from this curious fact, I have also noticed that people take suicide to be a kind of verdict on the life, a refutation, even, of the life. The life and its works are seen in some way to have failed. Yet the word 'suicide', like most words, is an abstraction, and covers not one but many exits, many reasons, many relations to life and death. And I have always felt, in relation to Deleuze; even if I cannot state it clearly, even if I cannot exactly explain it, that his suicide was a suicide carried out precisely in the name of life. It is possible to say this in French, '*Une suicide faite au nom de la vie*,' or '*Se suicide au nom de la vie*,' and people will know what you mean and agree, but in English the phrase sounds forced. He could barely breathe, Deleuze, with his one lung, 'chained' to an oxygen machine, prevented from writing or thinking. Death held its pillow over his face. But Deleuze surprised death by jumping out of the window, he escaped. A last grab of life from under death's nose. The agility of the thief, the child snatching candy when the shopkeeper nods. I say again, however nonsensical it sounds, *a suicide carried out in the name of life*.

We took these two deaths, Carvell and I, as the condign and legitimate cue to move to London, to abandon our respective doctorates. Carvell hired a van and we took off down the A40. As we came into London, Carvell was panicking about manoeuvring the vehicle, which he was unaccustomed to driving. His cheeks were very red. I suggested he pull over. I told him about failing my driving test three times with a 60-year-old hardman who stank of smoke. Doubtless he wasn't even that hard, I said to Carvell. Doubtless I could have had him, could have knocked him out with a single punch, or at least inflicted significant damage on his face quite easily, for his skin had the texture of a paper bag, I told Carvell, smiling. But a hardness nonetheless, in his face. An absence of humour, of flexibility, of tolerance. And an underground anger. Parked in the underground car park, his anger, with the key in the ignition, I said to Carvell. Waiting for a pretext to slam its foot on the accelerator. To switch on the siren. You could see all this in his eyes. No doubt an ex-policeman. Absolutely the demeanour of an ex-copper, I said to Carvell, an ex-copper who's taken early retirement and works part-time as a driving examiner. Precisely the kind of job an ex-copper does. You can see them a mile off. His face in fact was the cold physiognomy of the Law. Three fucking consecutive times over a period of eighteen months it was him. Brian. Some grizzled agent of fate sent to torment me, I joked to Carvell. 'I'm afraid you haven't passed,' in his thin cockney voice with the strange whistle in the tail of it. And the third time, when I thought I was doing fine but got stuck behind a funeral cortège. That's when it seemed like a conspiracy, all the demons sat around in their depot laughing, I continued to Carvell. Suddenly sending a funeral cortège into the road out of nowhere. One of them spits out his tea, laughing, high-fiving the other demon who thought of this prank.

We both laughed at this story, and Carvell was OK to drive the van after that, though puzzled that I was so unflustered. Several people tell me that I have a calm and calming presence. This calmness is, I take it, supposed to be a good thing. Perhaps it is for them. But they do not know that this calmness has always been the calmness of the spectator, and that beneath or behind the spectator are unquiet violent spirits, something I myself realised only later.

Carvell lost his way and his mind in London – which is perhaps why he, and I, moved there, to get lost and go insane in relative anonymity, to succumb to the objective madness of the metropolis rather than make our own from nothing – and spent much of his time roaming through the city in search of the perfect café, in search of some busy enclave where writers and thinkers flourished. 'Wrong country,' I told him. 'Wrong fucking country.' He would announce great discoveries, such as Shepherd Market, a miraculous village in the midst of central London, he said, or Bonnington Square, a kind of communistic micro-community tucked away in Kennington, he reported. But they were all false dawns. Finally, he had found a café in Soho, on Old Compton Street, where a cadre of intellectuals met to play chess and talk about philosophy. However, he failed to secure access to this circle and remained a furtive spectator, rereading Debord in the corner. He then claimed to have befriended the professional hardman Lenny 'the Guv'nor' McLean. The two of them played chess every fortnight, he said, in an Irish pub off the Holloway Road. He relayed many anecdotes which, he said, McLean had told him, about various fights and knocking various people 'into the second row'. He told me that a *Guardian* journalist had contacted McLean about an article on 'contemporary masculinity', thinking he'd be a good editorial fit, to which McLean had replied, 'My fist'll make a good editorial fit for your fucking marf'. But despite many of these stories being subsequently published in McLean's biography, I remained unconvinced that Carvell had ever in fact met McLean, who died shortly afterwards of brain cancer.

I too lost my self after Oxford. At first, and for nearly two years, I lived on benefits and went to bed at 4 a.m. I relished the sweet silence that only descends, or rises, when everyone else, or almost everyone, is asleep. But I was forced into work by penury, and in particular one night when I realised that all I had left for supper was a bag of apples. I ate the apples and woke at dawn with cramps and racked with wind. And so it was that I was forced into work. So from 1997 and for ten desperate years (oddly coinciding with the tenure of Tony Blair at Downing Street) I worked at Belsham Media, a telesales office near Plaistow, making a hundred or more phone calls a day, one after the other, the phones rigged up so that as soon as you put the phone down it automatically dialled the next number on the list. Imagine. I would rather not write about Belsham, in so far as writing about it confirms its existence. For the writer is, among other things, someone who cannot shake off the idea that until you've dragged your experience into writing it does not fully exist. And so I do not want to complete Belsham's existence. It would be better to leave it out, so that it would fade, its existence would deteriorate into pixels and then disappear. But I cannot.

So, Belsham. Needless to say, if the company itself was a hell, it was first of all a hell of Money and the pursuit of Money. Amounts of money were written every day on a massive wipe board at the front of the office. These represented the 'deals' people had brought in. 'Fucking five grander,' Liam or Reg or Nicholson would shout, red and rigid. 'There's no feeling like getting a deal,' the unhealthily red and rigid Reg would exclaim, full of angry triumph. 'Fucking get in.' People would judge themselves and others by the monthly and yearly money total on the wipe board, people who were initially timorous would be inflated with confidence and transformed beyond recognition after bringing in a string of deals, and similarly diminished by a blank week or month. They, we, were inflated and deflated by Money, subordinate to the comings and goings of Money, and our qualitative affections reduced to weak facsimiles of Money's bodiless magnitude. I'm ashamed to say that this, the money, is why I stayed, meanwhile leading a life 'as solitary as an oyster', as Dickens put it. I delighted in hoarding money, with a view, perhaps, to a year of leisure, or oblivion. But no, more than money, it was an act of spiritual self-harm. I decided to rub out everything I thought I'd achieved, which had in any case only been achieved through imposture, as I thought; I decided to numb and punish myself for having abandoned my paradise. I would engineer the death of my soul, one fucking phone call at a time.

The script was a concatenation of sales phrases; I was forced to speak of 'business models' and 'target audiences' and 'rare commercial opportunities' and 'prestigious vehicles' and 'showcasing best practice' and 'proactive approaches' to x, y and z, and 'solution-led companies' and 'tangible returns' and 'leveraging the advantages of the medium' and 'brand association' and 'building a profile' and so on and so forth, and forced also to say things like 'you'll be positioned as a leader in the field' and 'you'll be aligned with a prestigious campaign'.

All of this vacuous jargon returned to haunt me, years later, of course, when I heard Cahun on his phone. In order to say anything meaningful it is necessary also to let language speak, but such phrases not only gagged language but also performed on language an immediate and fatal glossectomy. It is not possible to personalise such language, it is not possible to put your finger- or thumbprint on such language, such Teflon language, it is not possible to impart or import onto this language your native vitality without infecting that vitality, without depersonalising and debasing it, it is not possible to use such language unscathed, it is not possible to stand apart from such language and use it at a distance, for it is this very distance which also corrupts and bisects the soul. And just as in biochemistry we speak of precursors, such as L-Tyrosine being a precursor of dopamine, so are these insincere and empty sales words precursors of insincerity and emptiness in the soul of the speaker, so that incrementally and over a period of time the salesperson becomes a mere husk of a human being, a vendor of their own devalued self, and only some sudden and peremptory intervention will stop this.

This vapourhouse, this jargonbelch factory, was also a place of flagrant imposture. Each of us, in fact, operated via pretence and deception, for we did not, at Belsham, use our real names but hid behind invented names to conceal and protect ourselves. From the name – its flavours, its connotations – a persona grew, a throwaway facsimile of a person that could be discarded at close of day. Mine was Harrison, Nigel Harrison. His voice was not my voice at all. It was in fact a voice modelled, unconsciously at first, but then with increasing deliberation and art, on the essayist and 'commentator' Christopher Hitchens, who I had seen on television many times, engaged in divers polemical spats and speaking always with the same mannered eloquence. I found it easy to imitate his speech patterns and inflections, as I did the portentous accents of the omnimath George Steiner and, oddly, the esoteric mumbling of Brando in *Apocalypse Now*. It would have been ridiculous, of course, to speak on the telephone as either Steiner or Brando, albeit tempting, so that Hitchens was the only serious contender. His voice contained the silent proposition 'This is how it is, wake up and smell the coffee', but in an envelope of bonhomie. In any voice there is always such a proposition. My father said 'that's how it's going to be, end of story'. And accompanying this proposition is an affect, for example, of warm reassurance, which exists between speaker and listener as a kind of flow.

In any case, under the sign of a borrowed name, and with stolen eloquence, grew a character, slippery and plausible, who, over time, extracted hundreds and thousands of pounds from the gullible and self-deceived, which is to say the people we phoned up and flattered. Nigel Harrison is certainly a criminal, a fraudster and swindler, and the crusts of Nigel Harrison, which are the crusts of shame and self-revulsion, still cling to me, despite my several stratagems for absolution. This character, this persona, was, I fancied at first, something that could be slung away like an integument at 5.30, something I could shrug off and then run away from. But instead the name, like all names, nibbles into the flesh; the voice begins to nag at the soul. Nigel Harrison, that facile fiction, with his prosthetic voice, with his cod biography, his aristocratic pretensions, his winks and handshakes… it is true to say that his chemical blood was transfused into my veins and reached all avenues of my body and brain. It is true also that I have been morally compromised and can never undo what Harrison did and the money he made at others' expense. I have written to some and apologised, as the philosopher Wittgenstein apologised to the parents of children he'd hit. But 'in the finish', as we say in Yorkshire, Wittgenstein will always be – like my father – someone who hit children in anger, and I will always be someone who conned the almost innocent.

It seems to me now, looking back, that Belsham was less a hell than a kind of necessary purgatory, or at least a chamber of

Purgatory, where, surrounded by rough demons, by sightless milky-eyed gremlins and pot-bellied pigs in human attire, grotesques of the vilest sort, by wizened pensioners both impotent and priapic, shrivelled and unshriven, I was compelled to repeat endlessly the same actions – picking up the phone, reading a script, inputting leads. Belsham was peopled by men who had failed at their chosen profession or failed to choose a profession, people either devoid of vocation or whose only vocation was money and the making of money. Liam, the thick-necked onanist, already has a urinal reserved in hell, but as for the rest of them, I liked to imagine that one day, as they pitched, some stray phrase, some random lie, would, unbeknown to the speakers, contain a Kabbalistic formula that opened the trapdoor into hell, where they would, like Dante's swindlers, be consigned to some burning cauldron, their heads submerged, like feeding ducks, bums bobbing above the chunky soup. They would be forced to speak, as they did in life, the blaggers and frauds, out of their arseholes, which, lacking a tongue, would squash their words to pongs and whistles. And because they deceived others with made-up drivel, they would be assailed at night by a marathon of misfortunes, harpies and other fictional beings, whizzing through one ear and out of the other.

My escape from this purgatory of money and blokes, of anti-language and fifth-form sniggering, came about through a sudden unaccountable act, as all my escapes and forward leaps have come about. At certain points you must overtake yourself, so to speak, lunge or veer in an unanticipated direction. So it was with my resignation from this Belsham hellhole, a few years after my father's death, having arrived at work with no notion at all, no expectation that I would resign. I'd been called to a 'disciplinary hearing' by McCann. The disciplinary hearing had nothing to do with locking McCann in the toilet, another tale entirely, which may one day appear in the unexpurgated version of this story. No, the 'hearing' was for time-wasting. They, the company, kept logs of all numbers dialled and had discovered that I had repeatedly dialled a particular number around eleven each morning. Each morning, just after morning break, I would dial this number, which unlocked a sound, the aria from the *Barber of Seville*. I discovered it by accident, the hold music of some obscure college if you pressed option 4 for the Engineering department. Nobody answered, the music just kept playing, and in my mind I'd be in the Enoteca De Macci in Florence, with the old men and their small patient dogs, or I'd be sipping dark espresso in Naples's Caffè Gambrinus. I'd parachuted into Italy but left my body in the office, lit by ugly functional lights. But I was remiss, and frankly stupid, in thinking the company had no log of the calls, or didn't inspect the logs.

McCann invited me for 'coffee' at a dive called El Greco's round the corner, a small shithole of a café in the larger shithole called 'Plaistow' — a name and a place empty of beauty or inspiration, such that anyone who chooses to settle in Plaistow has chosen to fail, to surrender and walk among the ill and the spiritually defeated. Every time I walked through Plaistow, I breathed in a depressive vapour, and every time I left Plaistow this vapour would dissipate. El Greco's, with its threadbare awning and decor unchanged since the eighties (likewise its menu, which contained items like 'prawn cocktail' and 'breaded mushrooms' and 'white coffee') was symptomatic of everything that was soul-destroying about Plaistow. Only in Plaistow can a place like this continue to exist, only in a place where people have given up, removed themselves from time and history and yielded instead to mechanical routine. They have forgotten beauty, the denizens of Plaistow, living in a place where, uniquely, not one thing is beautiful; and they have likewise forgotten pleasure, for here nothing pleases the eye or the palate or the ear. The pubs are busy, of course, for people seek consolation in drinking, but failing to find it they drink too much and wake to the hangover also called Plaistow, which is like a catheter attached to the soul.

In any case, I laughed at his stratagem of meeting me in the café so as to 'take off his boss's hat' and have a man-to-man talk, to 'show his human side' and so on. Any boss *must* periodically perform this gesture of taking off his boss's hat and addressing you as a friend, or 'man to man', he must 'show his human side'. But the boss is never more boss-like than when 'taking off his boss's hat', when 'showing his human side'. Suddenly he's all disarming frankness; suddenly he's all 'no bullshit' bullshit. 'I like you as an individual,' he intoned. 'I think we get on, so I want to do you the courtesy of addressing you as a peer. At the same time, it would be difficult to understate the gravity of this matter. Nicholson's furious. I thought we had not just a good working relationship, to use the cliché, but a personal rapport. I see you as a friend first, employee second.' It is worth adding, parenthetically, and as I have already indicated, that McCann had always imagined that we had a 'rapport', that we'd get on because of his first editions and his botched facade of 'culture', his smattering of culture he wore only as a badge and a mark of distinction, like flying first class and collecting fine wines. In fact, all of the first editions he'd accumulated I regarded as stolen items, stolen and misappropriated by a fuckwit using his fraudulently gotten money. One day, I imagined, golden letters would appear above him and instruct him, as God did to the blasphemers at the feast, but also as Brian Clough did to his charges at Leeds United, albeit unjustly, to throw away all your medals and trophies, *because you got them only by cheating*. There could be no sense in which a collection of Samuel Beckett's letters properly belonged with McCann, and, conversely, it would have been an ethical act of the highest order to steal them back from him and donate them to a true scholar or a museum. And so I had in fact repelled McCann's attempt to befriend me just as I had repelled the Tanner cretin at Shawcross. In each case some pure arsehole, someone who was the opposite of everything I admired or wanted, an enemy of magic and language, infringed on my life for no reason and tried to contaminate it.

So there I was, crouched inside my head, observing the scene from outside, watching the 'outer self', the self bound by social rules, go through the motions, mouth the platitudes, the formalities, the 'how terribly sorry I am' and the 'I'd just like to say…' The 'outer self' is our compromised diplomat, with a mastery of such points of etiquette. And yet… this so-called 'outer self', having delivered his propitiatory speech, having listened to a good bit of the 'I'll be honest with you' waffle from the incontinent director, took it upon himself to announce his resignation from the company, taking by surprise not only the director, who was only a quarter way into his slowly soporific peroration, but the inner self, who was thereby knocked off his stool. I was flabbergasted, and it's fair to say that until I uttered the words 'I'd like to resign with immediate effect', I had no idea I was resigning, just as, famously – at least in some quarters – Bertrand Russell did not realise he was in love until he uttered 'I love you'. But with those words I was freed and had also uncoupled myself from Belsham and from the director, who, at that instant, ceased to be the director and was instead only one human being facing another. Not that he realised this of course, still trying to implore me to be reasonable and so on, to reconsider before making such a rash decision. But the director had misunderstood, he had not realised that the form of words 'I resign' had magically dissolved his director title, and that he was now only a human being with no claims on me at all. After delivering a brief coda, as reported already, I headed for the exit. And as far as Belsham was concerned, I took leave of those defeated souls and left them there to broil and blather.

Some eight or so years have passed since that incident. But nonetheless, I will never outlive the ignominy of having worked there, the ethically and intellectually demeaning work, which I chose over poverty and practised, week after week. I had belonged in effect to a criminal organisation founded on fraud and deception but operating within the law. And it is to my eternal shame and regret that my father died whilst I was working at Belsham, only five years into the present century, and that the last image he had of me was not as a scholar or academic but as a telesales person doing valueless work, and I can cling only to the belief that since dying he has sat beside me, or greeted me in a dream, and seen me as I now am, teaching at the university and writing books.

Quitting the infernal Belsham created a small arbour of freedom wherein I was able to at least breathe, and savour the notes of my peculiar life, to listen to them coming across the arc of intervening years from before the idiotic Belsham, from Jericho and Port Meadow.

Only after leaving Belsham was I able to complete my thesis, albeit at Birkbeck in London rather than back in Oxford, and in fact I conceived and wrote an altogether new thesis, and, having completed it, got the job at the American university. The mellifluous Marxist MacGregor was now an emeritus at Birkbeck and happy to supervise my work, partly on account of our – supposedly – shared class origins. I seldom went into Birkbeck itself, but met with MacGregor at the Lord John Russell on Marchmont Street and drank strawberry beer outside. In the corner, always, a scouser with a single sunburned ear entertained various pale clients, regaling them with anecdotes about, for example, robbing 'fucking students' in 'Sefton Park', wherever that was. But this was merely, to use T.S. Eliot's image, the meat thrown to the guard dog, whilst more meaningful exchanges happened under the table with cash and small brown parcels. But I mention him, this scouser, firstly because I had been reading Yeats in Senate House Library and came across a line about 'a phantom hound / All pearly white, save one red ear', and learned how this in turn referred to Chaucer's *Book of the Duchess*, where an elusive hunt passes through the forest of a dreamer's mind as he searches for some way of dealing with loss; and it amused and consoled me, in part, to think of this Scouser, hereby capitalised, as an enigmatic allegorical figure, there to guide me at a not dissimilar time of mourning and bewilderment; and then, despite my mildly condescending image of him, this Scouser, I bizarrely came to envy his life, ensconced in his chair outside the law, a life of unstructured leisure, the pub his cosy fiefdom.

Mostly, though, I studied in Senate House, which was easily walkable from my flat in St Anne's Court. And because it was an ill-lit and functional place utterly unlike the Radcliffe Camera or the Taylorian, I cracked on with my work, and by October 2009 the thesis was complete and passed without corrections. I met MacGregor for a pint afterwards in the pub, and was unnerved to see that the Scouser's chair was empty. But he'd merely gone for a piss.

My thesis was inspired partly by a sentence in Wittgenstein, who says that in doing philosophy he is also *expressing* his peculiar form of life. He suggested, Wittgenstein, that even in the most austere, or seemingly austere propositional landscape, there is also an expressive path, an element which is not simply to do with the truth or falsehood of the propositions, but the unfolding of a form of life. And Nietzsche too says that philosophy is, inter alia, also the creative signature of some particular being, the expanding and growth of a force of life designated by the proper name 'Nietzsche' or whatever that might be. We are always expressing our form of life in everything we do. Whether we are writing philosophy, or poetry, or painting in acrylics, or something altogether more quotidian. In particular I discussed the theory of expression in Spinoza, his idea of God as being the very activity of expression rather than a something which is then expressed. And this was my final and counter-intuitive conclusion: that what is expressed does not precede its expression. Indeed, the thesis that I explicitly combatted and refuted was the idea that expression was about finding some apt vehicle for an already existing content. Rather than the litany of examples I provided and discussed, this can easily be illustrated in actual fact with reference to the making of espresso, which literally means 'expressed', from *esprimere*, which means to express or to force out. There are many factors of course in making a perfect espresso: the grind, the temperature, the water pressure and also the pressure with which the grains are compacted. If all these align it will produce a certain combination of flavours and sensations in the mouth and beyond. Do these flavours pre-exist their 'expression'? No, they do not. They are present only, we might say, *in potentia*. Expression is always about making something actual which exists only *in potentia*. In some sense, the espresso in the cup, the line of poetry on the page, the paint on canvas, come into being for the first time on the page, on the canvas or in the cup. That, *in nuce*, was my thesis, when eventually I was able to return to it and finish it, after that long and largely morbid interregnum.

My thesis, *On the Notion of Expression*, is now a received work of reference on the subject, as far as I'm concerned, and I am frequently asked to give papers on the subject at various terminally boring academic conferences, albeit in beautiful cities such as Prague or Budapest or of course Rome. Likewise have I been offered a number of jobs at a variety of English universities, including the University of South East London, where Carvell teaches, all of which I have refused and preferred instead my three days a week at the American satellite university in London, which has an extraterritorial status like an embassy, and where the students, who have made the conscious choice to come here for the semester, rather than stay in Minnesota or Tennessee, have an appetite and openness so often lacking in their English counterparts, and certainly lacking in Carvell's students.

When I heard Cahun speaking about identity and the face, this was the only time I listened to him with anything more than incipient rage, although there was something of that of course, and it was the only time also that his words had bent towards philosophy. For philosophy is not so much a discipline itself as the qualitative destination of each and every discipline. If you speak of something with sufficient intellectual rigour, then at a certain pitch, a certain limit it simply *becomes* philosophy. However, this forgiving impression was reversed immediately by the next – and penultimate – time I saw Cahun. He was talking to a man in the café. It was the first time he had ever brought other people into the café and the two of them, with laptops and other accoutrements, occupied a good third of the space. It was completely unacceptable that Cahun had brought someone into the café and was effectively using the café to conduct an interview, as if it were his office, and with no regard for the other patrons – only me, in actual fact – nor for the staff. No doubt this interview could easily have been conducted in Cahun's office, which I knew to be on Beak Street, having followed him more than once and established where he was 'based' – as he would doubtless have put it.

'Our office is staffed almost exclusively by millennials,' Cahun was telling the young man. 'As per yourself, they've spent at least their whole adult life swimming in the digital. They're connected, plugged in, reachable, social. They're also suspicious of rigid corporate structures.' 'What are your core qualities?' he was asking the young man. 'Your core behaviours?' The young man said he was creative and passionate. 'Great, great,' Cahun replied, and asked the man what his 'drivers' were... 'Finding solutions, solving problems,' the young man proffered. 'I see things in terms of problems and solutions.' Cahun told the man that he wanted people who were 'Innovative, Passionate, Agile, Collaborative. IPAC, we say for short.' 'What you also need to know is that we play hardball,' said Cahun, smiling and with raised eyebrows. 'Sure, sure,' said the young man, slightly nervous. 'I mean we literally play hardball,' said Cahun, with a smug and childish laugh. 'We literally go and play hardball once a month. The bats, the balls, the venue... It's team building. There's this company that arranges a hardball league – a lot of the tech and digital start-ups do it. It's a whole lot of fun, but it's fantastic for the team...' 'So look... We're doing some work with local councils. It's the government's Smart Councils initiative. We won the contract, and it's all about helping councils navigate digital disruption. I mean, traditionally, they've not been that open to change, right?... public sector bureaucracy blah blah. But like everything else at the moment, there's no alternative. It's an exciting time. It's about optimising the emerging technologies for public benefit. Whether you're talking about artificial intelligence, wearables, internet of things: all these can benefit local authorities just as much as industry. There's already lots of really interesting stuff going on. Some councils are already experimenting with, like, chatbots and virtual assistant systems to handle basic enquiries more efficiently. There's some really interesting software and robot technology being used to tackle residents' questions or do admin. It's about using AI and cognitive computing to reduce the burden of bureaucracy. It leaves the council with more time to think of creative solutions for residents and citizens, plus your employees will be happier if they don't have to do all the boring stuff, right?' This was of course wilfully naïve shit from Cahun, who thought he was talking about something revolutionary and new, whereas he was talking about automatisation being used to cut back on labour, the old stupidities through the new speakers as Brecht put it. In any case it was at this point I left the café, unable to tolerate this nonsense any longer and determined to remove Cahun from the picture; Cahun with his grubby business hands on the Councils. Cahun, 'swimming in the digital', playing hardball, being a dickhead.

For the next two weeks I was forced to drink coffee at one of the 'new wave' or so-called 'artisan' independent coffee shops on Wardour Street. The Naked Portafilter it was called. They had an array of 'single origin' coffees, from Tanzania and Ethiopia and Guatemala, with 'notes of pineapple and sherbet, butterscotch and lime'. 'What do you think of our new Rwandan single origin?' the barista would ask me, assuring me it had 'really interesting bergamot and watermelon notes'. 'Interesting in the same way as an apple that tastes of haddock,' I replied. This was where I was forced into exile after seeing and hearing Cahun occupy the café, plotting his infiltration of various councils, invading them with his 'business model'. Cahun would have been entirely at home in the single-origin coffee shop, which was in agreement with his mindset and expressed it in every and each particular. Amato, by contrast, was quintessentially an old Italian café and made coffee as the Italians make it. The Italian espresso is like a punctuation mark. An exclamation, or a colon, sometimes even a paragraph break; occasionally only a comma. In any case, it pauses time only to then speed things up. Just as the day's first coffee turns you from the dream world and towards the daylight, so does each coffee dissolve the accumulated dregs of time and begin again. It says: the next bit of time starts here. In the artisan coffee shop, with their single-origin coffees, there is much talk of 'notes', notes of grapefruit, dates, tobacco, molasses, butterscotch, maple or lime. But all that is shrapnel, it fails to hit the mark. A good Italian espresso always lands in the right place. This has little to do with caffeine content, which is often greater in the cardboard buckets of sloshing lattes that churls buy from chains. It is, rather, like grappa, to do with intensity and localisation. In Rome, that lucent summer with Julia, we went into a church off the Piazza Navona. A middle-aged woman, a businesswoman perhaps, very smart and elegant, very precise, on a break perhaps, came in and kneeled and prayed. She was there only very briefly. I imagine she went back to the office, the boardroom. This, I thought, was a spiritual espresso, the equivalent of an espresso. It washed her clothes and sent her back out into the world afresh.

In the two weeks I drank at Naked Portafilter I did not shave and grew a decent beard, and my intentions for Cahun, a nebulous and spiteful fantasy some months ago, were now condensed into a careful and exact stratagem.

The following Monday I left my flat on St Anne's Court and walked slowly to Amato. I was wearing the blue baseball cap that Alex had left behind, a thick blue tracksuit, and of course my grandfather's welding goggles that lent the world an old-world, blood-orange tint. It was a dark December morning and I walked past Amato, where I could see Cahun. Exceptionally, he was reading a newspaper as the wall lamp shone across his face and onto the page. It reminded me, this image, of someone's description of the poet Cavafy, who *stood absolutely motionless at a slight angle to the universe*. A beautiful description and a state to which all poets – and intermittently all of us – should aspire. A photographer, seeing the similarly motionless Cahun, might have been tempted to take out his camera. The sideways light, the downward gaze, both cascading onto the page. It was a composition drawn by chance. The photographer, as opposed to the obsessive snapper, is one who recognises the composition drawn by chance and saves it from oblivion. As it happens, it's been rescued only by these words here.

I lingered and strolled for a few minutes until Cahun left the café. He went up Green's Court, the narrow piss-splashed alley that leads onto Peter Street, then walked up Hopkins Street and left into Ingestre Place. This was the spot I chose, despite its risks. For it was overlooked by the big tower block where Jeffrey Bernard used to live, and a bit further along there was some red-brick social housing. This, incidentally, was a miraculous survival in contemporary central London, where everything is destroyed, levelled and replaced purely on the basis of monetary value, regardless of neighbourhood, justice or history.

Anyway, there is, or was, a blind corner, or half blind, on Ingestre Place. This is where he was intercepted. As he entered Hopkins Street, I moved towards him quickly and silently. His phone rang. He stopped to take the call. 'We need to action it asap,' I heard him say. I took this snatch of jargon to be a condign and legitimate cue. I was just around the corner, nose to the wall, just in case someone looked out and saw my albeit half-concealed face. As it was, they'd probably just think I was urinating, a fairly standard sight in these parts. Anyway, I started to repeat to myself my phrase, a meaningless phrase: 'We're all interested now.' This phrase had lodged in my mind when I was a child. I don't know where it came from. Perhaps from the television. Maybe a politician said it. For some reason I think it was David Steel. It doesn't matter. It was a phrase which stoked my anger after I'd been hit and sent to bed, for instance. 'We're all interested now,' I'd snarl and punch the mattress hard, 'we're all interested now.' The correct emphasis falls firmly on 'all' and 'now', and the latter word is slightly elongated. It was a broken bit of language that I could stab the air with, stab the mattress with. And now, if I say these words, I am angry, rage follows these words so closely that the two are inseparable.

I heard him finish his call: 'OK, I'm gonna sign off. OK, bye, bye, bye... bye.' The *diminuendo* of his 'byes' infuriated me, inviting a fast and brutal riposte. I ran towards him and made a screech in the back of my throat. He swivelled nervously round and with almost balletic grace I punched him square in the nose. It cracked. 'I'll take your fucking jaw off,' I snarled at him, 'I'll take your fucking jaw off. Absolute fucking twat.' 'No, no,' he was crying, his palms up. He doubled over as people often do, and as the Lawrence boy had at school, so that I was able to hit him hard in the bony face with a series of wild yet exact uppercuts. 'Are you interested in violence,' I asked him, or whispered to him through gritted teeth. 'Are you interested in violence, are you interested in violence, are you interested in violence? Because we're *all* interested now. We're *all* interested now.' Each stressed syllable was in fact an extension of the punch, each punch an instant illustration of the words. 'You need. To stop. Speaking. Shit.' As his legs buckled, he made a noise that surprised, I think, even himself, childlike and desperate, or the caw of a bird, as if he was aiming for language but missed, as if his body had burst through. What I couldn't have foreseen was that he fell backwards and cracked his head on the wall, falling to the floor with a bump. There is always something which escapes our intention, of course. He lay motionless on the floor. 'Shut the fuck up,' I said with audacious and final triumph, breaking my own prohibition by kicking him then in the ribs. Not once but twice. And he did, of course. He shut the fuck up. He certainly shut the fuck up.

I'd been on the verge of asking him 'What's the value proposition?' but it carried too many risks. In any case he seemed unresponsive. As it was, the phrase 'We're all interested now' would baffle both him and the police to whom he would of course report the incident. It would be their only clue, but empty of meaning, the ultimate false trail, leading back to the belly button of my childhood but known and open only to me. It would be burned on his brain, as it is on mine, with a little corona of affects, as with me. That much at least we would have in common, like the secret sign that the evil dentist drills on the back of the tooth.

Cahun, Cahun the business goon, crawls back home by the light of the moon. Cahun, Cahun, lying in a swoon, jerked into life by a spastic tune.

During the attack, I really had been 'living in the moment', a facile phrase which we use ordinarily to signal peace and beatitude and so on; but this phrase is more properly explicated in the heat of violence, the collision of knuckle and flesh. And then, afterwards, there was a wonderful decompression, a slackening, a return to time and consciousness. The world reassembled around me, the sky and pavement fell into place, and the aftertaste of violence in the world of thought and recollection was sweet and innervating at once.

I left him there on the pavement and made my way to the river. I imagined myself a Mesopotamian demon or Blake's 'Ghost of a Flea': implacable, gleeful, prickling with hate, strung between animal and divine, outside the human community. 'Shut the fuck up,' I kept saying, for there is a savage pleasure in saying 'shut the fuck up' *after* the person has fallen silent, just as some footballers scream 'get in' after the ball is in the net... 'get the fuck in'... there I was buoyed by conquest, I walked along the river with rocking iambic stride, for my walk was powered and sustained by the rush of externalised violence. I gravitated to the river as I always have, since being a child, and I walked along the Thames, yes, 'Wide as an arm of the sea', remembering that the Thames, with its other name, Isis, flows as well through Oxford, and down I went to Battersea, where I had walked joyously with William and Julia, through Putney and eventually to the wetlands near Barnes, place of marshes and narrow paths, and patches of unclaimed nature, where I sat as my quick speech slowly subsided, subsided softly and ceded to silence.

For I had been speaking non-stop since Soho. Yes, when I was on my walk... I was not, as one might expect, mute and thoughtful, I did not, as you might expect, ally myself with the silent flow of the water or the barely audible godlike wind, as in those films where the wind in the trees is an augur of something uncontainably divine and typically apocalyptic. I was talking in fact, delightedly talking, a great phosphorescence of language in fact... go to mudland, you babbling *twat*... all the quotations queuing up, queuing up to be stroked and mangled. Rash intruding garrulous fool, alack, alack, alack. Fleabuzz the fuckwit, a farting dud, his skin scraped off with an iceblade. All my voices queuing up, my Brando voice, for example: 'Are you an assassin?' Well, it seems, in the finish, I am an assassin. 'Of course I'm a fucking assassin,' I said. 'I'll thrash you right down to an inch of your life, I'll thrash you right down to an inch of your life... *I'll* give you "I won't eat it"'... do as you're do as you're do as you're told... the sausages covered in glass... the old gate, dry and dead on the floor... the red peeling paint of the wooden door in which the key had broken, the rest of the key in my child-small hand...

all my albums were stashed inside there in that outhouse... *The Dark Side of The Moon*, for example. 'It's funny music is this,' Dad said. 'I've always been mad, I know I've been mad'... Act right in your head, act right in your head; I won't act right in my head, I'll never act right in my head... or wind my neck in, no, never again... I'll do as I please.. my neck will uncoil, and the light of my eyes will shine fully... I'll play my peculiar music, I said, as I walked by the water on Wednesday. Don't you dare insult it, Cahun, I'll play my intuitive music, what's the value of being on this earth, being on this frequently beautiful earth, with its pink and purple geraniums, and acres of pine trees, and rivulets clear and cold over stone, what's the value of water and light and blueness – *hers* in particular, the value of my blue-eyed lady of the sofa, becalmed and absorbing, whose words alone melted my permafrost silence, for whom I'd destroy ten thousand Cahuns... I'm on your fucking case alright... I've chased off death's breathless messengers... cold needle points of rain on my skin when I was indoors. Absolutely fuck off. And then the racing shadows themselves, level with my eyes and therefore out of focus... scuttling around the dry perimeter of vision... they came for me as they came for Dad but I fought them off, not forever, of course, because no one does... but I ducked down a ginnel with a bag full of creatures... And him on the floor of the ocean, crying... Nobody, nobody, nobody understands... Then later, in Jericho, in the dark twilight staring backwards at the golden lost days... 'With me you could blossom into a flower and not be a creature of night'... 'Cheekbones pointy like a child's elbows,' Julia said, after I sent her my photo. 'I saw you fading away in a dream,' she said, 'your pale face almost transparent.' I wrote to her: 'I brought back the shadow of death from a dream, not death itself but the *swooning*,' and I kept the dream under my pillow, along with the small rock from

Delos she gave me... a piece of us both after all that rock... it lives in a small glass jar... I open it sometimes to fill the air with the clearest blue dawn you can get in this world, Greece of course, from right before history started, and winged mortals, like tiny floaters in front of the sun, dropping fast unnoticed, and Skaros encrusted with ruins... the small white and blue church on the end of the promontory, whiter than swans or sea foam, as blue as the blue in the top of the sky... high up on the caldera, the clouds low, so low down, we walked outside and touched the cool and tumbling clouds after midnight, and before that at midnight the lone praying mantis, one of God's incredible finger sketches, Julia said, and Thira's chalky moon-made walls at midnight... all that much is certainly true... but I remember reading Beckett, when doing the Oxford entrance exam, *It was not midnight. It was not raining*... such a beautiful two sentences and also the beauty of literature, to subtract the ostensible so-called truth and make words sing and ring out all the more, all the more fully and sadly and mortal against that pure leftover silence. For silence it is, poetry too is silence not words, a silence *in* words, just like the wind in these trees by the Thames that makes them wave and pregnant with meaning... but 'pregnant with meaning' is itself enough, you don't have to wait for Meaning to come, it's always *about to occur*, it's best when *about to occur*, it's most present when *about to occur*, and if that sounds like nonsense, fuck off. The 'soul's silent adventure', someone said about poetry, the breeze of silence that sets words singing. Is this your own work? Of course it is, you gingerbread fucking dunce, I am mine own work, but language is not my own work, in any case, language is a public letterpress imposed on the private soul, and poetry is what happens when the mute soul rebels against that ruling power, and words are set moving by silence, by its great and previous plenitude. What do I mean?

Fuck off, shut the fuck up and fuck off is what I mean, Cahun, fuck off and get some wings, prise yourself up off the pavement. I'm tired of pedestrian whining. We all have these wings of course, we all have a surplus vitality of course, an unrelenting and vexing force which bubbles through into words and also gestures, if the two can be separated.

… and actually, all of the words I spoke by the Thames, all of these words and so many more, multiple flames of the selfsame tongue, were accompanied by the body's exclamation marks and underlining and bold type, by grimaces, tics and twitches, my hand screwing in an imaginary light bulb, fingers pinched together in desperate entreaty, like a grubby street kid, like the mortals of Trastevere playing their aces, and through these words and gestures, through these voices and quotations and ellipses it bubbled up and through, a surplus vitality, it began to flow in all its invisible brilliance… which we all have of course, we all have it, we have it of course as children especially, it comes from the body, its drives, appetites, spikes of energy, its dum-dumming rhythmic insistence, though of course, like me, we lock it back inside. It never quite fits into language, even as it requisitions language, even as it requires language, just as the sun needs the pale desert stone to know its own heat, and so it, we, are constantly trying to break out of language, amplifying words with gestures or pulverising them to pure sound, snapping them open as children do, turning them slowly to notes… and poets, as I said, out loud, out loud to the old Father Thames, are of course the most attuned to this vitality, they are in an ongoing state of escape from language, contrary to what people think, the poem left behind is the remnant of this escape, like a gate snapped and bent by the wind. It exceeds, this vitality, who we've been trained to be, and words are part of this training – the word 'boy', for example, commands: 'be a boy'. 'No, not a boy! I am William!' It is rebellious to instruction, our vitality, and so *as well as* being unambiguously positive, therefore, it is *also* always saying 'fuck off', but a great life-affirming 'fuck off'. 'Fuck off, not a Man, I am Henry!'

... I saw as well and finally that the jerks and spasms and tics and spikes of energy that the psychoanalyst perceives as 'symptoms', the manifestations of hidden 'issues' and so forth, each *fuck off* and *of course* and *in fact*, are in fact and of course the energetic signatures, the crests or prickles, of this vitality, and that the worst thing we could do is cure ourselves of these so-called symptoms, cure ourselves of our great original ceaseless appetency. I realised that I did not have to cure myself, no, I did not have to 'deal with' or resolve anything, I did not have to cure myself, or 'sort myself out', for this cure would in fact have been a poison cancelling life itself, and I realised too that although over the years I may have neglected myself completely, and waylaid myself as well, and imprisoned myself in my bowel, and shrunk myself into a creature, I had, most recently, and now in eliminating Cahun, opened myself, redeemed myself tenfold, and all my precious madness. Fold it all into that one phase: *all my precious madness*.

Say it with me, be on my side, as I know you are: *Fuck off.*

EPILOGUE

My Father, a Short Monograph

After my walk by the river, I took public transport to the Barbican and spent some of the evening in a café there, a place that was empty and tatty and furnished with seventies regalia. There I was, sitting in the Barbican, in a curious capsule removed from time and reality, the bored bartender reading her book, the half-drunk glass of beer. There are some places so soulless, so emptied of soul, as in certain paintings of Hopper of course, and as in this café in the upper Barbican, that they are then flooded in melancholy, which is nothing but another kind of soulfulness. I looked down at the page; it was blank, not littered with cliches or scrawl, blank and inviting me in. I wrote down two words, and sat and looked at them as if I had just completed a novel, or a house: *My Father*.

My father died before I was ready. My father died early in the morning on the hottest day of the year. He was ambushed in the bathroom. We personify Death so we have someone to blame. Death waiting in the bathroom for an old man to go for a wee, the coward Death. He'd slunk in at night and waited, his wrinkly pale body behind the door. My father didn't stand a chance.

I got a call when I was at work. Midway through a sales pitch to some cleaning company. The shame of it. That the news of his death was so sullied, so defiled. That I was doing what so grievously disappointed him. My hatred of the sales office doubtless has something to do with this. Their role in defiling my father's death. What were you doing when your father died? 'I was talking absolute shit.' Shamed by the cruel juxtaposition.

I have never been able to 'metabolise', as they say, the sight of my father's dead body, like a figure in wax. Not looking heavy, as you might expect, but somehow light, in transit, in parenthesis. The signature of a departure. When I saw my father's body I wept, or better to say 'I was wept' – weeping happened to me, and I struggled to deal with it; just as I have since struggled to deal with this image ever since. No matter how much intellectually we are able to grasp something, to think something, there is another level at which we simply cannot integrate something into our world. Nor should we, *pace* the psychotherapists, integrate such things. A part of us will be lost to melancholia, that afterlife of grief, which tries to find some trace, glimpse or reflection of what is buried too deep ever to be recalled.

Sometimes, still, and doubtless forever, I listen to my father's death. Listening to my father's death: to the untutored ear, or to the English ear, it might sound pretentious to say that I was listening to my father's death. But in fact it makes complete sense. For I was not thinking about my father's death, I was not applying my mind to my father's death, in so far as I was not turning it over, pondering what might otherwise have been, reconstructing how my mother might have felt finding him lifeless on the floor, or listening to his scarcely human choking immediately before that, or reimagining the scorching blue summer day in question of course, when I was taken completely unawares and had to get the first train back to Bradford. I was not thinking about any of this. I was just sitting with the wordless fact of his death, listening to the note sounded by my father's death. And to do this, to listen to a death, one has to, of course, eliminate all external sounds, to tune in to this faint note which we might call an afternote, a note that only rings out after death. And one sits and listens to this note when all the world's lights have been turned off and there is nothing else to listen to. For perhaps when you reach a stage in your life where the necessary loves begin to die, one realises that there is no longer silence, in so far as any silence is only a kind of prelude, a pause before the notes of the dead begin to move towards you, like shapes from the mist, becoming clearer and clearer. So yes, I will carry on listening to my father's death for as long as I am alive.

There is perhaps a violence inherent in all expression. A force emerges which destroys the existing state of things. Yes, there's a violence in me, of course, which first of all consists in a feeling that there's something in me more than myself, that I can't contain. There is no point trying to contain it; it overflows. That's just what it does. Its essence is to overflow. And my infirmities, my ill health exist only in relation to this greater violence for which my body is insufficient. Those who enjoy good health do so only because there is no corresponding violence, no force that is too great for their body.

In my father's case, violence was primarily physical, although of course with emotional shrapnel, and it was remarkable how completely his violence departed following his breakdown. This violence that had characterised his actions and his language: it went. My father, after he retired, was granted an amnesty of ten years before death robbed him in the middle of the night, in the cruellest fashion. But in those years, he experienced a strange rebirth. He experienced a refulgence; or rather a parcel or pocket of him underwent a refulgence. Pockets of eccentricity and kindness were opened, as a flower opens, a humble flower hidden under the bridge or in a small dormant pocket. These were opened by his breakdown, and flooded his whole being, or rather, and better, irrigated it, for new and different things flourished: shoots and fruits which had not before seen the light of day, or only fitfully, or had been locked up, as in a shed, and had waited patiently inside the seed packet, although the packet itself was faded with age, the letters no longer distinct. Up until that point one might have accurately described my father as a violent man and not without evidence said that he was *essentially* a violent man, who brought with him his own violent weather, sometimes directly and loudly overhead, sometimes trailing in the distance, and most often inside the house. But our so-called essence can be knocked out of us by accident and circumstances, by winds and objects that collide with us from an Outside we cannot control. This violence of my father, far from being his essence, was a force blocking other forces from emerging. In any case, something inside him had snapped, a tight string of anger vibrating as long as I'd known him. It snapped. And he went with it. Whereas he had been a solitary man who spoke little and to few people, he became a loquacious man who spoke with many people including strangers, and asked them about their business. He made up songs and read about Ancient Egypt. He bought rare seeds and flowering bulbs from a man named Bob in Devon. Whereas he had always caged his emotions and often exploded in rage, he now told people how much he cared about them and was amused and easy-going. He tenderly held my mother's hand and sent her unforeseen flowers. Everything had been folded inside out. Nothing really remained except a mad dance of eccentricity, an eccentricity that up to that point had surfaced only now and then through little fumaroles when work and routine subsided. Call it his essence if you want, except it wouldn't have seen the light of day, it wouldn't have been the dominant note of the late years, the 'late style' as I like to call it, had he not changed jobs and had the breakdown. The breakdown gave his mad dance permission to be, to flourish. All the knots unravelled. History is an accident which happens to all of us, and his eccentric dance might have been there his whole life, might have been, in fact, at the centre of his whole life had he been born in a different era, a different class, to a different mother. Instead, it only began to live and breathe in the last years.

Yes, my father's violence departed and cleared with his breakdown so that a new sun rose on my mother's life and on ours, although I had by that time departed. And so, when one expects to wizen and diminish, a new era opens and new light shines through the unlikeliest of portals. When one expects to begin the slow decline, the decrease and diminution, instead a new line is scored on the canvas and the bright vermilion blooms.

Some people, conversely, pluck the fruit of their life too soon, or blossom too soon, and spend the rest of their days withering and dying. Some people spend up to threescore years slowly dying after having blossomed and dropped their fruit, they spend forty years on the ropes being pummelled by time. It is better slowly to ripen, to garner and collect, and bear your best thoughts and actions at the age of sixty, like Kant of course, or the underrated Kurtág. It is odd that this late rebirth had happened to my grandfather, who, after my white-haired invalid grandmother died, found another love and went on adventures, driving to distant lakes and forests, and kept this a secret till after his death. An album full of photos opened and amazed us. And, although not so late in life, I believe it has happened to me, who blossomed briefly at Oxford only to sink, as I thought irrevocably, and then re-emerge from the unlikeliest of places, the darkest of holes, triumphant by the Thames and bathed in aureate dawn.

It was in this phase of my father's refulgence that I would sit, when I visited, sit with him on the bench outside the bungalow. My grandfather had bought that scruffy plot of land and learned from library books the basic principles of construction. Everyone raves of course about Wittgenstein designing and building a house for his sister, as if this were some remarkable feat for the philosopher, except Wittgenstein was a well-educated man of impossibly rich parentage, placed already far, far, ahead of the pack to begin with, and trained also as an engineer. He thus possessed all the necessary tools and expertise to design and put together a house, having only to think through the design and the shape of, for example, the radiators and door handles – both of which are admittedly beautiful. If you go to Wittgenstein's house, on the Kundmanngasse in

Vienna, you can see them, form married perfectly to function. But my grandfather, before he could start thinking about door handles, or radiators, or in any way constructing his house, had before that to master all the principles and rules of construction, had to learn about foundations and materials and stresses and in fact everything else to do with constructing a house. To do this he had first of all to visit the municipal library and take out a number of books on architecture, and building and plumbing and wiring, while Wittgenstein by the same stage was doubtless already laying the first stone. My grandfather has been born before the welfare state and had been granted only a rudimentary education, growing up at a time of obscene social injustice. His construction of a house, therefore, not simply from scratch but from a stage even prior to that, so that he had to labour arduously in the evenings, after finishing his welding job, just to *reach scratch*, the point from which others began, must be seen, I assert, as a feat certainly greater than Wittgenstein's construction, given the relative starting positions of the two builders, Wittgenstein and my grandfather. For in measuring someone's achievement, of course, one must always take account of where they began. Someone who climbs Everest from the base camp and someone who is parachuted in near the summit (disregarding for the time being whether such a thing is physically possible) cannot be judged by the same measure, even though this is what, socially, we do all the time. Wittgenstein certainly performed some impressive flourishes at the summit, but he was also dropped by helicopter only a few feet away. And similarly, for decades, most of those at the summit of social and political life, certainly, were dropped there by the helicopter of privilege, and imagine that their elevation, above those that began from base camp, is due entirely to merit, a palpably stupid claim as soon as one uses a simple analogy, which of course no one does, and nor do people any longer understand analogies.

And so, on this bench outside the house, we would sit for hours exchanging the odd word. That is all, the odd word. Where you were probably expecting me to say 'intimacies of the heart'. But no, it was not that, finally, we had the great long exploratory chats crossing the silence of years. No, nothing of that kind occurred. It is more like the two of us, sat side by side, each opened the door of our solitude to each other. I opened the door in his direction and he opened his in mine. This had always in fact been our mode of communication, in so far as we communicated. We knew, tacitly, that it was possible, in each other's company, to share our solitudes, which were made of the same timbre, a sharing that was deeper and more trusting than the sharing of any secret. This is how it was on the banks of the Aire or on the rocky shores of Blea Tarn, waiting for the first bite, or not really waiting at all but sitting and experiencing pure time, time which had put aside its horological clothes and was sitting with us by the lake simply combing its hair.

Nonetheless and occasionally, through this silence, when we sat on the bench, stray words would appear, words which perhaps needed this silence to feel secure in appearing, little badger words, emerging as into a clearing. One time my father turned to me and asked, puzzled, 'Why do folk have kids?' You might think that this was a strange and insensitive thing for a father to say to his child, to ask the child, in a sense, what reason was there for him to be born. And I grant I have laughed when I have thought of him asking this question, with its pure Beckettian humour, and its cadence of genuine Yorkshire incredulity, which I remember exactly and can exactly reproduce if asked, a mode of incredulity one finds only in Yorkshire, or perhaps only in my family. Doubtless it is a question for late in life, a question which drops from the tree very late, and it was indeed very near the end of my father's life, if not the very last visit that sweet, warm April, after he had made a point of asking me to visit, for I think my father had received, although he did not directly divulge it, certain premonitory signs of and from Death. How they presented themselves to my father I do not know, only that he insisted I visit him that April, the month before he died. 'Make sure you come up in April,' he said over the phone, but giving no particular reason. And I promised him and did indeed come up, which is when I sat on that bench outside the house, in that unseasonable warm April weekend, a weekend seemingly interpolated from another season.

But let me say that those words, 'Why do folk have kids?', were the best thing he could have said to me, for he was addressing me not as a Father to a Son, having to think of what might or might not be appropriate for that particular symbolic and scripted interaction, but only as one human being to another, throwing off his Father mantle and speaking to me as he might have spoken, for example, to Peter, his one remaining friend, who he saw every second Tuesday at the pub. Father and Sons, he'd done with all that, in the last months, he'd dropped all that palaver and so was able to address me in a way that was free and careless, which was fine and more than fine.

We both looked out over his garden, one portion of which was for growing turnips, cabbages, raspberries and strawberries, and one portion of which was for flowers. My father talked about the turnips at some length, the Half-Long Croissy and the Norfolk Red Top, and also of the Early St John cabbage. My father's delight in these turnips and cabbages was also a delight in their names, for they were very rare varieties which dated back to Victorian England and as such were also the seeds and signs of a lost world. His ambition, he told me, was to have the best garden in Bradford, which was certainly a possibility, for it was a beautiful garden. But the last time I sat with my father on the bench he had revised this aspiration. 'I no longer want to have the best garden in Bradford,' he announced, whereupon I looked slightly disappointed. 'I want,' he said with a twinkle in his eye, 'to have the best garden in Britain!' At this point we both started to laugh heartily and continued laughing joyously and unstoppably for several minutes. It is hard to say in what that laughter consisted, or rather it is easy to say: it consisted in joy, a pure kind of joy, the sheer exorbitance of the claim breaking out in laughter, as it were. We were not, and in no way, laughing self-deprecatingly at the hubris of this claim, for there was no hubris to the claim in actual fact. Rather it was a great swelling and rolling 'Why not', crashing waves of 'Why the hell not?!' And of course in one sense it was certainly the best garden in Britain, being the best at permitting my father to flourish, the best garden at expressing my father's peculiar form of life, so to speak. And to talk of the best garden in Britain in the abstract is fairly meaningless, since we need to colour that in with the particular desires and needs of individual human beings and their eccentricities and foibles. It is not only that I remember that laughter still, as an echo, that laughter when we sat side by side with the doors of our solitude open. No, it is also that it is still there, that laughter, and cannot be extinguished, and sometimes, unexpectedly, I will hear myself laughing with that exact same laughter and welcome it back into my body and allow myself to tremble and shake as I did back then on the bench with my father who, a month or so after that laughter, was dead. He was ambushed by a brain haemorrhage, having woken in the middle of the night and made his way to the bathroom. I can only imagine what it must have been like, and I do, I do imagine it, yes, I imagine it often.

It was the punching out of Cahun that has allowed me to return to my own childhood and to my father and write about these things. The destructive and the creative, the violent and the poetic, imbricated and inseparable, and all of these things, and the writing that ensued, are segments in the arc of my blossoming: the stamens, calyxes, petals unfolding. And in the calm vacated space of the page of course, I've gravitated towards my childhood and written of many things, such as the stubdog, and the light bulb exploding at home when I was a child. But to really finish writing I needed to return, I had to go back. For writing is not self-sufficient; it has to be plugged into something. Most obviously, for example, a pen, a fine-nibbed fountain pen to write in microscopic script, an espresso, the sound of the silver spoon against the white saucer, a table, a window, a strict esoteric routine but wide open to improvisation, the light of the sun at daybreak, the light of the sun at evening, the sound of footsteps on an empty street, a jazz band, a rain shower thrown against the window, a sudden breeze from a yellow-blossomed tree, the skeleton of a hare, a scuffle with a stranger on a bus, the vignette of an alley through which Soho Square can be glimpsed as a rectangle of greenery and sunshine, Beethoven's Ninth and its kernel of resilience, an armed insurrection, a revolutionary war, a civil war, a disused shed in County Wexford, a defaced burial stone, the rising of the waters, a conspicuously uneventful childhood like a fallow field beneath the hot summer sun, the smoke from the fire at Christmas in Naples, the shudder and creak as the century stops, a sea cave woozy with music, a lark, an albatross, the antiquities of Rome, the flame of life under the skin, the seventies upholstery in the Barbican, the gentle trickle of the water fountain at night, savage disappointment lacerating the heart, the empty coffee cup into which the barista pours a thimbleful of grappa, the frog as an object of infant cruelty, copper bells ringing out in a small rural town, aching bones, the field of fresh snow on New Year's Day, a faded photo retaining the dead, a blossom tree's springtime confetti, crashing waves beneath tall Cornish skies, the colour purple clotting into a blackberry, the unrelenting viciousness of humanity, the unrelenting variousness of what exists. But to finish the monograph I needed a river. I needed to place my mill wheel in the brown, imperturbable Aire.

I have for a long time visited my mother, at the bungalow, in the years after my father's death. If I sit on the bench near the porch, I am careful to sit on the left, for he always sat on the right. And if by mistake I do sit on the right I say 'Sorry, Dad' and move over. Still, today, if I were to go there, and someone forced me to sit on the right, I wouldn't be comfortable. If you ask me 'Do you believe your father is beside you on the bench?' I would say 'Of course not.' Nonetheless. Back home in my London flat also, sometimes his presence is very strong. He sits on the sofa, silent; he never used to say much and he doesn't now. It's a tender silence. Of course, as a formulated opinion I do not believe in the afterlife, but I am happy he is there on the sofa. To say 'I am happy he is there on the sofa', insolently *in the face of my own beliefs*, lifts me, makes me hover, in defiance even of myself. He visits me also in dreams, those great and extraterritorial embassies of the dead, through which the dead reach out to the living. But there was one dream, perhaps a year ago, which has since crossed over completely into my waking existence, when I dreamed that my father lived in a modest house by the river. I saw his face pale and silent behind the double glazing. When he saw me, his face broke into a beaming smile, and he came to the door and walked down to the river where I was stood. 'Ah, you've come then,' he said, and I realised he'd been waiting by the window for me 'all this time', as the dream put it, without specifying how long, though of course in the dream it was understood, just as it was understood that I was simultaneously my adult self but also a child with a cowboy hat. Everything in a dream is replete with significance, but 'significance' not as our waking self knows. It was a tender reconciliation, anyway, in the dream, with my father and myself. It was the Aire, I realised, on waking. That spot we used to fish in just above Keighley. It was just before visiting my mother.

I resolved, after that dream, to go there, to go to the spot that I'd visited in my dream and meet with my father, and return with this to my writing, so as to finish my writing, my monograph. I would meet with my father's ghost as Joyce did – to wrap it also in a literary mantle – when he emerged from the wood of words, the densely woven wood with its roots and branches and bristling buds, and saw his *cold mad feary father*, although Joyce is perhaps talking about the river. But mine, in my dream, was not cold or mad but warm and calm and reconciled.

And so, not long after attacking Cahun, I headed north. I had not walked by the Aire for many years, but I knew that if I did, I would smell my childhood. Specifically in the reeds and hogweed of the Aire at Keighley, in the nettles and cuckoo spit. Sat on the muddy bank, me and Dad, waiting for trout to bite; midges and – their supposed antidote – tobacco smoke from Dad's meerschaum pipe. 'Where's the back of beyond, Dad?' 'North of the middle of nowhere.' A tatty unattractive spot on the slow brown river. A rogue band of teenagers smoking and swearing downstream. Dad told them to clear off, and they did, apologetic, for there was something in his voice which made people do what he said. From time to time, after long drifting intervals, we pulled life out of the waters. Then we unhooked it and put it back, and watched that silver blade return to the depths. Perhaps I would cross paths with him there, my father. I would go there on a Wednesday morning, in honour of him. For my father had set up a walking club called Walking by Water on Wednesdays, a series of walks by the River Aire and the Wharfe and the Nidd and the Calder, and also along the many canals that traverse Bradford and Bingley. He was always immensely proud of this mellifluous phrase, *Walking by water on Wednesdays*, this alliterative flourish, which he would intone endlessly with a gleeful smile, just as he repeated everything which delighted him with a kind of surplus of joy, the joy of a small dancing child. Every Wednesday for years he would run this walking club, until his very last year when he was no longer able to walk very fast and they all fell away, his fellow walkers, they all fell away, as people do (and as my people did), after deciding that my father was too slow. The only one left was a very old man called Arnold, who, my father said, would 'bore him to death' with tales of disappointing lunches at Morrisons supermarket and other places. I do not know why my father's walking slowed down so dramatically in his final year, for there was no obvious or organic reason, unless it was one of those inconspicuous heralds that Death sends us in advance so that we might turn the rudder and drift towards the low, candescent sun.

In any case, it was very early that I set out to the river, with my thick greatcoat and leather gloves and woolly hat. The landscape was empty and beautiful, mist like cold steam rising from the earth. I passed the ruined abbey, and various buildings and stiles and drystone walls that were each the marker of some half-rubbed-out memory. This world belonged to my father and me, my first and original country, at ease in that silence that held us both, my father and I, when we fished in the incomparable Aire. A part of me will always exist in the Aire, and I know I can always go back to that part, for the river will always be here, its mixture of murky enchantment and careless childlike freedom. I was outside myself again, as Beckett had been when he spoke of receding mist, the mist that *was* his melancholy, just as this *was* the sense memory of my childhood, and my childish shyness and wonder, it was all there waiting for me, and no intensity of introspection could arrive at where my legs had taken me, at what the trees and grass offered me, and the remarkable thing is of course that nature can host these things, can host our body's deepest sensations and thoughts, Beckett's melancholy or my youthful reserve, being as it is indifferent and inhuman. Nature, with its own intelligence which is not ours, although that's probably why it can hold them, its inhuman intelligence, which means it retains, immaculately, the shapes of our past, without human infidelity, without leaching and contaminating our past selves with subsequent human wishes. These were the thoughts that came to mind as I walked by the water, these were the thoughts that suggested themselves, buoyed and sustained by the rhythm of walking, and these thoughts, this rocking iambic stride, this landscape which was not distant enough to be 'landscape', together combined to welcome the ghost of my father, together combined to open the space where he might appear, some crease in the skin of the visible world which might allow him access.

I didn't see his ghost, I didn't see the ghost of my father, because firstly of course ghosts don't exist, outside their life support of metaphor, and also because it's a misconception that ghosts are something you *see,* that they float in the field of vision. Rather, they infiltrate the sense of touch and smell and hearing, the more internal senses, they creep inside you, they prickle and creak and bristle and hum, or at least my father did, once I'd found it. It was not difficult to find, the spot, our spot, where we'd fished for chub. It was the same spot, I was sure of that, the grass worn away and the soil firm and smooth and a piece of red brick protruding, the same as before, and the pool beneath the tree where we fished for chub. All the same, the same as before.

I knew how I'd get there. To him, I mean. I thought, first of all, about the first time I went back, after the funeral. I'd watered the tomatoes, the garden, retracing my father's steps, trying to revive, however faintly, my father's life. The smell of the wooden slats of the fence in the sun, the smell of the watered compost, the vegetable odour of green tomatoes inside the small humid greenhouse, the smells that composed my father's world, I'd wanted to breathe them again. I'd sat and watched a spaghetti western because my father loved these and watched them over and over and quoted from them with glee. 'My mule don't like people laughing.' I was watching it but was also sharing my father's watching, watching his watching, *becoming* his watching. And I'd surveyed the garden as my father (and his) had surveyed the garden, with proprietary pride, one of the emotions he had experienced now imitated by me, I'd repeated the words my dad had pronounced after victory over the chair shop, and felt the same eccentric glee, albeit ten times diluted, and when the phone rang unexpectedly I'd exclaimed, as Dad did, 'Who the hell's that?', and for the briefest duration the pop and fizzle of annoyance that still clung to those words, so pronounced, burned through me, an echo and rebound of a life no longer here.

And it was this strange necromancy I would use again, at the river's edge. As I sat down on that bare brown bank, as my father had sat, the sensation of the cold soil against the seat of my pants was, or must have been, exactly the same sensation that my father felt when he sat there, so that in a way it was his sensation, or a *likeness* thereof. And as I sat there, enjoying this sensation that belonged to my father, I took out the meerschaum pipe from my pocket and pressed my thumb against the bowl as my father had done and so did I feel what my father had felt and got a brief taste of what it must have been like to *be* him, and I took from my pocket a packet of Gold Leaf, which I had bought especially from the shop from which my father bought his, and rubbed that loamy, soft tobacco between my fingers as my father did, and sniffed my tobacco-infused fingers as he doubtless had, once again tasting his very existence from the inside. And, as I had never done before, I lit the pipe, only so the smoke could rise and mingle with the air, as it had done all those years ago, time and again, and it passed into my nose and I tasted it in my mouth, secure in the knowledge that I was smelling and tasting exactly what he had smelled and tasted, and that these things were weak but authentic echoes of his soul, if you believe, as I do, that the soul is no or little more than a composite of sensations and thoughts; but actually all these things were only the prelude to his language, the voice which is the *true* expression of the soul... it was language, his language, with tobacco and soil as its compost perhaps, and it began within *me*, as faint as fairy footsteps on felt, I heard it and felt it, the dum-dum beat of his breakdown first, dim as anything, but I tuned in, tuned in to the words and the rhythm emanating from inside: *nobody, nobody, nobody understands; nobody, nobody, nobody understands*, a pulse that ran through us, me and him, and more words came and I gave them voice, my own voice but his words, and increasingly his own accent, which I found easy to reproduce, with his characteristic turns of phrase, the signatures of his being, such as *you're a funny lad, what's wrong with normal milk?* And *What have you got to show for that bloody degree?* And *why do folk have kids?* of course, and *when me and Piggy were at school a fella in Peel Park showed us his dick and we came back with the police and they gave us each some chocolate, which was a right treat in them days* and *if I'd have told me grandad that I'd have a son that went to Oxford, he'd have thought I was bloody daft* and *that Arnold doesn't know how many beans make five* and *are you one of those fellas who likes cooking his own food?* And *all day bloody long drinking bloody fancy water* and *what the hell are chickpeas?* and *when I was at school we had a teacher called Mr Dooley and when he turned to write on the board we'd all start singing in whispers 'hang down your head Tom Dooley, hang down your head and cry' and as soon as he turned round we'd stop* and *then there was Charley O'Dowd the maths teacher and he had a fist like a bunch of pork sausages,* and *I didn't know me dad until I was five, when he got back from the war, and this fella walks in and your grandma says this is your dad, and his eyes brimmed up,* and *I don't think I've got long left lad, it's just a feeling I've got, I don't think I've got long left, I felt it when I was driving down from the Lakes with your mum and I asked if she'd drive instead. I didn't feel right. I don't feel right. Just a feeling I don't have long left. Come up and see me in April, son, do you promise?* Whereupon this voice began to weaken, to escape, and hovered at arm's length outside me in the form of a reedy note, in the form of a faint hint of smoke, in the form of a kiss on the crown of the head, and I said simply, 'I love you, Dad,' and there it was. 'I love you, Dad.' All that red sputum turned into ragged evening pink, or like when we walked back from Blea Tarn with the trout that we cooked for breakfast, and its flesh the colour of dawn. And where there had once been rage – and fear – there was now only love. How lovely to say the word! How *lovely* to say the word, to *arrive* finally at the word 'love' and not have to travel further.

Acknowledgements

Thank you first of all to my wife Gemma, who read everything and kept faith and encouraged me at every stage. To my children, Hector and Arno, for more than I could mention, but for William's words in particular.

To Lars Iyer, who read various versions, for his advice and enthusiasm; to Terry Eagleton and Stephen Mitchelmore who read early drafts.

Thank you to Sophie Lewis for translation assistance.

To Sam Jordison and Eloise Millar, my publishers, for believing in the book, and for reading it with such care and love. And thanks also to Alex Billington, who typeset the manuscript.

Why Be a Galley Buddy?

At Galley Beggar Press we don't want to compromise on the excellence of the writing we put out, or the physical quality of our books. We've also enjoyed numerous successes and prize nominations since we set up in 2012. Almost all of our authors have gone on to be longlisted for, shortlisted for, or the winners of over twenty of the world's most prestigious literary awards.

But publishing for the sake of art is a risky commercial strategy. In order to keep putting out the very best books we can, and to continue to support talented writers, we need your help. The money we receive from our Galley Buddy scheme is an essential part of keeping us going.

By becoming a Galley Buddy, you help us to launch and foster a new generation of writers.

To join today, head to:
https://www.galleybeggar.co.uk/subscribe

GALLEY BEGGAR PRESS

We hope that you've enjoyed *All My Precious Madness*. If you would like to find out more about Mark, along with some of his fellow authors, head to www.galleybeggar.co.uk.

There, you will also find information about our subscription scheme, 'Galley Buddies', which is there to ensure we can continue to put out ambitious and unusual books like *All My Precious Madness*.

Subscribers to Galley Beggar Press:
- Receive limited black-cover editions of our future titles (printed in a one-time run of 600).
- Have their names included in a special acknowledgement section at the back of our books.
- Are sent regular updates and invitations to our book launches, talks and other events.
- Enjoy a 20% discount code for the purchase of any of our backlist (as well as for general use throughout our online shop).

FRIENDS OF GALLEY BEGGAR PRESS

Galley Beggar Press would like to thank the following individuals, without the generous support of whom our books would not be possible:

Cameron Adams	Andrew Bailey	Nick Black
Kémy Ade	Tom Bailey	Mark Blackburn
David Anderson	Edward Baines	Peter Blackett
Darryl Adie	Timothy Baker	Michael Blissett
Timothy Ahern	John Balfour	Charlie Bloor
Liz Aiken	Maggie Ballistreri	Blue and Kat
Andrew Ainscough	Christopher Ball	Lynne Blundell
Sam Ainsworth	David Ball	David Boddy
Jez Aitchison	Andrew Ballantyne	Sophie Boden
Elizabeth Allen	Sarah Balstrup	Rich Boden
Richard Allen	Paul Bangert	John Bogg
Lulu Allison	Victoria Barkas	Kalina Borisova
Anna Andreou	Chad Barnes	Poppy Boutell
Natalia Anjaparidze	Edward Barnfield	Tom Bowden
Kirk Annett	Kevin Barrett	Edwina Bowen
Deborah Arata	Tony Barrett	Mark Bowles
Robert Armiger	Morgan Baxley	Michelle Bowles
Eloise Armstrong	Perry Beadsworth	David Bowman
Kate Armstrong	Rebecca Bealey	Joanna Bowman
Alba Arnau Prado	Lauren Beattie	Alexander Bown
Sean Arnold	Rachel Bedder	Judith Box
Curt Arnson	Georgia Beddoe	Matthew Boyd
Xanthe Ashburner	Joseph Bell	Astrid Bracke
Robert Ashton	Angel Belsey	Sean Bradley
Emma Ashton-Pain	Madeline Bennett	David Brady
Rachel Atkin	Felicity Bentham	Debby Brady
Edmund Attrill	Jean Bergin	Andrew J. Bremner
Valda Aviks	Michelle Best	Chris Brewer
Jo Ayoubi	Gary Betts	Dean Brooks
Kerim Aytac	David Bevan	John Brooks
Sam Bachy	Alison Bianchi	Sheila Browse
Claire Back	Gavin Bingham	Marcus Brujstens
Thomas Badyna	Sandra Birnie	Carrie Brunt

Richard Bryant
Laura Bui
Kevin Burrell
Alister Burton
Tamsin Bury
Joe Butler
Esther van Buul
Kester Brewin
Jorien Caers
Alan Calder
June Caldwell
Gabriel Calin
Matt Callow
Francesca Cambridge Mallen
Gordon Cameron
Lucy Campbell
Mark Campbell
Laura Canning
Annette Capel
Andrew Cardus
Elettra Carini
Leona Carpenter
Daniel Carr
Sean Carroll
Leigh Chambers
Lina Christopoulou
Neal Chuang
Gemma Church
Neil Churchill
Deborah Ann Clarke
Simon Clarke
Douglas Clarke-Williams
Steve Clough
Gwendoline Coates
Matthew Cocker
Emily Coghill
Steven Coghill
Daniel Cohen
Paul Cole
Jennifer Coles

John Coles
Emma Coley
Sam Coley
Ruby Colley
Wayne Connolly
Jess Conway
Joe Cooney
Kenneth Cooper
Sarah Corbett
Paul Corry
Andy Corsham
Mary Costello
Sally Cott
Nick Coupe
Diarmuid Cowan
Colette Cox
Isabelle Coy-Dibley
Matthew Craig
Anne-Marie Creamer
Joanna Crispin
Brenda Croskery
Alasdair Cross
James Cross
Thomas Crossley
Kate Crowcroft
Stephen Cuckney
Rebecca Cullen
John Cullinane
Damian Cummings
Stephen Cummins
Andrew Cupples
Effie and Tim Currell
Patrick Curry
Emma Curtis Lake
Chris Cusack
Will Dady
Rehab Dahy
Jon Dalladay
Rupert Dastur
Maurizio Dattilo
Claudia Daventry
Andrew Davies

Julie Davies
Linda Davies
Nickey Davies
William Davies
James Daviss
Emilie Day
Sarah Deacon
Ann Debono
Liam Dee
Paul Dettmann
Angelica Diehn
Bartholomeus Johannes Diels
Kasper Dijk
Belinda Dillon
Gary Dixon
Turner Docherty
William Dobson
Mark Dolan
Freda Donoghue
Laura Donovan
Kirsty Doole
Ilana Doran
Oliver Dorostkar
David Douce
Carol Dow
Janet Dowling
Maurice Down
Jamie Downs
Iain Doyle
Ian Dudley
Gordon Duncan
Fiona Duffy
Gwilym Eades
Lauren Eames
Matthew Eatough
Nicola Edwards
Lance Ehrman
Elizabeth Elliott
Thomas Ellmer
Theresa Emig
Stefan Erhardt

Fiona Erskine	Richard Furniss	Benjamin Hamilton
Frances Evangelista	John Gallagher	Paul Handley
Gareth Evans	Marc Galvin	Paul Hanson
Kieran Evans	Gonzalo C. Garcia	Jill Harrison
Paul Ewen	Annabel Gaskell	Greg Harrowing
Sarah Farley	Elke Geerlings	Pearl Hawke
Fin Fearn	Nolan Geoghegan	Lewis Hayes
Emma Feather	Pia Ghosh Roy	Robbie Hearn
Lori Feathers	Phil Gibby	Rachel Heath
Gerard Feehily	Alison Gibson	David Hebblethwaite
Jeremy Felt	Luke Gibson	Clare Hegarty
Maria Guilliana Fenech	Sonya Gildea	Andy Helliwell
Michael Fenton	James Goddard	Richard Hemmings
Edward J. Field	Stephanie Golding	Petra Hendrickson
Paul Fielder	Elizabeth Goldman	Padraig J. Heneghan
Catriona Firth	Pippa Goldschmidt	Adam Saiz Abo
Becky Fisher	Mark Goldthorpe	Henriksen
Cheryl Fisher	Morgan Golf-French	Steven Hess
Duncan Fisher	Anil Gomes	Matt Hewes
Nicholas Fisher	Bryonny	Felix Hewison-Carter
Caitlin Fitzgerald	Goodwin-Hawkins	Sophia Hibbery
Mark Flaum	Sakura Gooneratne	Simon Higgins
Hayley Flockhart	Judy Gordon	Annette Higgs
Nicholas Flower	Nikheel Gorolay	Alexander Highfield
Patrick Foley	Sara Gorton	Jennifer Hill
Mathilde Fourie	Simon Goudie	Daniel Hillman
James Fourniere	Amber Graci	James Hilton
Ceriel Fousert	Seb Gray	David Hirons
Kathleen Fox	Becky Greer	Snusu Hirvonen-Kowal
Richard Fradgley	Helen Griffith	Marcus Hobson
Matthew Francis	Judith Griffith	Jamie Hodder-Williams
Mimi Francis	Ben Griffiths	Stephenjohn Holgate
Nigel Francis	Neil Griffiths	Turan Holland
Bridget Fraser	Vicki Grimshaw	Ben Holloway
Charlotte Frears	Miriam Guastalia	David Holmes
Emma French	Dave Gunning	Deborah Homden
Gill Fryzer	Jack Haden	Ellis Hough
Graham Fulcher	Ian Hagues	Adrian Howe
Paul Fulcher	Daniel Hahn	William Hsieh
Jane Fuller	Nikki Hall	Steve Hubbard
Stephen Furlong	Robin Hall	Hugh Hudson
Michael Furness	Peter Halliwell	Anna Jean Hughes

Richard Hughes
Robert Hughes
Kim-ling Humphrey
Raven Hurste
Simone Hutchison
Louise Hussey
LJ Hutchins
Lori Inglis Hall
Jarkko Inkinen
Grace Iredale
Joseph Jackson
Ryan Jackson
Jane Jakeman
Briley James
Helen James
Mel James
Michael James
Graeme Jarvie
Daniel Jean
Gareth Jelley
Rachel John
PJ Johnson
Alice Jolly
Alex Jones
Bevan Jones
David Jones
Deborah Jones
Jupiter Jones
Rebecca Jones
Anna Jordison
Diana Jordison
Diane Josefowicz
Sapna Joshi
Claire Jost
Benjamin Judge
Andrew Jupp
Gary Kaill
Darren Kane
Martin Kerry
Michael Ketchum
Vijay Khurana
Ross Kilpatrick

Anna Kime
Fran Kime
Philip King
Xanath King
Euan Kitson
Clara Knight
Joshua Knights
Jacqueline Knott
Zuz Kopecka
Asli Korkmaz
David Krakauer
Emily Kubisiak
Elisabeth Kumar
Navpreet Kundal
Candida Lacey
Geves Lafosse
Rachel Lalchan
David Lamont
Cliona Lane
Dominique
  Lane-Osherov
Kathy Lanzarotti
Shira Lappin
Denis Larose
Aimee Lauezzari
Jo Lawrence
Lorraine Lawrence
Elizabeth Eva Leach
Stephen Leach
Rick Le Coyte
Carley Lee
David Lee
Tracey Lee
Jessica Leggett
Chiara Levorato
Sara Levy
Oliver Lewis
Chris Lilly
Chris Lintott
Clayton Lister
Amy Lloyd
Lyn Lockwood

Kate Lockwood Jefford
Tracey Longworth
Nikyta Loraine
Lele Lucas
John Lutz
Mark Lynch
Marc Lyth
James McCann
Seona McClintock
Paul McCombs
Emma McConnell
Jon McGregor
Alan McIntyre
Eleanor McIntyre
Sarah McIntyre
Laura McKenzie
Lucie McKnight Hardy
Chris McLaren
Tom McLean
Jane McSherry
Gerald McWilliams
Ewan MacDonald
Andrea MacLeod
Victoria Mackenzie
Eric MacLennan
William Macey
Shelby Maddock
Joseph Maffey
Sean Maguire
Eleanor Maier
Philip Makatrewicz
Sarah Male
Anil Malhotra
Joshua Mandel
Venetia Manning
Cheryl-lynne Mansell
Kyren Marshall
Paul Marshall
Harriet Martin
Christine Martin
William Mascioli
Lewis Mash

Adrian Masters
Rebecca Masterman
Sarah Maxted
Dan Mayers
Kellie Mayes-Barwick
Sally Mayor
Rod Mearing
Andy Merrills
Sarah Messerschmidt
Tina Meyer
Chris Miles
Lindsey Millen
Ali Millar
Phillipa Mills
Sally Minogue
Lindsay Mitchell
Adam Moliver
Ian Mond
Fiona Mongredien
Alexander Monker
Denise Monroe
Alex Moore
Clare Moore
Gary Moore
Michelle Moorhouse
Jonathan Moreland
Nigel J. Morgan
James Morran
Harriet Mossop
Farid Motamed
Carlos Eduardo Morreo
Elizabeth Morris
Joanne Morris
Julie Morris
Patrick Morris
Paul Morris
Clive Morrison
Catriona Morrison
Donald Morrison
Penny Morrison
Jennifer Mulholland
Christian Murphy

Ben Myers
Zosha Nash
Linda Nathan
Tim Neighbour
Marie Laure Neulet
Natalie Newman
Kate Newton
Catherine Nicholson
Chris Neill
Sophia Nixon
Mariah de Nor
Emma Norman
Sam North
Max Novak
Anna Nsubuga
Arif Nurmohamed
Simon Nurse
Rachel Nye
Eli Oakes
Caroline O'Brien
Christopher O'Brien
James O'Brien
Martha O'Brien
Alec Olsen
Siobhaan O'Neill
Ruby Opalka
Valerie O'Riordan
Sam Osborne
Sally Osborn
Sebastien Ohsan-Berthelsen
Liz O'Sullivan
Hassan Otsmane-Elhaou
Kate Packwood
Marta Palandri
Steven Palter
Chris Parker
David Parker
Gilly Parrott
Dave Parry
Simon Parsons

Gary Partington
Debra Patek
Ian Patterson
Adam Paxton
Mark Payne
Tom Payne
Stephen Pearsall
Rosie Pendlebury
Jonathan Perks
Tom Perrin
Robert Perry
Tony Pettigrew
Nicolas Petty
Joshua Philips
Dan Phillips
Sandra Pickford
Hannah Piekarz
Steven Pilling
Robert Pisani
Ben Plouviez
Alex Pointon Melville
Erin Polmear
Dan Pope
Jonathan Pool
Christopher Potter
David Prince
Laurence Pritchard
Victoria Proctor
James Puddephatt
Damian Pugh
Alan Pulverness
Thom Punton
Lisa Quattromini
Leng Leng Quek
Ian Raby
Zoe Radley
Jane Rainbow
Sim Ralph
Polly Randall
Ian Redfern
Dawn Rees
Sam Reese

Padraid Reidy	Benedict Schofield	Lauren Stephens
Susie Renshaw	Jan Schoones	Gillian Stern
Vasco Resende	Ros Schwartz	Jack Stevens
William Richards	Craig Scott	Zac Stevens
Caroline Riddell	Emily Scott	Mark Stevenson
Thea Marie Rishovd	Stephen Robert Scott	Joe Stewart
Chris Roberts	Luke Seaber	Dagmara Stoic
Stephen Roberts	Darren Seeley	Jamie Stone
Emily Robinsonb	Carl Sefton	Zoé Stone
Ada Robinson	Adrian Selby	Justina Stonyte
Joanna Robinson	Darren Semple	Elizabeth Stott
Joyce Lillie Robinson	Henry Settle	Madeleine Stottor
Neil Robinson	Siobhan Shea	Renuka Sornarajah
Lee Rodwell	Nicola Shepherd	Julia Stringwell
Lizz Roe	Emma Shore	Andrew Stuart
Barbara Roether	Deborah Siddoway	Daryl Sullivan
Lorraine Rogerson	Anna Siebach-Larsen	Jesse Surridge
Kalina Rose	Kate Simpson	Helen Swain
Lillie Rosen	Mohini Singh	Felicity Swainston
Andrew Rothschild	Lauren Skene	Elizabeth Symonds
Nathan Rowley	Ann Slack	Lydia Syson
Martin Rowsell	Mark Slater	Ashley Tame
Beverly Rudy	Sarah Slowe	David Tang
Giles Ruffer	Ben Smith	Ewan Tant
Paul Ryan	Catherine Smith	Justine Taylor
Souryantanu Saha	Chris Smith	Kate Taylor
Floriane Sajdak	Hazel Smith	Nicholas Taylor-Collins
Alison Sakai	Kieron Smith	Darren Theakstone
Himanshu Kamal Saliya	Michael Smith	Cennin Thomas
Peeter Sällström Randsalu	Nicola Smith	Sue Thomas
	Arabella Spencer	Susannah Thompson
Bairbre Samh	Levi Stahl	James Thomson
Robert Sanderson	Conor Stait	Julian Thorne
Benedict Sangster	Ellie Staite	Geoff Thrower
Nicky Sargent	Karl Stange	Alexander Tilston Fleming
Steven Savile	Daniel Staniforth	
Natalie Saxon	Jeannie Stanley	Stella Töpfer
Lior Sayada	Phil Starling	Amie Tolson
Liam Scallon	Sarah Starr Murphy	Eloise Touni
Amy Scarrott	Peter Steadman	Geoffrey Travis
Linde Schaafsma	Cathryn Steele	Kate Triggs
Robert Scheffel	Jakub Stehlik	Jojo Tulloh

Steve Tuffnell	Christopher Walthorne	Gary Wilks
Devin Tupper		Andrea Willett
Charlie Turnbull	Zhen Wang	Gareth Williams
C.X. Turner	Tahia Warda	G Williams
Mike Turner	Jerry Ward	Richard Williams
Neil Turner	Kate Ward	Sarah Wiltshire
Aisling Twomey	Peter Ward	Kyle Winkler
Eleanor Updegraff	Rachael Wardell	Bianca Winter
Geoffrey Urland	Guy Ware	Lucie Winter
Raminta Uselyte	Darren Waring	Sheena Winter
Joris van Veeren	Emma Warnock	Stephen Witkowski
Symon Vegro	Susan Warren	Michael Wohl
Francesca Veneziano	Daniel Waterfield	Naomi Wood
Essi Viding	Chris Watts	Nathan Wood
Julia Wait	Sarah Webb	Emma Woolerton
Susan Walby	Ian Webster	Lorna Wright
Chris Walker	Joanna Wellings	Lydia Wynn
Craig Walker	Ian Wells	Lindsay Yates
Phoebe Walker	Karl Ruben Weseth	Gideon York
Stephen Walker	Jo West-Moore	Ian Young
Ben Waller	Wendy Whidden	Juliano Zaffino
Kevin Walsh	Robert White	Vanessa Zampiga
Sinead Walsh	Nayela Wickramasuriya	Sylvie Zannier
Steve Walsh		Rupert Ziziros
Louise Walters	Ben Wilder	Carsten Zwaaneveld